The Lowborn Lady

Books by

PEGGY TROTTER

Year of Jubilee
Reviving Jules

~Unchained Souls Series~
The Secret Things
The Secret Storm

~Society of Outcasts~
The Misfit Bride
The Lowborn Lady
The Spellbound Schoolmarm (6/1/22)

The Lowborn Lady

Society of Outcasts

Book Two

PEGGY TROTTER

The Lowborn Lady

Visit the author's website at: www.peggytrotter.com

Published by Ransomed-Ever-After Books

First Edition, 2021
ISBN-578-31815-6
ISBN 978-0-578-31815-8
Library of Congress Control Number: 2021922027
Printed in Seattle, WA, United States of America

All Scriptures used with this work are from the King James Version (KJV).

Cover Illustration © 2021 by Zanne Davis
Edited by Nancy Clark

No one abides as a member of the Society of Outcasts.

For, to God there are no misfits, only those who thirst to be Redeemed.

"And Jesus put forth his hand, and touched him, saying, I will; be thou clean. And immediately his leprosy was cleansed."

Matthew 8:3

“If the Son therefore shall make you free, ye shall be free indeed.”

John 8:36

Chapter One

1853~New Albany, Indiana

R*emember ladies. Grace…at all costs.*

Miss Bickle's finishing school mantra berated Rhapsody Hasting's brain while the hand of her dead husband weighed on her shoulder. Rhapsody tightened her grip on the armchair to repress the instinctual recoil. Surely the woman who'd dispensed such wisdom had never—never sat for a mourning portrait.

"Mrs. Hastings, please move your head a bit to the right. And here," the brown tweed-coated man appeared from beneath a black sheet shielding the back of the camera, "if you could reach up with your right hand and lay it over his."

Rhapsody shifted her chin slightly, bringing her husband's pale rigor mortis fingers into her peripheral vision. Nothing gleaned from Miss Bickle's Ladies' Etiquette and Finishing School had prepared her for this. Mindful of the twitch that tended to pulsate below her left eye, Rhapsody tensed her jaw. Miss Bickle intruded into her thoughts again.

A true lady never reveals any distress or disappointment. Your countenance remains unimpassioned, imprisoning all the uncouth, lowly desires of the commoner. Miss Lennox, still that tic near your eye. Miss Bickle would snap her waspish figure to attention in front of Rhapsody, making sure the terrible malady had been controlled. *Always remember, Ladies. You are to be graceful, elegant, and refined. Sacrificing everything for dignity.*

Yes, Miss Bickle. All girls had promptly replied in low, controlled tones. Too loud and one earned a wooden spoon to the head.

Reality pressed the fog of childhood away. The brown tweed coat approached her. The best photographer in the city, she'd been told. His downtown, spacious office perched near the Ohio River amongst the thriving businesses of New Albany, Indiana, catered to the elite of the city, both here and in Louisville. The man had the latest and best equipment money could buy in 1853. But that did not stop him from grasping Rhapsody's wrist most unwelcomely.

"If you could just clasp this area of your husband's hand, it would make such a…fine picture."

In other words, make the dead appear alive. The photographer pressed her fingers against the lifeless hand. Rhapsody blinked only once. But revulsion still burned an acid trail up her throat.

"Right here, Mrs. Hastings. Lovely."

The photographer's platform pole exploded, bringing a burst of light into the air. Rhapsody wasted no time dropping Devlin's cold, stiff extremity and shrugging from beneath him to a standing position. She brought her wrist to her nose, inhaling the smelling salts in the hanky tucked in her sleeve.

"Brilliant. Now, I will leave Mr. Hastings in the stand for group photos. I believe the rest of the family are to assemble soon?"

"No, please remove him." She couldn't get to the door fast enough.

"Ma'am?"

A hesitation and a slight turn at the door brought her husband's accusatory stare into her eyes. Her breath hitched. She pressed a palm to her throat. "No. Remove him immediately and return him to the casket."

She spun to avoid any more dialogue and headed toward the gleaming cherry stairway. *Feet progress slowly, grasp the rail with firm yet gentle pressure, slight hitch to the skirt, chin averted, but not up.* Miss Bickle's voice nagged away. Right now Rhapsody loathed this lesson. Better to scurry up the stairs, slam the door, and never reappear. Ever.

But she directed her delicate shoes to promenade to her room, toward the master at the end of the lengthy hallway. Eight bedrooms. She'd insisted. Why, Rhapsody had stipulated every item. Specially crafted, delivered, no cost considered for perfection. The small hallway table she passed came from France. Worth a small fortune. The ivory statue, *Genteel Lady in Garden* rested atop the unique table. Carved from the ivory of Africa, the figurine had traveled the great Atlantic Ocean to adorn this specific location.

She paused beside the lady, swathed in a beautiful frozen robe, clutching a flower to her nose. A surge swelled inside Rhapsody's breast, and it was all she could do not to swat the French-made table down the stairway and watch the ivory figure explode into a million shards.

Instead, Miss Bickle returned. *If you must, stab your nails into your palms. But you shall squelch all emotion. A lady of class never allows it to be shown.*

Rhapsody's hands clenched. The proper way, only allowing the pinky and ring finger to dig while leaving the others lax. All appeared calm. She jabbed her nails into her soft flesh and strolled to the last door on the left. Yes, she had insisted on the left with its ornate door and crystal doorknob.

Once inside she pushed the solid slab closed and turned the skeleton key. How to escape the next twenty-four hours was beyond her. She inched forward, grabbed one of the four columns of the ridiculously huge four-poster bed and pressed her cheek to the cool mahogany.

After a few deep breaths, drawn short by the overly tight corset, she settled on the edge of the ruffled bedspread. Then she decided to stand. It proved much more difficult to breathe sitting down.

A knock sounded at the door. "Who is it?"

Had her voice always been so harsh and demanding?

"Maid, Ma'am."

"I have no use for you now."

Silence.

Her gaze met the daguerreotype of Devlin and her hanging near the door. Such a handsome couple, oozing confidence and luxury. It had been taken at a much different time and a much different circumstance. She plucked it from the wall. Even from a still photo his stare shamed her soul. She stomped to the desk near the window to thrust the castigating image into the drawer. Another knock, sharper and insistent, rattled the door.

"Rhapsody. Open this door."

Mother. The one who insisted on niceties rarely followed them herself. Rhapsody's reluctant feet slipped across the Oriental rug. She twisted the key in the lock and the massive door opened with a rush.

"Your presence is required downstairs. Family photos."

"I'm feeling under the weather."

Her mother's eyes narrowed. "Of course you are. Laying your husband to rest is an unpleasant, but necessary task. Come."

The family matriarch rotated her imposing black hoop skirt and brushed through the doorway, her freshly coifed hair swept back in an intricate, low-set bun. Not a hair out of place, as usual. Nothing defied Mother. The woman turned outside the door, her profile stiff with fine breeding. "Five minutes. No more."

Irritation. Rhapsody used her old trick and tightened the muscles running to her ears, causing them to move only slightly. It always produced a soft rushing sound that she imagined as her temper, simmering. Anything to relieve tension. "Send Lissy up."

Her mother blinked and nodded once, like always, and disappeared like a ghoul. Rhapsody rushed forward to shut the door. She gripped the crystal knob and closed her eyes. How? How could she draw this torture to an end? The shallow breaths she panted inspired inspiration.

At the tentative knock, Rhapsody whipped the door open, earning a flash of the whites of Lissy's eyes glowing in her dark-skinned face.

"Yes, Mum?"

"I need tightening." Rhapsody stepped back and allowed the servant to enter and eased the door closed. She turned and gripped the post once more.

"Mum?"

Rhapsody spun and slung her hands to her hips. "What is it, Lissy? I'm needed downstairs without delay."

The obedient servant nodded, her little dust cap bobbing as she curtsied. "I done strung you to twenty this morning."

"And?"

Again the whites of her eyes bugged as she looked left then right. "Well, that's the tightest you ever gone."

"I want nineteen and a half. Or possibly nineteen. I need to look my best for my husband today."

Lissy blinked a quick succession of flutters, but nodded. Rhapsody once again set herself against the pole while the woman undid the buttons down the back of her black satin dress.

"Lock the door first."

More hesitation from the seasoned maid.

"Now."

"Yes, Mum."

Rhapsody took the last deep breath she was liable to have for the rest of the day as the lock tumbled into place behind her. Then the maid resumed, yanking and pulling. Moisture popped out along Rhapsody's brow.

"Mum, I can't—"

"Tighter!"

A foot landed against her backside as the sturdy maid tugged. Rhapsody tried to relax and allow the stays to pull her smaller, but it was a battle of pain. At last the corset held and Lissy let go. Rhapsody rested against the column for just a moment, taking silent puffs of air through her nose. She pushed away and stood. "Now, my hair."

The broad servant nodded and hurried to the dressing table. A rush of fogginess crept into Rhapsody's vision, and she clutched a hand to the post. "No, you imbecile. I can't sit."

"Yes, Mum."

The maid rushed behind Rhapsody and adjusted the curls at her nape. A crisp knock brought everything to a halt.

"Rhapsody. Come."

Lissy hustled to the door and turned the key. The portly maid opened the door with an odd, perhaps sympathetic, look on her wide face.

"Mum—"

Rhapsody held up a finger. "Speak when spoken to, Lissy."

The woman nodded and cast her gaze to the floor. Rhapsody glided past. Indeed, this was perfect. A shadowy mist threatening her vision pulsated to the beat of her runaway heart. She grasped the rail with new meaning. It was her only means to safely reach the bottom of the stairway. Chin up, face emptied of the agony she carried not only beneath her corset, but in her heart.

Ah, the family milled about the entryway and spilled into the drawing room where Devlin still stiffly stood. His mother and father hovered near the casket, broken at the loss of their son. Mrs. Hastings dabbed her eyes with a fine lace hanky. She'd give anything to avoid them. Anything.

Hesitating at the bottom of the stairs, she took several shallow breaths. Why had it come to this? But she knew. Selfishness, greed, pride, conceit…she could go on, but she could barely breathe and tears threatened. Tears for all she'd lost and all she'd ruined. She glanced up for one last look. Her husband stood, propped upright in his finest silk suit, his empty gaze staring through her. Condemnation seared her soul. She squeezed her eyes shut and darkness closed in around her.

What splendid timing. Her knees buckled and the finely woven carpet runner rose up to greet her. Her left eye gave a slight twitch. Sorry, Mother. Family picture time was over. The room disappeared into a hazy, distorted blur.

Rhapsody jerked from the pungent smell of salts and fluttered her eyes open. A circle of faces hovered above her including Mother, Lissy—looking guilty, and Father, with a worried crease across his brow. So, they'd placed her on the fainting couch in the downstairs guest room. How apropos.

The tin ceiling glared at her. Someone spoke, but she only heard her memories. *Tin ceilings are meant only for parlors or dining rooms, I believe. Much too extravagant for the entire home.* Gertrude Smidely, mother's affluent neighbor, had assured her outside the church house one hot morning.

Rhapsody had been draped in her sky-blue day dress. The large hoop, multiple crinolines, and the daring dip beneath her chin garnered the attention of every male in the congregation. She remembered giving a snide tinkle of laughter. "Perhaps, but Devlin will deny me nothing."

Nothing. Except his very presence.

Someone slapped her hand.

"Rhapsody, dear, are you well?"

Again, Mother. Little had she cared a mere twenty minutes earlier. Or had it been longer than that? Had they already conducted the funeral? Buried her husband in the cold spring ground?

Rhapsody struggled to sit up. But Father, and her accessory to the crime, her corset, pressed her down.

"Lissy, run get a cold cloth." Motherly tones. Stiff and disapproving.

"Dear girl, answer me. Can you speak?"

Darling Father. At least a smidgen of sympathy had found its way into his voice.

"Yes."

The neat salt and pepper beard parted to allow a gentle smile. He looked older today.

Mother straightened. "Never mind, Lissy. Let's get her into the parlor."

Father also rose. "You can't be serious, Minerva. She's only just awakened."

However, Mother whisked away, gathering the distant males of the family to carry the entire couch into what Mother called the parlor. Rhapsody ignored the men lifting her couch and the sputtering of her father while stilling her tongue. She'd personally made sure the room was larger than a parlor. Therefore, clearly, it could only be christened a drawing room. Yet, Mother's house would never be outdone, even when the truth was in the blueprints.

"Here, here. Set her next to Devlin." Mother's voice carried a slight twinge of enjoyment, carefully veiled. How she did love to be in charge.

"No. Stop." A family photo of her on a fainting couch, reclining like some saloon wench? Indeed not. "Set me down. Immediately."

Her cousins acquiesced and lowered the chaise lounge near the door.

Mother leaned over her. "My dear. You're revived. Irvin, Gotwald, grasp her arms. Perhaps we can have a decent family photo after all."

Her two distant cousins clamped her elbows and drew her from the couch. Once standing, the dizziness threatened again. But since Mother seemed so insistent on these photos, even fainting dead away would not change the woman's mind.

Her two bodyguards remained at her side as Mother and the photographer situated everyone in their places. The men all but carried Rhapsody toward her upright, deceased husband, his blank stare encompassing the entire room and denouncing her at the same time. She pressed her eyes shut until they had rotated her away from his accusatory stare.

"And now, stand here, Mrs. Hastings. Men, can you back her up, right against her husband? That's it. Perfect."

Perfect? Nothing about this was perfect. A sob threatened to rise up her windpipe, but the corset kept it at bay. All she'd wanted was to establish her place in society, to outshine her contemporaries with a successful man by her side, a home others would envy, and a future that transcended all others.

What drivel.

The truth? She hadn't loved him. He'd only been a means to an end. She'd literally run him to the ground, and guilt lay heavier than the weight of the earth that would soon cover her pitiful, deceased husband.

At least the photographer didn't insist on crooking his hand around her arm. Still, she leaned away. What she deserved was a proper reckoning. It would serve her right if they'd wrap Devlin's arm around her neck, and he suddenly roused from his lifeless pose to squeeze the life from her.

"We need to be in haste. I feel my daughter is still quite unwell." Father, her knight.

"Yes, yes, of course. All eyes here." The photographer retreated behind the camera and pointed to the circular lens on the front.

Rhapsody lifted her chin, set her teeth, and pulled her ears back. The rushing sound simmered inside her head as the flash exploded once more. Then, a slight indention convulsed in record pace below her left eye. Miss Bickle would be horrified. Nevertheless, a slight satisfied sigh escaped Rhapsody's lips. This unpleasantness would soon be over.

As unconsciousness rose up in a black fog, she hoped above all hopes she would never awaken. For in reality, she envied Devlin. He had the pleasure of physical death while she remained nothing more than a walking cadaver.

"Pleasssse…"

The word exhaled from her as she crumpled to the floor.

Chapter Two

1854~New Albany, Indiana

Cavanaugh Blackledge scrubbed his hand through the two-week-old beard. Scruffy mess. A man nearby grabbed another chunk of wood to throw beneath the huge vat boiling the long oak planks. Even in the spring Indiana weather, with both doors open to the huge building, the fires made Cav sweat like a grave digger on a sweltering August day.

He cast his eyes out the nearby doors. Blevan's Foundry lined up on the Ohio River with Lennox's Steamboat Wharf. Down the hill, the hull of the next steamboat stood like a massive skeleton. The base carpenters would soon have the planks hammered onto the frame and the vessel lowered into the Ohio. Then the boat would press against Lennox's spacious wharf to be fitted for its steam machinery and finally its frippery, the carved salons, the costly velvet upholstery, and the imposing pilot house equipped with its mammoth steering wheel.

He appreciated the mechanics of the build. Rigorous studies of law at Yale had lent much patience and appreciation, not to the subject of choice, but to Cav's hobby interest in the dissection of the great steamers' configurations. His slant into the sciences nurtured his interest in the various phases and details of actual construction.

Given this beauty was a mighty side-wheeler, two handsome paddles, now in construction farther down the wharf, would grace the sides of the two hundred-footer. At least, that is what he'd estimated it to be.

The first two of the four decks, the main and the boiler, were already beginning to take shape in the ribs of the structure. Soon the hurricane and the Texas deck would climb the stacked ship. Of course she'd be floating by then.

Yes, he'd thought much about swapping his father's study preference for engineering. But other collegiate fascinations had stolen his attention. So now, he observed when he could. Even though he lacked the degree those in charge possessed, he'd often seen them flounder in small matters and watched boat sections topple into the water. Not that it mattered now anyway. He'd abandoned such dreams in exchange for—

"You."

He tugged his wandering mind into reality. "Yeah?"

"More wood." The soot-covered man disappeared back into the bowels of the huge building.

Cav grunted his assent. Not his job, but worth the breeze across his skin to pass on the command. The wharf towered with wood. Beech, oak, poplar, pine. Cav knew them all by touch. Perhaps he should shoot for a job with Lennox. Work his way to the top and build steamers.

But with the Blevans and Lennoxes in cahoots with respects to steamboat production, he doubted he could change his overheated employ. Rejecting one meant rejecting them both. Besides, what did it matter? In another life, he might have taken on such a company, if only for a hobby. But now, he only desired to camouflage his true activities. He would remain here while it suited him. Then move on to the next masquerade.

Cav welcomed the rush of cool air across his cheeks as he birthed through the huge doors. He pivoted toward the wood lot, a towering pile of scraps lying a hundred and fifty yards away on the bluff of the sandy bank. He motioned the nearest dark-skinned man wielding a wheelbarrow full of kindling.

With a lazy stride, Cav nodded to halt Lazarus. 'Course he dare not speak his name. Cav resurrected his clandestine accent. "Y'all bring more wood. Y'hear?"

The long-boned man bobbled his head. "Yes, Sah."

"And get yer feet stepping, boy." He earned a wink from Lazarus for his southern drawl. Brave soul. He'd get caught for sure if he didn't watch himself. Cav acknowledged with a mere swipe of his hand, as if hurrying him. "Middle furnace."

The sound of the hog chain wagon rolling across the wharf snagged Cav's focus as Lazarus rumbled away. Two workers directed the long rods toward the new boat. No doubt the introduction of hogging the side-wheeler with the long chains, thick rods that ran from bow to stern to keep the center hull from sagging in the center, would be coupled with the older design of cross chains from side to side.

He shook his head. Nothing but trifle information at this point. He'd forged a different route. One much more compelling than building steamboats. And much more dangerous. A course with far-reaching consequences that may very well change the country. At least he hoped so.

Cav tugged his attention away. His own commoner's job may be in jeopardy if he didn't get back to his station. Farlin, his partner, had the crucible red hot. Despite Cav's meanderings, he needed to step back into Hades and accomplish his current assignment. He spun and cut back to the molds.

Back at the iron winch, Cav followed his partner's hand gestures and tipped the cauldron of glowing orange liquid brass. The molten metal flowed into each of the little holes across the ten foot molds. Once they cooled, there would be twenty new steam-release knobs. The crucible righted and he stepped back. Cav wound the wench and brought it back to the furnace.

His partner jumped up. Most likely to find someone to fetch more fuel to heat the furnace. Poor Lazarus would be transporting more wood as he himself would be doing this evening. For an entirely different reason. One that had become Cav's life mission. Though it would look like he delivered wood, he would in fact be delivering freedom. The thought kicked in his adrenaline. Best to save it for tonight though, when his and others' lives would be on the line.

Moisture dripped from Cav's brow and he let out a sigh. Farlin, lucky devil. It was his turn to feel the cool breeze on his face. Working as a commoner had its disadvantages for sure. But the camouflage was necessary if he wanted to lay low. Cav turned his hope to lunch and much more important matters.

Tonight was operation night.

Cav tugged the strap on the horse's back. Number Two held out pretty well. Number One had been an old horse when he'd purchased him. Keeled over during the night in Preacher Dubber's rickety stable after a late night of transportation. Should've gone lighter on that load, he supposed. Shame to lose the old thing. But Number Two was young enough to still eye the mares on trips through town.

The horse was plain brown, which matched his unfortunate name. Nothing remarkable with this animal. And that's just the way Cav liked it. He ran his hand over the wood frame of the worn wagon bed and then cast a gaze down at his commoner's wool britches and work shirt. Average Joe. Average horse. Average farm cart. Ideal for blending in. The dark helped, too.

Tonight's load came from Louisville way. He checked under the seat. Two extra canteens, filled, and a loaf of bread. And the ever-present basket of Tiger Lilies.

He checked his load of chopped wood before boarding the wagon and steering Number Two toward the River Jordan, or in this case, the Ohio River. Time was slipping by and he couldn't allow that. Lives were at stake. Some very important baggage to pick up. Cav let out a cheerful whistle as the wagon ambled down the streets.

As the river drew nearer, he could hear the musicians at the pub nearby. He shook his head with a slight grin, glad the darkness hid the crack in his discretion. If he wasn't near on positive, he heard 'ole Lazarus singing bass.

At the back of the establishment, he halted the horse. Cav jumped to the ground, strode to the dilapidated building, and rapped on the sturdy oak at the back entry. A dark face appeared at the door.

"I gots me a load of wood," Cav intoned in his best commoner's lingo.

The man's profile nodded, eyes bespeaking his understanding. "Yes, sah. I'll gets the loaders to take care of it."

"Sure 'nuff." Cavanaugh faded back toward the wagon and kept a sharp eye on his surroundings.

The first three that came were young men. They grasped armloads of the rough wood and headed toward the light coming from the back door. The music swelled louder. Right on time. Cav dropped the tailgate. Daylight would have revealed a hidden storage area beneath the load of wood.

The stomping and hollering to the heavy beat throbbing from the pub coincided with three individuals who slipped up from the opposite direction. Slick as wet ice, three stair-stepped dark figures shimmied into the tight space. Cavanaugh whistled a meandering tune as he slipped his hand into his pocket. Before securing the back section, he tossed the red powder at the feet of his charges, and then shut and chained the gate.

He waved at the man still at the back door and yanked himself up on the wagon seat. Full darkness would be here soon. Best head on to the Knobs of freedom. His tune drifted into *Go Down, Moses.* He finished one verse and then addressed Number Two, "Forward, old nag. We've got another station to get to before the night is done."

Cav took up his tune again, knowing *forward*, *station*, and his song would help calm and reassure the precious parcels he contained in the wagon's sarcophagus.

Lord, part the waters.

"I said prepare me a buggy." Was she, Rhapsody Hastings, not mistress of her own home and the carriage house? Could she not take a phaeton out alone if she so preferred? Surely no one would perish if she were seen driving unchaperoned.

"Mum, I'd be glad to drive you wherever you'd like. It's just that—"

"I don't want or need you to drive me anywhere, Barton. I wish to be alone. Is that clear?" Rhapsody's voice mounted in shrill tones. Her eye twitched, and she squeezed her ring and pinky fingernails into the soft flesh of her hands. "And you will not summon my father on this matter. Do you understand? I'm a grown woman who can take care of herself."

The servant's head, frosted in white, nodded once, but he said no more. Not even mentioning how close it was to dusk. Actually, Rhapsody preferred eventide. Less whispers if she were seen unaccompanied. The stable hand assisted her aboard the sleek phaeton, and she tilted her chin at the rash wildness of her decision.

Once seated, the reins in hand, a thrill of power surged through her. No one, not even her father knew she'd often driven after begging and pleading her many escorts. Silly men. Besides, if she ran the horse out of control, and screamed to her last breath, would it really matter?

She flicked the leather straps onto the animal's rump, a mild brown mare. Rhapsody preferred the black stallion that Devlin had driven. That animal combined with the newest, flashiest phaeton in town had drawn the stares of envy. But a bit of wisdom pecked through her rash behavior. The mare would be adventure enough.

Nothing but open country prodded Rhapsody's mind as she guided the animal down the lane. The Knobs were not well known amongst her society friends. Mostly a place where freed slaves dwelt. Not an area she'd normally be seen in, but for decency's sake, that's where she headed. The less attention she garnered, the better.

The air gusted against her cheeks, and she closed her eyes for the joy of it. If only the events of the recent past would rush by like the breeze, far behind her, never to be seen or felt again. Her mistakes and guilt whisked away as if they had never been. All the weight of society's condolences yet hidden smirks of her current predicament, disappeared into the growing dusk.

The farther she went, the more wooded it became. The green moist tunnels of trees balmed her soul, fed her hungry heart, cleansed her mind.

"Hmmm." She sighed as the phaeton zipped on, the little brown mare's hooves striking crisp thumps on the dirt road. Wouldn't it be lovely to get lost? To be set adrift and never have to return? To be a totally new person with a new future? A smile played at her mouth, and she pressed her eyelids closed.

A jolt dashed the comforting thoughts from her mind. The phaeton shifted precariously, and the mare slowed. Rhapsody cried out, dropped the reins, and clutched the buggy seat. A scraping racket permeated her startled thoughts. The seat leaned so terribly to the left that she struggled to grab the harness leads flopping at her feet.

"Stop…stop!"

The gentle mare did indeed halt and tossed her head to glare at her.

"Oh, my." Rhapsody pressed a hand to her thumping heart and gingerly navigated herself and her stubborn hooped skirt from the cockeyed carriage.

Once she stepped away, she let out a gasp. The wheel had sheered in two. She glanced back. The other half remained a good fifty yards back. The mare again shifted her sleek neck to eye her, tossing her nose and jingling the bridle.

"Yes, yes, I know." Not certain why she spoke to the animal. Perhaps because there was no one else to blame.

"Imbeciles. I'll get rid of every one of those stable boys." She parked her hands upon her hips. What an idiot she was. She'd already dismissed everyone but Barton since Devlin's funeral. Besides, laying guilt upon the servants? How could that possibly undo this damage? She stomped the hard-pressed earth. Seemed it had always worked for her before. But right now, the rote behavior appeared childish.

She let out an unladylike growl. Miss Bickle would be quite unhappy with her behavior, which made her growl once more. Perhaps she'd picked up the habit from attending the local grammar school. Plenty of country bumpkins to stain a perfectly schooled fourteen-year-old future debutante trained at the best finishing establishment in New York. She pressed her chilled fingers to the twitching spot beneath her eye.

Enough assessments of proper behavior. Somehow she had to get back into town. Even in the slight clearing beyond the tree tunnel, the sun had obviously dipped far below the tree line. Not only that, but she hadn't seen a house in some time.

She paced up the road, arms in a tight knot. Infuriating. Devlin's face popped to mind. "Rash decisions are often relived indefinitely." He'd said it more than once. All she could think of at the time of his ridiculous quoting was applying it to her decision to marry him. Poor dull Devlin.

She sniffed, brought her chin up, and spun to pace back to the mare. Why? Why had her life slid into the slop bucket? Mother seemed to handle all the bumps in the road with a nose as stern as a rudder. Unruffled. Perhaps uncaring. But she? Seethed with anger at every turn.

She stomped. “Absolutely vexing.”

The mare snorted as if in agreeance. Then sounds echoed through the tree tunnel behind her. Could it be? Would she be so lucky that another soul would actually be out on this road? Hope soared in her heart. Yes, now this is what life should be. A series of good fortunes.

A horse and wagon came into view with a lone man in the driver’s seat. Perfect. A smile lit her face. Maybe it would have been slightly more advantageous to have a pair of gentlemen, and certainly less scandalous, but she was sure she’d be on her way in a matter of minutes.

She parked herself near the back of the phaeton as the farm wagon drove up. The man’s appearance narrowed her eyes a touch. A bear of a man, bedraggled beard and unkempt hair. No mind. They often were the easiest to convert to her will.

He slowed the cart to a stop. She noted the wood piled in the back. A common laborer. All the better.

“Howdy, Ma’am. Got some trouble do ya?”

She almost purred. Such a simpleton would soon be dancing at her feet. “Why, yes. I’ve had a bit of a mishap.”

“Your man head back to town?”

The reply set a small frown between her brows. She inhaled to erase it. “No, I’m afraid I’m unaccompanied.”

“That’s a shame.”

A shame? “Please, kind sir, I need a lift back into town, if it wouldn’t trouble you so.”

A grunt escaped him and she almost rolled her eyes. It would probably take him ten minutes to gather a thought in his jug head. “Can’t do that, Miss.”

“Pardon me?”

“Got a load to take out to the Knobs and it can’t wait.”

How dare he leave her to the dangers of the impending darkness? “Listen, Mister—”

“Valprid.”

She sniffed at being interrupted and began again. “Mr. Valprid, you surely cannot assuage your conscience by leaving a defenseless female on a lonely road at night. Have you no chivalry?”

He turned to face her full on, an elevated brow and a shrewd smile waiting at the corner of his mouth she hadn’t been quite prepared for. “Perhaps one, of a female persuasion, might avoid encountering such a quandary, should have had the forethought to have procured a driver to accompany her. One versed in the novelty of mending fragmented wheels.”

Her mouth dropped. “How dare—”

The yip of a dog cut her scornful tirade. Alas! She would not have to deal with this insolent thug. More rescuers, from the opposite direction, rounded the bend into the tunnel.

“Blast.” The man in the wagon dismounted and wedged up close. “Follow my lead,” he whispered.

Mr. Valprid leaned precariously close, and her mind struggled to catch up with his sudden change of attitude. As she stuttered-stepped backward, he reached forth to enclose her in a bear hug, effectively trapping her arms at her sides. She gasped at the assault, her words of indignation swallowed as his head dipped and his lips fastened to hers.

Chapter Three

The kiss, instead of repulsiveness, sent flaming warmth through her. The definite masculine woodsy-leather smell enveloped her, sending her into a clouded daze. His lips roamed, first firm, then softening.

She struggled a moment but he continued like a gentle caress, exploring her mouth like no other had. Certainly not Devlin. Rhapsody stilled and released any resistance, leaning into the unexpected pleasure of intimacy, enjoying the rasp of his rough beard. Floating, suspended as if in mid-air. As brusquely as it had begun, the kiss jolted to an end and the stranger wrenched from her.

The cool air of early evening on her heated cheeks prodded an awareness of reality. With a sharp intake of breath, humiliation washed over her. A complete stranger had lip-locked her. She shoved down the odd, yet pleasant sensation. What was she thinking? He'd violated her. And she'd pressed toward him. Had she lost her mind? Why hadn't she cried out? It all seemed to happen in a snap.

The next thing she knew, he'd pulled her back to his side and pressed a basket of flowers into her hands. He shoved his other hand into his pocket.

"You heathen dolt—"

His hand flew from his pocket to her cheek, and his mouth pressed on hers again. His touch was not forceful, but felt almost as if he…cared. Then the moment passed and through gritted teeth he muttered, "It's a matter of life and death."

A gurgle was all she could force from her lips with his head so close to her own. Heat seemed to blaze from his mouth. Now, intermingled with the male scent that had taken her hostage earlier, the faint smell of cayenne pepper drifted to her nose. Even in the shadows, the stranger's dark eyes bore into hers, pleading with an intelligent gleam. But what was he pleading for?

Instead of answers, he pulled from her. A lewd whistle split the air.

"Well lookey here, Smitty. A pair of lovers."

Rhapsody caught sight of the three men, hardly more than vague silhouettes. The scrape of a match cleared the dimness and grew brighter when the man on horseback touched it to a lantern's wick. He held it up to illuminate the area. The men clutched shotguns across their laps, and a string of bloodhounds on leather leashes sniffed the ground. One bayed at them, causing the others to join in the cacophony.

As peculiar as it was to be in this stranger's arms, who had not only denied her request for help, but had blatantly kissed her, something about the new arrivals made her eye twitch.

"Shuddup, ya idjits." The floppy-hatted man's reprimand quieted the jumpy dogs. "There ain't no darkies."

Even through the haze of ambiguity, Rhapsody recognized slave hunters. She was sure her father had dealt with these men before. Mr. Bowles? Yes, she was sure that was the heavyset man's name who seemed to take the lead.

"Sorry fellas. You surprised us." The slight tremor in Mr. Valprid's arm suggested otherwise.

Bowles guffawed. "Well, what do we got here, Smitty? Ain't that Mr. Lennox's daughter? Devlin Hastings' widow? Gutsy young buck, you are. Wouldn't be good for her pa to spot ya." The other two laughed as if he'd shared a witty joke.

Something shrank and died in Rhapsody. Caught on a road, distant from town, in a tryst with a scruffy man. Devlin had been right. Rash decisions were often relived indefinitely.

Above all, ladies, you must always, always appear chaste, unblemished from wagging and prattling tongues. Oh, Miss Bickle, why had you appeared amongst this mayhem? Devlin's quotes were more than enough.

"It's not like that at all. This is my fiancée…"

Rhapsody's tongue could only let out a slight squeak as Mr. Valprid continued.

"We haven't announced it yet, but we're merely waiting for her mourning time to pass. You know how it is, don't you boys?"

As he spoke he eased Rhapsody forward, toward the sniffing dogs. Fear of the huge animals sent all alarms of her tarnished reputation to the wind.

Again, raucous laughter. “Oh, we know.”

The one named Smitty, the slender one, held up the lantern and leaned closer. His eyes worked their way down her body. She shivered and Mr. Valprid’s arm tightened. A snuff brought her head down. The dogs had their noses in the flower basket she held.

“Oh.” A startled exclamation broke from her frozen lips.

“Don’t you mind there, pretty thing. Them dogs got a mind to sniff ever’thing. They won’t hurt ya.” Bowles grinned and then spat tobacco. “That is, unless we tell ’em to.”

He, Smitty, and the third man who spoke not, snickered.

“Well, we’d appreciate it if you’d keep this under your hat. We haven’t even broken the news to her folks.”

“Them things have a way of getting around before you want it, eh?” Mr. Bowles, his sweat-stained clothes visible even by lantern light, relaxed back in his saddle. “We’re just out prowling for runaways. Ya ain’t seen none has ya?”

Mr. Valprid stepped forward, brought a hand up, and rubbed his knuckles against his beard. Then, he seemed to think better of it and yanked his hand away. The smell of cayenne returned to Rhapsody’s nose.

The rest of the dogs plunged their noses into the flowers, and Rhapsody stifled a shriek. She huddled toward Mr. Valprid and pressed her head against his shoulder. The sturdy stranger next to her was much preferred to the teeth and claws of the powerful snapping hounds. What if those creatures decided to latch onto her? The deep resonance of the stranger's voice vibrated against her cheek.

"Nice visiting with you gents. Sorry we couldn't be of more help."

"Reckon we'd best be pressing on and let you two commence the smooching."

Rhapsody elicited a fearful cry when the two men wrestled the lunging dogs' muzzles from her bouquet. She waited only a few moments as the slave catchers meandered on their way before she launched away from the crazy stranger. Oh. He. Would. Be. Sorry.

A sound slap caught Cavanaugh squinting at the darkness. Fire and lightning lit through his right eye.

"Mr. Valprid, how dare you manhandle me? I'll have you incarcerated for your blatant attack on my reputation as a lady."

He brought his cayenne-free hand up to rub his cheek. "Man, you pack a punch."

"You had no right whatsoever to—to—"

"Smooch you?" The humor he inserted into his reply didn't keep him from seeing her fists form in the darkness.

"Those derelicts will saunter into town and tell my father what they saw. You have ruined my honor. I'll be the scandal of society, shunned and whispered about. Not fit for proper associations. And then to tell them we're betrothed…"

She spun and marched toward her phaeton.

"Ma'am, I assure you it was for good reason."

She flew out from behind the dilapidated carriage. "Good reason? Is there any such thing?"

Her hand flashed forward once more, and he captured her wrist before it made contact once again. He'd overstepped his bounds for sure, but he wouldn't take another slap because of it. Cav held her easily as she panted in rage.

"Let's get back to our original conversation. Since I cannot take you back to town, you'll have to accompany me."

"What?" She snatched her hand from him. "Are you insane? You've already made me a scourge of society and now you intend to kidnap me?"

He liked her. Even in the precarious moment of nearly being discovered, Cavanaugh couldn't help but admire her spunk. She could be quite useful indeed. It wasn't how he wanted to conduct the operation, but perhaps this was providence staring him in the face. Or slapping him in the face as the case was. A late night romantic rendezvous? What better cover was there? The fiancée fabrication was probably a bit over the top, but it couldn't be helped. He couldn't risk any trouble with the catchers.

"Ma'am, I will return you to the city, safe and sound, I assure you. But first I must make a delivery."

He clutched her arm and pulled her toward the wagon.

The woman set her heels. "I refuse to accompany you."

She tugged and tugged until he was sure she'd dislodge her shoulder. Her other hand flew up and swatted at him. The fiery thing got in a few good smacks before he snagged her other arm. Then a stomp to his foot. Instead of howling in pain, he gritted his teeth and bent to flop her over his shoulder. She beat at his back.

"Let me go, you oaf. Help, help!"

He slung her to the wagon seat and captured her flying hands. Quite a feat in the dark. "If you'll just hold still, we can get underway."

"Never."

"I promise I won't hurt you."

"I—"

A sneeze interrupted their tussle. The woman's head pivoted back and forth. "Who's there?"

"We've got to go." He heaved himself up on the seat and slid her over. "Just trust me? Please."

For once she held her peace and seemed to settle, yet her gaze searched the darkness to identify the author of the sneeze who must lay hidden somewhere in the wagon. Still, he kept her in the corner of his eyes. In the darkness, she could easily cold-cock him out of the seat. And knowing her fierce disposition, he wouldn't put it past her.

"I think I hear someone crying," she whispered, laying a hand on his arm.

He heard it, too. His cargo needed to work on being incognito if they were to make it to safety. "Just your imagination."

He could tell she glared at him, but he kept Number Two moving. A little faster than he should. Those slave hunters had been too close for comfort.

In the distance, Pastor Dubber's home was a sight for sore eyes. The lantern hung on a pole near the front porch of the dilapidated cabin. Good. These parcels needed gentle protection. He jumped down, fetched the lantern, and pulled around back. When he dismounted a second time, he patted the wagon. "All clear."

That should give the hidden parcels some courage. Soon they would be fed, housed, and safe. For now, anyway. The back door to the shamble shack opened. There stood Pastor Dubber, a large man with big hands, clutching his door.

"Who's there?"

Cavanaugh smiled as he fiddled with the wood. "A friend of a friend."

That fired up the old man. He came loping through the yard. "Zat you, Mr. Cav?"

"The wind's blowing from the south today, wouldn't you say, Pastor Dubber?"

His voice came strong, full of hope. "Yes, sah. Right fine breeze."

And then his well-kissed, counterfeit fiancée was there. Standing between him and the pastor.

"Mr. Cav?" Her head took a jaunty tilt, and her voice carried more than a hint of censure.

How to explain to the preacher that he carried more than three escaping slaves? He knew no memorized codes for an untrusted friend.

"Sorry, Pastor. Picked up a stray on my way." He glanced toward her in the lantern light. Mrs. Hastings, was it? Handsome woman, given this was the first time he'd gotten a good look at her. Blond hair, maybe green eyes? He couldn't tell in the low light. She was decked to the nines with a black silk dress and gloves, hair encased in a lace cover. "You can wait in the wagon seat."

She tightened her crossed arms. "I'll wait right here."

His mouth twitched. Cussed stubbornness right there. "As you wish. Where do you want the wood, Pastor?"

"Tonight, might be best if'n you piled it near the shed."

With a nod Cav couldn't help but throw out a jab. "You up for helping, Ma'am?"

Her eyes narrowed in the lantern light. "You accost me and then think I'll resort to servant's chores?"

Cav glanced at the good preacher. "Then you might step back."

With a sniff, she spun and strode into the darkness. Cav hurried to the back and unlatched the back gate. Dubber hung the lantern on the wagon's hook, stepped forward, and pulled the three from the bottom of the woodpile. He glimpsed a flash of tears on the youngest face. Dubber wrapped his arms around them and rushed them toward the barn.

"What's going on here?" His unwanted hitchhiker stepped forward, eyeing the four as they disappeared inside.

He grabbed some wood. "Unloading."

She scampered after him as he flung the wood to a growing pile near the shed. "No, those people. They're escaped slav—"

A huge hand engulfed her mouth as he grabbed her. Mr. Valprid, or was it Mr. Cav, leaned into her ear. "You should have stayed in the wagon seat."

His gruff growl stilled her struggles. She would never outlast the man's strength. And escaped slaves? What had she gotten herself into?

"Now, I will let you go, if you promise to be calm. Got it?"

She nodded. He stepped away, watching her, as if she'd bolt like an untrained colt. Rhapsody heaved a breath and studied him. "That's why you kissed me."

"Yes."

"And why you smell like cayenne pepper."

"Again, correct."

Well, at least he didn't try to lie again. But there was still the uncertainty about his name. She let her eyes travel down him. Disheveled clothing, suspenders, work boots—yet a keenness shone bright in his eye. "Are you going to…ravish me?"

"No."

A trickle of relief oozed through her while anger mounted. "I could report you. Call those slave hunters back. My father's a powerful man."

His beard shifted slightly as if he clenched his jaw. "You've got bigger fish to fry."

Rhapsody's saucy attitude took a dive. Her dignity had been compromised, and he clearly understood the ramifications. "Thanks to you."

He shrugged. "I suggest we discuss a satisfactory solution as I drive you back into town."

"That's just it, Mr. Valprid or should I say, Mr. Cav? There is no satisfactory solution. The damage has been done."

Cav moved to snag the lantern from the back of the wagon, seemingly uncaring that her very life hung in the balance. "Here, hold this."

Why she took it, she had no clear idea. He shut the back gate on the wagon and retrieved the lantern from her hands. "May I assist you into the seat, Mrs. Hastings?"

Curse Mr. Bowles for mentioning her name. Chin aloft, she allowed him to lift her to the wagon's bench. Then he was next to her again. This was absolutely the most preposterous thing she'd ever been involved in.

The wagon circled the shack, and her escort stopped to rehang the lantern on a pole. Then he set a basket on the front stoop before heading back. Soon they were retracing their journey. They came abreast of her wrecked carriage, and he pulled back on the reins to halt the animal's progress.

"I'm just going to unharness the mare. No sense in her standing out here all night."

With the horse fastened to the back, Mr. Valprid jumped back in control of the wagon.

"Well, I hear no remedy for the fix I am in. And no apologies, as well."

He harrumphed next to her. "I do apologize, Mrs. Hastings. I, in no way, intended to include you on my journey this evening."

She almost indulged in an unladylike eye roll. “That is not what I am insinuating. I am referring to your outlandish vulgar behavior.”

An actual laugh popped from him. “I do apologize for overstepping my bounds as a gentleman. But it was, indeed, necessary.”

She snorted. Her hands flung to her face. How unseemly. And in mixed company. How had such a noise escaped her lips?

A muttered chuckle met her ears. “Mrs. Hastings, as much as your appearance may have thwarted my excursion this evening, it’s been a delight to encounter you.”

“Stop insulting me.”

“No, no. Certainly not an insult. I’ve enjoyed the tussle, so to speak.”

She glued her mouth shut on his choice of words. But, sadly enough, he wasn’t finished speaking.

“Seldom do I meet a woman who throws off the constraints of society to be who she really is. And I truly have enjoyed it.”

There hadn’t been too many times when Rhapsody had met her match in wits nor been complimented for her impulsive, brash behavior. But Mr. Valprid seemed quite adept at both, countering her while appreciating her impetuous nature, a personality quirk—or perhaps flaw—that Miss Bickle had failed to completely stamp out. And, apparently, this man relished the task. It bled a peculiar sensation in her middle.

He wove through town at her wordless directions and set the brake once parked next to Rhapsody’s house. A whistle emanated from her companion. Her house, a silent, regal sentinel, set off a welcoming air with the lanterns at each window. Yet, the carriage perched at the curb argued the point of a pleasurable welcome. Her parents awaited inside.

She gripped the seat, pushing away the desire to grab the reins and urge the horse to disappear into the night. Perhaps Mr. Valprid, or whoever he was, was a preferable distraction compared to a late-night clash with Mother and Father.

The stranger circled the wagon and reached up to hand her down. "Perhaps you have company?"

A gasp caught in her throat. Mother stood at the entry. She never answered the door. 'Twas beneath her. Rhapsody's shoulders stiffened and she tipped up her chin. Both her pinky and ring fingernail gouged her palm.

"Mrs. Hastings?"

She turned to her companion, noting the question that hung in his gaze. "Yes?"

"Are you quite all right?"

"My parents are here. I—" She stopped. No use explaining. Now, she'd face the thrashing that awaited her in the drawing room. Perhaps just a parlor to a woman scorned.

"Ah, excellent. I'll accompany you."

Excellent? Her jumbled brain could not decipher any excellence in the last couple of hours let alone facing her parents in a duel to the death. Mr. Valprid lifted his elbow as if dressed in an expensive suit and escorted her to the door. Mother met them there, the wedge of her angry face raking them both.

The house was awash in light as if she were entertaining. But Father stood within, grim-faced, with his attorney nearby. Perfect, he'd brought reinforcements.

"Explain yourself, young woman." Father's voice held an edge of contempt, his broad chest swollen in indignation below his frothy silk cravat. "Are you aware I've bounty hunters at my front step only moments ago, spilling news of your indiscretion?"

Cav bowed beside her. "A thousand apologies, sir. I bear the sole responsibility. She has behaved with the utmost chaste manner."

No matter how Rhapsody tried, she couldn't open her mouth.

Her father's flushed face swung to render his withering gaze at her companion. "I have no knowledge of who you are and what you are doing with my daughter."

"I, sir…"

Rhapsody both felt and heard the weighted sigh that left Mr. Valprid's chest as he forced a well-practiced smile to his face.

"…am the man who is going to marry her."

Chapter Four

A curse flew from her father's lips and Rhapsody froze. "Indeed you will. You have ruined the status of this family and my business." Father's gaze scoured her companion. "Unfortunately, you appear unfit to wed my only daughter, Rhapsody Marie Lennox Hastings."

Thoughts raced through Rhapsody's brain. Father was name-dropping. If she thought her life had left the rails before, she'd just now had a head-on crash.

"Please forgive my attire. I was working with my thoroughbreds. Allow me to introduce myself. I'm Cavanaugh Blackledge." He extended his hand.

Rhapsody blinked and lined her teeth in perfect order to check the reaction she wanted to express. *Grace…at all costs.*

And, she feared, this was going to cost a great deal.

"Blackledge, you say?" Father's lawyer, Tavin Lockwood, stepped forward and clutched his hand. "Of the Judge Blackledge family perchance?"

"The same."

Any noise in the room snuffed out. And Rhapsody's gatecrashing family immobilized into tree trunks. That is, until a smile meandered across Mr. Lockwood's face at the very same time her father's brows endeavored to reach his hairline. She, herself, restrained another unladylike noise that started somewhere in the pit of her stomach, which now rolled like a carriage wheel.

Mr. Valpid, or rather Mr. Cav, was Cavanaugh Blackledge? But she had lost track of the conversation given her mother's continued glare. The only one of her guests who remained quite unimpressed with her ill-dressed companion.

"—for an acceptable date. It need be soon, to avoid the damage of the gossip mongers, but not too soon, as it were, to avoid feeding speculations of this—rendezvous—if you approve, Mr. Lennox?"

Rhapsody watched her father nod.

"I am in total agreeance. We were merely waiting for an opportune time to announce our news—"

"Yet you did not wait." Mother materialized from her marginal stance at the edge of the room.

Cavanaugh Blackledge didn't hesitate a moment. "Hence why Rhapsody and I thought our rendezvous the perfect tactic to speed the marriage process."

Ignoring her faux financé's well-timed smile, her mother shifted her icy glare. Rhapsody lifted her chin and bore her glacial contempt. Any conceived story to survive her mother's exacting revenge would be embraced. Cavanaugh's hand slid around her waist before he spoke.

"Mrs. Lennox, could you deny your daughter radiates beauty and elegance? Given her splendid parentage, it's no surprise that even a sworn bachelor as myself wouldn't—couldn't—forgo her charms." Her companion tightened his hold on her.

Oh my, he laid it on thick. Mother's eyes narrowed only slightly before sliding to Rhapsody once more. "Nevertheless, it could have been handled in a much more appropriate manner. Rhapsody has only been widowed a little more than a year."

Cav nodded. Ahhh. One more vital piece to the puzzle. He inclined his head, feeling the stiffness of the woman at his side. She'd uttered not a word since entering the house. "I sympathize with your point, Mrs. Lennox, and apologize for any embarrassment I may have brought unto the family's name. But I can assure you, our meeting was quite chaste in our attempt to conceal our courtship."

But Mrs. Lennox refused to let go of the bone she gnawed on and stepped forward. "Requesting the right to court, Mr. Blackledge, should have been addressed to her father. Preferably in a year or two in the future."

Cav let a smile curve his mouth and a brow arch. "And therein lies the problem."

Rhapsody's mother inhaled so swiftly her nostrils squeezed in. Cav could sense her digging deeper to confront him once more, but Mr. Lennox cut in.

"My dear, it's much too late to mince words with Mr. Blackledge. Too late in terms of time of day and too late in the sense of propriety. I, therefore, believe since the details are yet to be reckoned with this binding oral agreement, we should take our leave for the evening and revisit the subject tomorrow."

"I so concur." Tavin Lockwood arose, collected his coat that had been slung to the leather Chesterfield, and took up his briefcase. "I will be in touch with your father."

Cav nodded. Mr. Lennox drew his and his wife's scattered jacket and shawl from the brocade chair near the fireplace. Indeed the disaster of the night could be read even in where the staunch family had discarded their outerwear.

He kept a tight hold on his companion as she made no move to extricate herself. Which rather surprised him. The feistiness he'd witnessed on the quiet dirt road was all but non-existent inside this house. At least he felt assured she could keep his clandestine operation confidential.

The three stepped to the door and Cav pressed Rhapsody forward until they stood on the porch. The trio marched to the family's carriage perched on the curb. Mr. Lennox secured his wife inside and then stood on the sidewalk conversing in low tones. Ah. They waited for his departure. Indeed. He must seem like a complete dolt as a suitor. To the right Cav turned the woman stuck tight to his side to backtrack his path to the driveway, thankfully parked at a right angle to her parents' sleek carriage.

"Would you walk me to my wagon, Mrs. Hastings?"

"I'd rather throw you into it, my dear sir."

He let a low chuckle emerge. There she was. "Well, Mrs. Hastings. It has been my great privilege, as a chivalrous gentleman, to escort a defenseless female, as yourself, safely home."

"Rot in—"

"Now, now, my dear fiancée, it is terribly late," he hesitated next to the wagon, "And I'm sure the shock appearance of your dear family members and loyal attorney has all but exhausted you. But let's not let our language get out of control."

As if waking from a nightmare, he could feel her seething beneath his arm, and she pulled from him. Her fists went to her hips and she squared up to him. "If you think I would marry the likes of you, Cavanaugh Blackledge, you are very much mis—"

His lips smothered the rest of the sentence. It was the only way he could think of to shut her up. He'd had such success with this maneuver earlier, he knew it was his best option. And he wouldn't deny he enjoyed her soft lips and shapely body that swayed toward him just a tad. But he kept his wits and held onto her wrists as he pulled her toward him. What he didn't expect was her trembling body.

A bit of remorse scraped at him. "Are you well, Mrs. Hastings?"

Only a pause before she answered. "I am fine. And I will be even better when you drive away."

"Then I shall oblige." He nodded, a smile returning to his face. "Au revoir, Madame."

"Bon débarras, Mr. Blackledge."

He let a low laugh trickle out. Good riddance? She didn't know the half of what was to happen. Their lives would now be changed forever.

Rhapsody watched both the departing carriage as well as Mr. Blackledge's farm wagon, splicing into two different directions. What had happened, she could barely comprehend. Did her lips indeed have knowledge of that stranger's kiss? Had her father been proposing a marriage arrangement as she had drifted in a stupor? She closed the front door and secured it.

Mabel, her maid, drifted in from the back of the house, wringing her hands, her dark face in a scrunch. "Ma'am?"

Rhapsody took a deep breath, ready to construct some sort of story that would send the usually mindful maid back to her servants' quarters. But her mind replayed the hunched figures scurrying toward the pastor's barn. Escaping slaves. Running from a miserable life? Rhapsody understood more about that than she cared to admit.

With new understanding, she leaned against the pillar of the entryway and let her body slump. She turned her head to study the ebony-skinned woman. Tall, gangly, cooking genius in those big hands, and a sleepy softness to her gaze. What must it be like to be ordered about one's entire life? To have no pleasure to plan a lifetime of dreams? To merely be at the beck and call of a superior? And then, to die. A new ache started deep within Rhapsody, knowing she and Mabel were more alike than either would ever fully explore.

Mabel had the wretched task of answering the door to find her livid parents this night. No doubt they'd been demanding, callous, uncaring in their hunt for retribution. Cruel. In her mind she imagined Mabel scurrying around to light the lamps, responding to demanding questions she didn't know the answers to.

And now, all the lights but one near the stairway had been blown out, casting the room in shadow. Another task done yet unappreciated. Tiredness soaked to the marrow of Rhapsody's very bones. A strange twist made her stomach cringe.

"It's nothing, Mabel," she whispered, "you may go back to bed."

The woman stood only a moment before bobbing her head. Then she turned to complete the task her mistress had bade her. And such was life.

Once the room was empty, Rhapsody wrapped her arm around the pillar and pressed her forehead to the white wood. Blackledge, a name that tumbled about Louisville high society, had secretly assisted runaways. The same Blackledge had kissed her. Not once but three times. And now, nothing seemed the same.

She tiptoed to the stairway and took the lantern from the table. With a glance around her opulent drawing room, she turned away and crept up the stairs.

Cavanaugh stared at his father, wondering at the fact the man had taken twenty minutes from his busy schedule to bother with him.

"He was quite wroth, son. What in the Dickens occurred?"

"'Twas a slight indiscretion. A mere kiss. Nothing more."

Only, a lot more.

His father robed in black stood to pace his quarters. Surely the man had a trial to judge beyond the massive cherry door? "Could you not control your urges, dear boy? It's likened unto a workman of the lower crust. Surely my offspring has a tighter rein on his bodily impulses."

Lawd, as Lazarus would say like a short breath of prayer. Cav kept his hands clutched behind his back, feet spread apart in an intimidating stance. His stalwart father seemed forgetful of his own feminine indiscretions, which made Cav grit his jaw. To be thrown in among the courtesan-exploiting, powerful ruling class of the city appalled him.

"No matter." His father paused at the long window and gazed down at the downtown melee of Louisville. "These things have a way of being expunged."

No doubt. "I intend to marry her."

Judge Blackledge's cotton-haired head swung so quickly, the loose skin beneath his chin quivered. "Don't be mad, Cavanaugh. You barely know the wench."

“She’s heir to the Lennox Steamboat Works, dear Father. It would be a bold and wise union.” Disgust filled Cav’s belly to bend so low as to throw the financial benefits at his father’s feet. It cheapened the woman who shook in her shoes merely a week past. And he despised the image he wove for his father’s benefit. Because for some reason, Cav had taken a shine to Rhapsody Lennox Hastings. And he would speak his father’s language to make the marriage happen. Though, if he had any sense, he ought to run in the opposite direction.

White, cloudlike brows mounted in his father’s wrinkled head. “Interesting. Though, steamers are sure to find their demise soon. Bigger faster transportation has commenced to inroad America. Soon the nation will be crisscrossed with railroads. Businesses will boom. And that is the future.”

Cav merely inclined his head, noting how the subject of female entanglement slid off the page to converse of business. Pray Jesus he didn’t have to witness yet another clandestine lecture on the future of American freighting. “Nevertheless, Mr. Lennox seems to have padded his bank accounts nicely as of now. And he is nearly as shrewd as you, Father. I’m sure his investments will keep pace with advancements in transportation.”

His father huffed. “Fallen to flattery, lad? My, you’ve learned well from your mother.”

A small smile tucked in the corner of Cav’s mouth. Wise to keep still. Father’s time was surely up.

"I must go. Murder trial, you know. That's all I can say. Final arguments await me beyond the door. Do what you must. I dare say you will despite my reservations. As you were."

Cav nodded briskly to his father's typical military dismissal as the older man strode to the door.

"All rise," echoed in the chamber beyond.

Excellent. Full steam ahead. If he knew his father, the matter had already dropped from his mind.

He took the other mammoth wooden door and stepped into the echoing marble tiled hall. This strange little distraction worked perfectly for Cav. The woman would merely be a carefully constructed cover for his Underground Railroad operation. Why, even his astute father, steeped in the intricacies of the law, educated in the best universities, wouldn't even suspect him of journeying slaves to freedom.

He grinned. He couldn't help it. Leaving college and facing his father's condemnation and ostracizing manner were all worth it. He rubbed his jaw, already heavily shadowed with whiskers even though he'd shaven clean this morning in anticipation of this meeting.

There remained now only the woman herself. Yet, he didn't think it would take much convincing to navigate her into his plans. As his assistant at the bank had told him earlier today, the woman had become a recluse since the death of her first husband just a year ago. She'd spurned a farmer and married the accountant of her father's firm. Then she had proceeded to build the most stunning, albeit, expensive mansion in New Albany.

No husband. No money. Oh, sure she could get by with the handouts of her wealthy father. However, the chilly reception between Mrs. Hastings and her parental counterparts meant he could capitalize on that if need be.

His smile faded. Maybe he'd become more like his father than he'd like to think. Using people for his own purposes. When it suited.

He paused, his hand affixed to the stair railing at the limestone steps leading out of the courthouse. But there were lives at stake. Some things, and more sadly some beings, must be sacrificed in the betterment of mankind. His thoughts went to old Samby, his family's old carriage house slave. The poor man was so steeped in fear of white men, it had pained Cav deep inside. The uncertain light in the old man's eyes. The constant acquiescent attitude as he fetched the horses, cleaned the tack, leathered the horses. All while being belittled by those in authority.

His old friend. The only one who'd shown him a bit of patience. Kindness. And dreadful, long-suffering. He'd died and been disposed of like some old carriage horse, buried on the back side of the property without even a grave marker. Not one person had spoken of him again.

Cav's jaw clamped. Since then, his mission had become an emancipator of the oppressed. Why his father, versed in every law of the land, could be so blind to the collection of atrocities toward slaves was beyond him. Only that his father, like Samby on the opposite end of the gamut, had fissured, even embraced slavery of another human into an acceptable cultural norm. As repellent as the idea was to Cav, it revealed an inequality in a nation who prided itself on the exact opposite. And that could not continue. Not while he had breath within his body.

Cav rumbled his feet to the bottom of the of stairs and strode toward his horse. Well, he would happily sacrifice one woman's happiness as well as his own to allow his work to level the field of liberty for all people. Regardless of color.

And next to persuading the nation to accept the literal truth of liberty for all, convincing Mrs. Hastings to marry him would be a snap.

Chapter Five

"Marriage?" Rhapsody's mouth hung open like a choking goat. But she couldn't seem to fasten herself back into proper society mode. "Why it will be a cold day in—"

"Rhapsody Redemption." Her mother interrupted in a steely voice. "You will watch your manners."

Manners are the framework of grace. They must be impeccable. Rhapsody was beginning to resent Miss Bickle very much. She shoved memories of the severe matron and her trite maxims to the back of her mind.

For, more importantly, Mother had used her confidential middle name. One no one spoke of. Ever. And the only reason she knew was due to the document lying on her father's desk as she'd fetched his letter opener many years ago. The conversation following had seemed to go much like this one. Only Rhapsody had only been fourteen then. And the name had been sealed into the bulging invisible trunk of what not to say at dinner parties. Or anywhere.

"Why did you call me that?" She refused to ignore her mother's gaff.

Her mother lifted her chin. "Because when you act so uncivilized, I begin to believe you are a different child altogether."

"I'm not a child at all, and I refuse to marry that…that ruffian."

Mother stepped forward, her height a decided advantage, her black eyes snapping with controlled anger. "You will not bring shame to the family name. Is that clear? I will not socialize in high society and be witness to the scandalous gossip of a trollop that is my own daughter. You will marry Mr. Cavanaugh Blackledge. Your tryst in the darkened woods while unescorted made the decision clear for you. Do you understand?"

A need to scream grasped Rhapsody's entire body, trembling with exertion to hold it in. "Yes, dear Mother."

The two stood facing off a moment longer, for Rhapsody's answer bled with contempt.

Her mother spun on her heel. "I'll make all the arrangements. It will be a small affair, no pun intended."

Rhapsody dug her ring and pinky fingers deep into the flesh of her palms. She only hoped the blood that dripped would go unnoticed. Not that Mother would sympathize anyway. Besides, the real hemorrhage always stayed buried deep inside Rhapsody's soul.

Mabel's eyes widened as her mother approached the door. The servant handed Mrs. Lennox her shawl, but she wasn't done roasting her daughter. "I despise speaking of the base, but

Rhapsody, financially you have no recourse. Your father and I have no intention of funding all of this." Her hand indicated the huge drawing room. "Therefore, if nothing else, your Mr. Blackledge will be beneficial in that task."

The woman allowed the servant to wrap the dark wool scarf around her neck, and Mabel creaked the door open. Her mother lifted one finger. "Listen carefully, daughter. No more flitting about town. Or the next man you kiss may surely be a frog."

She stepped forward with a glare that could wilt flowers at five paces. "This marriage will be the apex of your life. It will be successful, fruitful, and proper. You will treat it as such. If anything scandalous occurs, I will disown you. Understood? Good day."

The door clicked closed on her mother's departure. Mabel scurried to parts unknown, leaving the room echoing in her mother's threats.

So, this was Rhapsody's punishment. A riptide of returning deeds as dreadful as the ones she had dished out. The guilt of her husband's untimely death, the last-minute spurning of another suitor before him. How would she bear the overwhelming weight of her vindictive life sentence?

The shriek, like a feral banshee whirling in her lungs, rose higher up her windpipe. Rhapsody rushed to the stairs. Yes, rushed, clearly ignoring how *Sedateness breeds ladylike refinement.* Curse Miss Bickle's axioms. She'd never rushed anywhere.

But if she couldn't scream very, very soon, she would begin destroying everything within reach until her hands were bloody.

She sped up the stairs. The statue of a genteel garden visitor mocked her speed. With a growl, Rhapsody slapped the delicate figurine and flung it shattering down the stairway.

She flew through the hand-carved doorway of her master bedroom, slammed it closed, grabbed a pillow, and screamed into it until she was exhausted and her throat grew raw. The black fogginess that had greeted her the day of the macabre family photos, her deceased husband's hand perched on her shoulder, rose up to greet her.

Rhapsody welcomed the swoon with relief. Finally, she would have a few moments of reprieve. No mother, no guilt, no impending, reputation-saving marriage. No… All thoughts ticked one by one from her mind.

Slowly she crumpled to the floor.

"You may kiss your bride."

Cav turned toward the thin statue at his left. A veil, several layers thick had shielded Rhapsody's face from him for the entire ceremony. Not that it mattered. Although he hadn't spoken to her since the night he kissed her six weeks ago, the arrangements had been nicely welded together by lawyers and assistants between the two families.

So, it greeted Cav with some surprise to lift the white shimmering shroud to find tears glistening in her baby blue eyes. Drat, if it didn't cause him some pause, which could be construed as a point of notice by the few who had gathered in what now, was his parlor. Nevertheless, he lowered his lips to her stiff ones. He stayed long enough to coerce her mouth to soften and then he broke away. Cav had but a glance at one tear spilling from her eye before she hastened the veil down over her face once more. He had no more time to contemplate the scene before the minister cupped his shoulder to turn them about.

"May I present Mr. and Mrs. Cavanaugh Blackledge."

The smattering of applause about the room that had been altered to resemble a chapel was of the politest type. For only near relatives and a few close family friends had attended. Most notably, was the lack of a girlish tribe to gush with the bride over such an event. Cav stored all these tidbits of knowledge in the back of his mind. Meanwhile, his father's lawyer approached with a smirk of amusement on his face.

He slapped Cav on the shoulder. "Congratulations, you old rake. Someone finally landed you."

As always. Way too informal. The only reason he remained his father's lawyer was a long-ago boyhood connection. Wilber Patton lived a life of blessed peace and seemed to revel in Cav's supposed escapades with great pleasure.

The gangly man with slightly bulging eyes leaned in. "I believe she's a looker. At least has all the right curves in all the right places, know what I mean?"

A simpleton could have deciphered his meaning. Thankfully, Rhapsody had evaporated from his side to nether regions. Cav just smiled because it was the expected response. He shook the man's hand and then milled about toward other connections in the room. A male servant wove his way through the crowd and stopped in front of Cav with a bow.

"Yes?"

"Your presence is needed in the library, sir. The photographer wishes to take the wedding photo."

He nodded. Excellent. No time wasted and he liked that. Wedding, photography, meal. Complete. At least it had been well planned. He followed the servant through the hallways of his yet unexplored home.

In the library, Mrs. Lennox pulled the veil from Rhapsody's head and snapped her fingers at a large-boned lady's maid to tame his bride's hair. Then, he stood beside the woman he'd just married. The photographer had them link hands and turn three-quarters of the way toward him. Not once did Rhapsody meet his gaze.

Flash. Now the family. Flash, flash. Soon the wedding party dismantled and headed to the meal. Cav trailed the family into one of the biggest dining halls he'd ever graced. The long ebony table, adorned with lace and silver, could have easily seated thirty people. As there were slightly more, a smaller table sat near the bay window with chairs only on the back side. This is where the servant guided him along with Rhapsody and their respective parents on either side.

Her father rose and took up a wine glass and smote it with his fork. "Here, here. I propose a toast."

Everyone raised their glasses. “To the couple. Many prosperous years.”

A bit short and very uninspiring but at least to the point. Cav feigned a smile, raised a glass, and pressed the liquid to his lips without taking a drink. He flicked his eyes to his bride to ensure the audience in attendance saw his false affection. To his surprise, she seemed to forgo a swig of alcohol as well. Interesting. Either she was a teetotaler as he was, or she refused to comply with the compulsory salute. He thought probably the last, given the steely gleam in her eye.

The afternoon passed with great sluggishness. Cav could feel his usual tolerance wearing thin. First the friends and associates left and then the parents dawdled near the door, discussing politics and investments. With a handshake to Rhapsody’s father and a nod from his own, the men wandered through the door, still talking stocks.

His mother, a glowing example of a properly reared woman, dressed in a flowing gown of plum, nodded and clutched Mrs. Lennox’s hands. Mrs. Lennox, slightly less miffed than the night of the indiscretion, still seemed molded of brittle steel, acknowledging but not smiling. Odd that the dark-haired woman contrasted against the pale beauty of her daughter. There seemed no similarities between the two women.

His mother broke away, blessed him with a smile, and embraced him. “I’m so pleased you’ve made your match at last, Cav. I’m thrilled to accept your beautiful bride into our family.”

And no doubt she meant it. In her own way.

She then leaned into Rhapsody, with a suitable hug. “Take care of my son. He will be good to you.”

Rhapsody bobbed her head. Then Mother swept from the room in all her charm. Cav let a grin tuck in the corner of his mouth. His mother proved always to be the pivot in every room. Mrs. Lennox merely blinked at both of them like a dash of cold water and then focused her attention on Rhapsody.

“Remember what I’ve said.”

And then the woman whisked from the room. A small sigh escaped his new wife, and she drew up a hand to cover her mouth. Then her hands were flung to her sides. The servant closed the door, and Rhapsody swept past him and climbed the stairs in lady’s fine fashion. Cav scraped a hand down a chin already bristled with whiskers.

Pausing only a second, he followed her with a soft step. She proceeded down the long hallway and reached for the knob before realizing his presence behind her.

She jumped and pressed a hand to her breast. “How dare you follow me?”

He treaded closer, pushed a hand into one pocket, and rested his shoulder against the wall. “Well, it is our wedding night.”

Her mouth popped open. “You sir, are a corrupt, vile, immoral being. If you think for one moment that I would welcome you into my boudoir for a romp to satisfy your masculine urges, you can think again.”

My, she was gorgeous when fired up. And truly, she nearly burst the seams of that becoming green gown with her rage. And although he'd been quite the flirt, romping hadn't been in his cards lately. Yet taming her amidst the bedcovers did have a certain lure.

"Romp?" He let a chuckle escape. He drew closer and her eyes grew wide. He found himself drawn to the proper woman who was most improper. "I dare say that is tempting. But, dear wife, Rhapsody," he let her name glide out with a lowered tone of voice, "I promise you, when I bed you, I can assure you, you will want it as much as I will."

He caught her hand in mid swing and expected the second. But she merely stood, eyes dark with anger, a tinge of fear, and most definitely disgust. Trusting his gut, he leaned forward, stroked her face and then cupped her chin with a touch as light as air. Her breath came in small gasps, but her other hand stayed still.

With leisurely slowness, he brought his mouth to hers. Resistance met him but soon dissolved and became a melting pool of need. Her surrender so surprised him that he pressed closer, dropping her hand and wrapping his arms around her, pulling her nearer. His hand slid behind her head to cradle it and find the silky tresses there.

The taste of her lips intoxicated him. He couldn't get enough as he deepened the kiss. Feeling her snug against him did indeed entice him to lift her and bump through the door. Instead, he drew away and stepped back. He wouldn't be a fool.

But to his surprise, she didn't initiate any fair maiden slaps toward his cheeks. She stood there, mouth parted, breathing in the most desirable way. So much so, he thought he might have made a mistake in breaking the intimacy. He had rather enjoyed it.

Without a word, she reached behind her, turned the knob and melted away through the crack in the door. Interesting. Frigid little Rhapsody appeared to hide a hidden passion deep inside. He'd noticed a yielding with his kisses before, but he'd assumed she'd been stunned he'd taken such a liberty. But perhaps the woman did have a furnace that roared within her chaste demeanor. It might be exhilarating to stoke such a fire.

Cav tugged on his tie and turned to stroll the hall. Meanwhile, he'd find his things. He'd only sent a small amount of luggage to get by for a few days. As much planning as the wedding had taken, he was thinking on his feet at this point. But for propriety's sake, he had to remain in the house for a week or so.

If he knew his bride, his things were in the farthest bedroom from hers. Down the next wing he found he'd guessed right. Last door on the right. Inside stood his luggage, not unpacked. She herself had probably lugged it down here to avoid the chatter of the servants. As if the secret would last long.

He pulled the black dinner jacket off and removed his linen shirt. Cav stretched his arms above his head to shake the formalness of the day from his bones. He glided to the long window and looked out over the courtyard, running his hands through the hair on his chest. He could make this work. He deserved a diversion, and maybe this was it.

Either way, he could probably shed his job at the foundry. Not that he'd miss it. Horrible, hard-working hours. Trading it to be a genteel gentleman in the largest mansion in New Albany was just as beneficial as a cover as a lowly worker. And he could still dress the part when he took out old Number Two.

He turned to look at the door. Rhapsody could very well be a most interesting distraction as well, but he would have to be careful. He needed her discretion. The woman knew too much already. Still, the feel of her curves stayed with him, and his heart swelled with a thirst to kiss her again. Kiss her and more.

He grunted. Perhaps he was vile and all the other names she'd called him. For her features haunted him much like the proverbial carrot in the donkey's face. Ah, but he was good at intrigue.

And little by little, bit by bit, he would find out what made his stunning wife tick.

Chapter Six

Rhapsody kept her ear pressed to that hand-carved door until she heard the footsteps disappear down the hallway. Doors opened and closed. He would soon find the room he sought. She fought to slow her breathing. What had just occurred, she wasn't sure she could label. True, the man had appeared, decked out in an expensive black dinner ensemble, face shaved, hair slicked down like a dandy. As much as it pained her, she had to admit, he was the most captivatingly handsome man she'd ever laid eyes to.

She spun from the door and clutched the neckline of her dress. Had she actually used the word romp? Oh, for a thousand knives to cut the tongue from her mouth. She stepped forward, yearning to perch on the bed but knowing the corset would not allow such movement. Instead she touched her hand to the corner of her writing desk as if she needed something to support her.

Something strange happened when that man had melded his lips with hers. As if her brain suddenly took leave of her head. She should have slapped him. Several times. A fine thought if he didn't possess the skill to capture her hand before it met its target.

Yet it was more than that. Something profound had…shifted. His agile hands had done something to awaken a dead place inside her. His embrace had made her feel safe and wanted. Desired even. And she'd craved more.

A noise of frustration cooed from her mouth. Then she tightened her lips. Well, it would never happen again. This was merely a marriage to save her reputation. To please the masses of high society. She could…

What? Run away? Live in a hovel? Start a new life in the western frontier, dragging water to a shack to wash her drawers? She balled up her fist and shook them. No.

This was her life. Her house. She could direct the tide where she wished it to go. And right now, it was to avoid Mr. Blackledge with all her heart. Horrible things could happen if that brute reached forth to touch her, or heaven forbid, pressed soft lips to hers. She closed her eyes, hating the need that rose up at the thought.

Had she lost her mind? She knew the game. She'd played with men's hearts since a young girl. Tossed them aside when she grew weary of them. Hadn't she spurned her first intended on the basis that he'd been a mere farmer instead of a wealthy philanthropist of the community?

She'd written a note of dismissal, claiming love for another and then disappeared in a carriage with her parents to marry his best friend, Devlin Hastings. Devlin, chosen by her father and much more the fledgling benevolent community pillar she'd sought. Besides, Devlin had been delightfully pliant. Anything she wanted, she got.

Now, however, she feared, someone had upped the stakes. She lifted her chin in the way her mother always did when she laid down the law about some sort of idiot thing. If she had anything to do with it, this marriage would stay parked in platonic mode.

She grabbed the tonic bottle and squeezed the bulb. A fine spray of water tinged with a hint of lavender cooled her flushed face. She patted her skin with her lacy handkerchief. For the immediate, she would retire to her bedstead and have the servants bring up some tea and a light snack.

With swift steps she returned to grasp the tasseled bell-pull near the door. Having only three servants now, due to the lack of, as her mother had mentioned, the base mentality of cutting corners financially, she would be taking Lissy's time away from helping Mabel the cook and Barton the carriage caretaker from organizing the few hired-on staff to clear the wedding muck away.

But she couldn't think of that now. In mere moments a tap came at her door.

"Enter," she bade.

Lissy hustled through, her face wet with a sheen of perspiration.

"I wish to dress for bed."

"Yes'm. You don't feel well, Mrs. Hast—Blackledge?"

Rhapsody clamped her jaw. "A headache. Come, hurry with this."

The maid shuffled over and began working the tiny buttons down the back of the silk dress. Next the chemise, and then Rhapsody stepped out of no less than a dozen flounced muslin petticoats. Then the unwinding of the corset. Rhapsody almost cried in glee as the last of its pinching claws relaxed around her ribs. She took a deep breath and loosened the drawers and dropped them.

The servant approached her with the satin nightclothes and held them high for Rhapsody to shrug into them, tamping down a coo of relief.

"I'll bring you some tea and some scones, mum."

"That would be lovely." Why did she have an overwhelming desire to cry? Silly.

Emotions merely impede the gracious living of the—

"Stop!" Rhapsody's rude bark brought Lissy's ministrations to an abrupt halt. The servant's mouth and eyes stretched wide. It was plain to see fear written on her features. "I…apologize. I merely spoke thoughtlessly to the pain in my head."

Oh, yes. The pain otherwise known as Miss Bickle. Or perhaps it was rather her own memory of lessons best left to the past.

Lissy scurried to pull the fine white lace comforter back on the four-poster bed. Then she stepped back as if too afraid to get too close to Rhapsody. She stifled a sigh and propped herself against the pillow as the servant tucked and pulled, assuring Rhapsody of the best comfort a lady's maid could impart. Then the dark woman turned and retrieved the bed jacket and night cap and hung them on a hook near her bed.

Rhapsody pondered her as the slave took up the dress and its fallen counterparts and hung them on the wardrobe pegs, taking the utmost care. What had gotten into Rhapsody? Noticing things about the help that she never had before. Perhaps it had been that night of being rescued. When dark figures had rushed to the barn at the old preacher man's shack. Rhapsody wondered vaguely if Lissy knew the slaves that ran. Or the man that hid them.

Either way, it had brought her an…awareness. That maybe not all of them desired to live as underlings just to serve the upper class.

"Lissy?"

The woman froze and turned toward her, the green silk live with flashes of the dying light from the window.

"Yes'm?"

She kept it well hidden, if Lissy had yearnings to be free. But then, what choice did she have? "Uh…could you light the lamp? It's getting dark."

The servant nodded, first laying down the dress of Rhapsody's scourge on the chair tucked under the writing desk before coming to her bedside to turn on the gas lamp. And just like that, the woman did a task Rhapsody herself could have easily leaned over and accomplished. Then Lissy returned, hung the dress, and quietly slipped from the room.

Cavanaugh Blackledge dabbled in the Underground Railroad, freeing those who were enslaved. Yes. That could be a much needed device to keep him at arms' length. A much needed thumb-screw to fashion his behavior. Yet, as she relaxed against the soft pillow, she had much doubt how intimidated her new husband would be should she choose to exploit her knowledge.

How could revulsion, anger, dread, and, yes, she must be honest…passion—for she refused to cave to the word lust—all reside in her heart for her new spouse? Something she'd never had for Devlin. Glory, she would need all the tools at her disposal to resist his advances. Or whatever else he had in mind.

Cav pulled on the reins. The old horse obeyed and stopped cold. The ferry paddles swashed through the Ohio, but sounded some distance away. Maybe halfway across? Either way, he had time to hunker down, lower the tailgate, and huddle near the river. A steam whistle trumpeted a ways off, more than likely indicating a steamer about to shoot the falls of the Ohio. Two miles of sheer terror of rocks and dropping ledges. He hoped an experienced pilot stood at the wheel.

"Best luck to you," Cav whispered, glad he wasn't aboard the flat-bottomed vessels as it circumvented the boulders and drops for nearly two miles.

But as fascinating as contemplating the steamboat's treacherous path was, he had other fish to fry. He could hear the murmurs of people down at the dock, waiting to board the ferry for the Kentucky side of the river. What concerned him was the hope that four packages would fit underneath his stack of wood. He'd never taken such a load before, but Lazarus had assured him two of them were wee. His heart wrenched. Children.

He leaned back against a sizable birch. Never did his thoughts stray so far as to exclude his new wife. She'd barely shown her face in the week he'd spent traversing in and out of her mansion. Correction. *His* front door.

At least her absence meant she seldom spoke to anyone. News of his dealings should stay mum, but he'd have to confront her about it soon. He couldn't risk being revealed. Striding down and bursting through her bedroom door had occurred to him. After all, it would be within his right. That and much more.

But he knew this needed to be a much softer touch, ironic as that description was. Because he most sincerely would love to touch her. Tame the tiger. He shook his head. He'd gone mush in the head. Keeping it on a business track was a much safer course.

Noises indicated below that the oversized flatboat had arrived. Loud thumps rang out as they moored the vessel. He stood and waited. Two forms circled into the woods below him and approached stealthily as the bulk of people continued past him, unaware two had virtually walked into the shadow of the trees. And he would wager the lone skirted figure in the back would also be his passenger. But where was the fourth?

The woman darted into the woods, once separated, and doubled back to him. The two figures from below stood just outside his line of sight.

Finally a fourth scrambled up alone from the bank. Not a passenger, though. A white man.

"Ah, Mr. Valprid, I assume?"

His contact. "Mr. Aaron. You have business for me I assume?"

The man shook his hand and then shoved both hands in his pockets. Out came a note from his right, and he handed it silently to him. With a belying casualness, he looked back and forth on the path to the landing.

"That's right. Some precious cargo, indeed."

The last of the late comers hurried down the lane to catch the ferry. Then he motioned to the woman. She scurried from the shadow of the trees. With dismay, Cav noticed a tiny babe tucked in her arms. Without a word she made quick work of shimmying into the wagon. How she did that clutching a child, he had no idea.

"Yes, beautiful night for a slow excursion across the great river."

The man let out a chuckle, which brought the last two forms from hiding. A tall man and a smaller boy. They too, slid into the concealed compartment. Cav quickly gated the back and reached to shake hands with the stranger.

"Guess I need to get on to my next station, Mr. Aaron. Thank you for the business." Cav rapped the wagon as a signal and leaped into the wagon seat.

The man waved as Cav slapped the reins.

"Anytime, my friend." The stranger's voice lowered with a touch of emotion. "Anytime."

Cav whistled *Go Down Moses* as he jostled onto the main street. Not much traffic this late at night. "Forward, Number Two."

The same soothing words he used every time. The tiger lilies lay in their basket up under the seat. Rhapsody would be a lovely addition to his little scheme. But also much more dangerous.

Cav continued to whistle through his task, delivered his packages safely, and returned without seeing a soul. He parked his old wagon behind Lazarus's rickety shack and rode his spirited black toward his new home.

Mostly dark, the mansion seemed to be waiting. Still he hadn't explored the entire building. Almost everyone would have gone to bed at this point. It had to be past midnight. He'd be sneaking up the stairway again tonight. He really needed to have someone empty his third story apartment in west Louisville. The dirty hole in the wall had been a great cover for Mr. Valprid. But now, he rather liked the mansion.

He stopped before the drive, got off, and led his horse up the lane, staying in the grass to avoid noises. Now the challenge was not to wake Barton in the upper chambers of the carriage house as well as Miss Mabel and…Miss Lissy. Was that her name? At least that's what he thought he'd heard. Rhapsody somehow ran the enormous house on a skeleton crew.

Of course, all the bedrooms not occupied had been swathed in sheets. Less cleaning. Still, he needed to go over the books once more. Surprisingly, there remained several deep debts. He'd taken care of them immediately. No need to be in arrears. But it did puzzle him that Mr. Hastings had allowed such a shortfall to occur. Not much had been spent in the year before. He would have to dig deeper.

Cav lit the lantern as he stepped inside his own shadowed stable and led the black to his new stall. In the dim light, Cav made quick work of unsaddling and rubbing down his best horse. With a corner net full of clover and fresh water in a tub, Cav latched the half door and crept from the building. With swift feet he hurried to the back door.

*

Rhapsody pulled the bed jacket closer as she crept through the library. Devlin had often hidden the financial records from her. In his way, forbidding her to be involved. Her late night jaunts to nose through the journal hadn't ceased when he passed. But it had made the journal easier to locate. At least, she thought so. With Blackledge around, she couldn't be sure.

Hardly breathing, she felt through the room, splashes of dim moonlight flickering on the walls with the wave of the leaves. She reached the desk and moved by memory to turn the wheel on the gas lamp. Easing it on, she only brightened it to a low light and checked the thick brocade curtains to be sure no crevices of light would project.

She circled the desk, opening the drawer containing Devlin's financial books. Still here. A sigh of relief escaped her. Discovering the book a few months before Devlin's death, she'd been dismayed to see the red totals, indicating a great sum in arrears.

It didn't take long to locate the page, and she sank to the padded chair. New writing, different from Devlin's tiny neat script filled the columns. Instead a bold, slanted cursive had recorded the payment of all debts.

Her breath snagged in her throat. Mr. Blackledge had already been here, seen the damage, and taken care of it. What else had this man put his hand to? She supposed she should be grateful, but instead it raised ire in her belly. To depend on him so immediately didn't bode well.

She licked her lips. How she wished Mabel were awake to fetch her some tea. Or even a glass of water. A slight flash of shame swept over her. Mabel and Lissy had brought her every meal in the weeks since the wedding. And as much as she tried to harden her heart at their weary faces, she knew the burden of caring for the house on their own had taken a toll. But she refused to talk to…*him*.

Pressing the journal closed, she rose. She placed everything back to rights and slipped through the door. She knew the house by memory. Still, she'd avoided treading the house in the dark. It spooked her. Brought bad memories. And she'd rather pace her bedroom in the light of the gas lamps.

She swung through the hallway into the dining room and then ventured toward the kitchen, a much less familiar room. Surely she could find a glass and fill it with water to wet her parched throat.

A huge shadow lurched toward her as she stepped through the doorway, normally trod by servants only. A shriek began and grew louder until the demon clutched her. A hand clapped over her mouth, and soft lips pressed close to her ear.

Chapter Seven

"It's me. Stop screaming."

Blackledge.

She froze. The smell of him enveloped her. Woodsy. Leathery. Soap and horse and… *Him.*

Shivers crept up her spine while the man's arms, bands of steel to be sure, held her immobile.

"Rhapsody. Did you hear me?" At her nod he continued. "I'm going to remove my hand from your mouth. Don't scream. You'll wake the household."

"Mmm-muh."

His hand slid away, his hold relaxed. But his fingers ran down her arms. "Are you cold? You're trembling."

She clenched her body. Curse her loose nerves. Always betraying her. The twitch under her eye. The trembling. But usually only when spooked. Miss Bickle had beaten her derriere for that many times.

"I'm...fine."

His low chuckle met her ears. "You feel fine."

She tugged from him, rubbing her seared skin where he'd caressed her arms. "Must you do that every time?"

"What?"

"Make comments that are so..." she paused, unsure how to proceed. There seemed no sense in trying to force him to be genteel. Obviously the man wouldn't know how.

"Carnal?"

"Yes," she breathed.

His finger stroked down her cheek. "I think you bring it out of me."

She spun her face away. He would not get the best of her tonight. A scrape of a match lit the space and Blackledge touched the wick of a candle sitting on the table. And there he was, a smirk upon his face. Much too close.

"You are a fine woman." The dimple in his right cheek grew deeper, hiding amongst the heavy rasp of whiskers.

She swallowed. He looked gorgeous, cavalier. And dangerous. With a sniff she lifted her chin. "I'm quite sure you wouldn't know."

He grinned as he broke off a hunk of bread from beneath cheesecloth and swiped the butter crock from the shelf. "We could remedy that."

The man sat and slathered a hunk of butter onto the bread. She pressed her hands down to her sides. He really was quite base. And despite his upper crust bearing, the lean chiseled chin and strong nose, he was beneath her. Judge Blackledge's youngest son perched in a servant's kitchen, dressed as a commoner, unshaven, hair much too long, chomping a hunk of bread and butter. Like a plain working-class man.

"Want some?" he mumbled around the generous bite gyrating in his mouth.

"I came for water. Nothing more." Including him. She looked around, at a loss as to how to begin.

He rose and pulled a clear glass from the hutch next to the deep porcelain sink. He poured some water into the top of the hand pump and jerked the handle several times. Water gushed out and filled the glass.

"Your wish is my command." He slid the glass and it stopped perfectly across from him on the work space. A stool stood right below. "Have a seat."

Well, it certainly hadn't taken him long to make himself at home. "I was just returning to my room."

"Actually, I think we need to discuss some things. If you don't mind." He stuffed the last of the soft bread into his mouth and brushed his hands off.

Staying in his presence wasn't wise. Though she'd managed to manipulate the men who'd previously wandered into her space, this man seemed a totally different breed. The mere size of him, hardened into muscle masses of a commoner slinging sledges was the first point to contend with. The spot beneath her eye twitched. Then, there was his demeanor. Master of all he surveyed, including her. His ribald comment of possessing her still echoed in her mind.

"Of what does it pertain?"

That dimple darkened again and a brow quirked ever so slightly. He relaxed back in the chair and propped one leg up on his other knee. Then he stretched back to intertwine his hands behind his head. Very much in charge.

"Sit down and you'll find out."

Her throat was parched. She tiptoed forward and grasped the stool. Such an unsteady little thing. A servant's seat. For peeling potatoes and such menial tasks. Surely her mother would have had her switched for even touching the lowly piece of furniture.

"I won't ravage you from across the table. Honest."

Her gaze flicked to his. A humorous gleam danced in his eyes. To shut down his jest at her expense, she perched on the edge of the vile stool.

He leaned forward, steepling his fingers on the table. "Now, about the household staff. I feel there is a need to add two here at the house, a scullery and a maid. Plus, I feel Barton would do to have an assistant to clean the stalls and do various work about the house. What do you think?"

She blinked. This man of arrogant action was asking her opinion? Even spineless Devlin would have never consulted her about anything concerning running the household. It had been a continual drone of her demanding to get anything she wanted. She let out a slow, unsteady breath. Pushed and pushed until she'd nagged Devlin into sickness. And then let him die. Rhapsody pressed her fingers to the twitch below her eye.

Cav narrowed his eyes as shadows fell across his new wife's face. Glimpsing a sadness there made him wish he bantered with her instead of bringing on such inner grief. He had to remember the woman had buried a husband not long ago. And now, she was aligning to a new one.

His eyes dropped and followed her form in the satin night jacket tied with a ribbon. If she knew what a vision she presented in her night clothes, he'd dare say she'd slap him and scurry from the room. Her thick blonde hair, braided down her back in simplicity, gave her a look of innocence. She had beautiful hair. Golden in its purest form like spun silk. Obviously long. The braid tumbled down to brush the stool as she balanced on its edge.

Thoughts of unraveling her mane filled his thoughts. Then he'd reach up and pull the velvet bow at the top of her white jacket. He sucked in a rush of air to clear the image from his mind, as fine as it was.

She started as if she'd forgotten his presence. Her lashes fluttered to her cheeks. "Whatever you think."

The demure comment did not ring true to her personality. "Really? Then I think I'll move my possessions to the master bedroom. I feel more of my needs will be met there."

Her mouth flew open and she stumbled back from the table. "How dare you, sir?"

A slow smile pulled at his mouth. "I dare because I know you're pretending to be meek when in reality, you are a spitfire. My first meeting with you settled that."

"That was because you violated me. A complete stranger. Which I may add, you still are."

"I'm your husband."

"Still a stranger."

"Touché. Therefore, we will need to hash through what needs to be done. But this is your home, Rhapsody. And I want your involvement. Agreed?"

She hesitated, assessed him, and inclined her head in agreement.

"So no more than three new staff to hire on?"

It seemed she always carried her hands clenched in fists. Which she did now. Her way of remaining proper, he supposed.

"That would be adequate."

He tapped the table. "See. That was painless. I also intended to extend a wage to each of them. I won't have servants who only receive room and board. I'll only keep hired servants, earning their own way. Given my interests in other matters, I feel it's my duty. Now, in other concerns, there were some outstanding debts, and I satisfied them."

At her nod, he continued. "And one more thing. It involves my late-night escapades."

"What you do is your own business. We're not really married."

He swore her face turned a deeper shade. Cav rose. He was exhausted and beyond wanting to dance around her appropriateness of everything. "You know full well what I do has nothing to do with fleshly indiscretion as you seem to be indicating. And we are indeed married, and I intend to honor our vows. What I am trying to explain is that I need your word that you will keep my underground activities secret. From everyone."

He met her eyes, soft in the low light, and he found himself wondering what she looked like beneath her night jacket in the shining white gown. She must have read something in his gaze for she stepped back.

"What you do, Mr. Blackledge, is entirely up to you. We are but two individual people sharing the same household."

How he was tempted to rattle her cage with a sly comment. Something about kissing her into submission, perhaps? But he had bigger concerns. "Promise me you will keep this knowledge of my doings confidential. Lives depend upon your silence."

She nodded, looking somber. "You have my word."

"And will you also honor our vows?" Why this seemed important to him, he couldn't say.

"I have found that what I want is quite unimportant. It's what society wants. What it demands." She edged closer and closer to the door. "And given my mother will disown me if I fail again, I have no desire to do so."

And then she disappeared through the door.

Rhapsody woke from nodding off, having dreams filled with a wide-shouldered man who much resembled Blackledge. She shook her head to clear it and wiped a hand across her eyes. Clearly from the way the light filled her bedroom, the dinner hour had not yet arrived. She tugged the sheet up higher. The breeze from the window helped slice the heat in the room. A tap sounded at the door.

"Enter."

Lissy's bright face popped in. "Mum?"

"Yes, yes, what is it?" She knew she shouldn't be short. She'd spent the entire day in bed. Much like the days before. But she had no wish to be disturbed. She wished only to doze another day away and read through the night.

"Mrs. Lennox is here."

Mother. Here. "I sent her a missive declining Mrs. Grafton's tea party. You sent it by courier, didn't you?" Her voice rang sharp.

Lissy entered without being bade to do so, but really, Rhapsody could have cared less. The servant's eyes grew large. "She ain't happy, Mum."

What else was new? Had she ever known her to be? Maybe Rhapsody had pleased her upon occasion like the morning she'd broken her engagement to Miles and married Devlin. Other than a few moments in time, every day was a fresh day to attain new heights in bad-temperedness.

"What does she want?"

"She be wantin' you to go to the tea."

"Tell her I am ill."

Lizzy bobbed her head. "Done did, Mum."

Footsteps rang out on the stairway. "Lock the door. Hurry."

Lissy lumbered to the door and threw the lock. Rhapsody tossed the coverlet from her legs just as the sharp knocks sounded on the door.

"Rhapsody."

"Yes?"

"Open this door. I have no wish to yell through solid wood."

No, chastising her to her face was much more effectual. "I'm unwell."

The knock came harder this time. "Let me in." Each word a hard staccato to the beat of her raps.

Hopeless. She'd never shed the woman. She flapped her hands at Lissy, and she rushed to open the door.

There she stood in her best brown dress, the color of mud, beaded at the bodice, flowing white lace at her wrists, and a straight skirt. Formal, stiffly pressed, fluffed with thousands of petticoats beneath. The severe low bun pulled her face tight and heavy amber jewelry hung at her lobes and neckline. A perfect ensemble. As always.

"You're still abed? Such uncouth behavior. Lissy, fetch the puce gown."

Puce. Of course. The color of dried bloodstains. How befitting.

"Now up, daughter. You've squandered the day. And the many before."

"Mother, I sent you my regrets that I couldn't accompany you."

Her mother snorted. "And I promptly ignored it. We must be up and about to offset this scandal you've committed. Thankfully, you transgressed with a man of good breeding stock, or all of our efforts would be in vain."

Yes, thank goodness she'd been forced to marry a high society ruffian as opposed to any other run-of-the-mill brute. A stab of remorse made her rise from the bed. Lissy lost no time switching her night clothes for her horrible gown. Mother stood there, inflexibly rigid, hands upon hips, making sure every detail was accomplished.

Rhapsody sat at the vanity as Lissy ran her fingers through her hair. Then the servant's experienced hands wound it up high and tight, making Rhapsody's cheeks feel as if they were in a vise.

At this point there was no battling her way free of her mother's will. Pearl jewelry was piled on. Rhapsody rose and snatched up her beaded purse and an alabaster parasol. Lissy laid a gossamer shawl across her shoulders. Rhapsody joined her mother at the door.

"Eau de cologne." Her mother's biting command.

Lissy snatched up the decorative, bulbed decanter and spritzed Rhapsody's hair. At her mother's brisk nod, she'd evidently passed muster. Rhapsody wrinkled her nose. She hated that smell. Like dead flowers. Much too overwhelming.

In the carriage, her mother gave her instructions. "Matronly representatives and their respective daughters in attendance will be from the Elmers, Vaughns, Broussards, Millertons, and

Youngbloods." She ran the names' list like a rollcall of a banking institution's most prolific investors.

Rhapsody ran the detestable list through her mind and counted first the amount. Eighteen ladies counting her mother and herself. Enough to not contribute to the conversation much. Besides, Philomena, Elsie, and Meredith were a club unto their own. They would be full of questions about her new husband, but only to regurgitate the answers among the trio later for spiteful entertainment. The Grafton sisters would be polite, as the hostesses of the party, but unwilling to chat much with her. She had already been ostracized with the breaking of her first engagement.

That left the infants. Those under twenty-one who giggled at nearly everything. No thank you. Except Gladys Vaughn, who toggled at twenty-one. Yet Gladys's younger sister was part of the infants and that usually dragged her downward. That and the giggling.

Which left her at the mercy of the mothers, seven strong including her own, who would willingly sacrifice her daughter to save face. No wonder she'd declined.

"Remember, you are to avoid any rumors concerning the inappropriate timing of your marriage. As your husband claims," with this her mother shot her a stern look, "it was always planned. This is what I informed Mrs. Grafton when she called to deliver her invitation. Instead we will focus on the charitable fund at the church, Neva's courtship, and Lona's news of being in the family way. Her seventh. Can you believe? Surely that will be of more interest than your hurried nuptials."

"I will need to be home fairly soon." Rhapsody flicked her gaze to the road. It made it easier to lie. "Blackledge will be home, and I have no wish to be gone when he arrives."

She felt, rather than saw, her mother swell next to her. Never a good sign.

"Blackledge?" The volume of her mother's voice gained strength. "Blackledge? If you refer to your husband in such a way by his last name only, it will be the end of me, Rhapsody Redemp—Marie. Is that clear?"

Chapter Eight

Rhapsody cringed. Again with the name Redemption. As sure as the sun shone, her mother surely thought Rhapsody needed redemption. Instead, she dug the pinky and ring fingers into the soft skin of her flesh. "Yes, Mother."

"You will completely mortify me. Either refer to your husband as Mr. Blackledge or by his first name. You behave as if you have no cultural training at all. The Lennoxes have a reputation to uphold. I thought you fathomed the importance of our family's dignity."

Wasn't that why she was married? To a stranger?

"It will simply shame me to the core should you break etiquette. You never excelled with decorum, Rhapsody. I wished I had talked your father into moving back to New York where we lived before you born. That country school ruined you. I should have insisted you stay at Miss Bickle's And almost marrying a farmer? I begged your father to not transfer his business to this God-forsaken place, but he would not listen. Then, he built a home on the edge of town amidst fields. Hay fields, corn fields. Such dirty people and squalid homes. It's a wonder our family gentility didn't completely disappear among the goats."

Rhapsody clenched her jaw.

"Thank goodness I convinced him to build a proper house here downtown. But it was too late to save you, I fear."

"I apologize, Mother. It was an oversight."

The carriage stopped, and her mother set a firm grasp on her arm. "Don't let it happen again. Not today, not ever."

The platitudes. So many, Rhapsody had lost count. Hence the puce-colored dress. She'd silently bled while her mother castigated her of her gaffes. They strode up the fine walk lined with intricate wrought-iron fencing to the three-story house, painted mellow blue highlighted with burgundy and white posts.

The servant whisked them into the foyer, decked in carved oak around the door casings and in the intricate design of the floor. Deloris, the eldest daughter who'd already embraced her thirtieth birthday, greeted them with a nod and an imperceptible smile.

Tall and lanky, the woman had never been overly pretty. Rhapsody had seen the green-eyed devil of jealousy in Deloris's eyes many times. And that used to make Rhapsody feel superior. Now, a sliver of shame pierced her seared soul. Despite this thought, Rhapsody couldn't help but notice Deloris's dress. The floral print seemed a bit pretentious, but at least it wasn't puce.

In the parlor, for Rhapsody refused to call the little box a drawing room, the quiet chatter bounced about the room punctuated with several giggles. The infants had arrived.

"Ah, Minerva and Rhapsody. How nice to see you." Mrs. Grafton stepped forward, tall like her eldest daughter, but better looking like her younger. Even with the wreaths of lines etching her face. Mrs. Grafton was rumored to be older than her husband. Even approaching her seventies, but none of it could be proven.

Instead she kept younger company perhaps to tamp down the rumor or the truth, whatever the case may be. And according to stories of Beryl Grafton's youth, she and Mother had been quite close. Though Rhapsody would never be able to guess such a thing from the hard snap in her eye as she beheld the two of them.

"Beryl, we're most grateful for the kind invitation," Rhapsody's mother intoned.

"And there is that married lady in tow. Mrs. Rhapsody Blackledge. I think it sounds quite nice together. And how is that handsome devil? Seems I saw him hereabouts not long ago. Quite a striking example of a man." Her assessing gaze would have seared a lesser woman.

Rhapsody inclined her head, ignoring the older woman's portentous scrutiny, ready with the next fib. "Yes, of course I think so."

Mrs. Grafton's eyebrow rose, mocking in its tilt. "Of course."

The reply was simple but implied an immoral connotation. Fabulous. A day filled with double meaning conversations. Nothing had changed. Of all the events she wished she could have avoided, it was the Grafton manor teas.

"And how is Lona? I wondered if she managed to make it. Her seventh, I believe?" Rhapsody batted her eyes at Mrs. Grafton and the old woman's face stiffened before she pulled a tight smile.

"Yes, she's here. Anxiously waiting to see you both." She indicated the floral chairs to the right near the fireplace that was actually burning. Mid-summer and a fire graced the hearth. "Here we are. Pardon my fixation with a welcoming fire, even in the summer. But I can't resist. Ladies, Minerva Lennox and Rhapsody Marie Lennox Hastings Blackledge."

Despite the windows being opened beyond the lacy curtains, the room boiled. It didn't help Rhapsody's internal temperature that the woman had used all and any name she'd ever been graced with. Except Redemption. Perhaps the prickly woman wasn't privy to such information. But from the calculating look on her face, Rhapsody doubted there was little the woman didn't know.

The women sat around wafting themselves with fans. The one thing Rhapsody had forgotten. Mother whipped her matching brown fan out and pressed it to her lips. Then hissed, "Who in their right mind lights a fire in late July?"

Rhapsody acknowledged the women, linked up just as she had thought. The infants were on the floral couch, giggling amongst themselves. Good thing Deloris hadn't chosen that spot. She would have disappeared into the pattern of the tacky piece of furniture. Rhapsody's gaze continued to fasten on the exotic collectibles Mrs. Grafton had collected on her travels. A lamp from China. Vases from many different countries. A walking stick from Cairo, the painting from France. Yes, she remembered all the woman had boasted about over the years.

Mrs. Grafton seated herself in a gold wingback chair and tucked her hands together in her lap. "Of course, all of us are dying to know how you met Mr. Blackledge, Rhapsody. Why don't we start there?"

Eyes riveted on her. Rhapsody gave her best, wide-fake smile. "It's all so romantic, ladies. I don't want to bore you with all the details." Titters went around, but the stares came back. "Actually he rescued me from being stranded several months back. That's how we met."

"Just like the night the…catchers found you? But weren't you alone? At least that's what I heard." Melvina Vaughn, a curly redhead and the youngest of the infants piped up.

She could feel her mother stiffen beside her. Rhapsody waved a careless hand. "Don't be silly. Why in the world would I be alone?"

The chunky girl crossed her arms and leaned back in the chair. "Well, that's what I was told."

"And it is quite poor timing, you have to admit," Elsie Millerton remarked, gaining the nods of most the ladies in the room. "Some of us even thought you might have known him before Devlin passed."

The room grew silent at the casual accusation. Rhapsody sniffed, but forced herself to remain unruffled. "Entirely incorrect. Devlin was an excellent man, and I will always harbor a deep love for him."

A few eyebrows rose. Philomena Youngblood stopped picking at her nails long enough to speak. “Even though you’re married to…”

“Cavanaugh,” she answered smoothly. More lies lining up in her mind. “Well, most of you ladies aren’t widows, so you can’t know how a little bit of your heart is stored up for your former husband. But even though Devlin will always reside in a small corner of my heart, I’m now, of course, fully in love with Cavanaugh.”

“But weren’t your parents quite surpris—” Imogene Broussard, mother of her brood began, but Rhapsody’s mother cut in like a drunken dance partner.

“I want to hear all about how Lona is faring.” Mrs. Lennox directed her gaze to the woman lounging in the matching golden chair. The pregnant woman’s fan flapped harder than the rest.

Apparently her mother could ignore proper etiquette when she so desired and interrupt people mid-sentence. But what did she care? Rhapsody released a quiet sigh of relief when the direction of conversation turned to Lona, who was only too happy to garner all the attention. Rhapsody leaned back and scooted her chair slightly out of the line of sight of most of the ladies in attendance. Unfortunately closer to the fire. A small price to pay to keep out of the circle of gossip. She dabbed her forehead with her lace-trimmed hanky.

It was definitely a day to sweat out unpleasantries.

Cavanaugh stood as the new maid showed his associate into the library. They shook hands, and Cav motioned for him to take one of the padded seats in front of the huge desk. Holden Albridge, dressed in a black jacket and pants, was a compact type of man. Neat, persnickety even. His dark hair lay sleek against his head and the round glasses befit a man of numbers. His physique fit the banking industry as well, and that had been precisely why Cav had chosen him. Well, that and his obvious flair for running his investments with a streak of genius.

Holden lost no time cracking the journal on his lap. "The debts are cleared with little collateral damage to the bottom line. Do you want to start with investments or returns?"

Cav tipped his head back in laughter. "Holden, you never cease to amaze me. How are the wife and kids?"

His associate nodded once, a content gleam in his eye. Then he flicked his eyes around the room. "All is well. And I see you've outgrown that disgusting apartment in Louisville?"

"Yes, and I turned in my resignation at Blevans. No more a common workman."

"Being as you are now a gentleman commanding much attention with a wife who is the daughter of one of the most prestigious families of New Albany, probably a wise choice not to let someone see you gallivanting around in your dirty work shirt and disheveled hair. Perhaps you will also trim that mop?"

"It's a possibility. But you know me, Holden. I've always been a bit too rugged. I prefer men like you to front my operations." Cav dipped a quill and signed the documents Holden laid before him.

"Ah, the ladies seem to go for that type of gent. Your new wife is no doubt thrilled to have such a," he cleared his throat with a smirk, "ruffian."

Cav eyed not only his partner in crime, but his best friend. "You know very well what this is. And it serves a purpose."

Holden placed the documents back in a file and secured them in his leather case. "Always for the purpose, Cav? Never something for the sake of living? For the sake of joy? After all, I hear your new wife is quite a looker. And from the rumors, quite absent from the social scene. There has to be a reason for that."

"Never you worry about my female involvements, my friend. There are more important matters to attend."

The dapper gent in front of his desk glanced toward the door and lowered his voice. "I know you, Cav. We go way back. I know your involvements with the fairer sex merely encompasses helping a few of the female persuasion to find freedom. Someday you'll grow old, my friend. You'll look back and wonder why you didn't bother to take time for those around you. And, worst of all, you'll be alone."

Cav narrowed his eyes. Rarely did Holden escape propriety, breaking from his dignified manner to speak so baldly.

His friend arose and shook his hand, a gleam of sincerity shining in his eyes. "I will get on the business of investing for our financial future, Cav. Diverse investments for the greatest gain. But you, get on the business of making a life."

Some moments later, he heard the click of the door, and Cav realized he'd been standing, lost in his thoughts while Holden had let himself out. He stepped from behind the desk and paced the room, rubbing his rough bearded chin. Passing each window between the wall to ceiling bookcases, he paused at each one, looking out, contemplating.

Holden had been married for some time with three kids. Never had he seen the bloke so delighted than when he spoke of them. What must it be like to have someone care for you to such a distraction? He tugged his thoughts away at that notion. Distraction. Exactly. Just what he didn't need. Rhapsody, and her beauty, would be nothing but a distraction. And he could ill afford that.

Still, she drew him like a magnet. Stirred not only longings, but his impish remarks. But he wouldn't be constrained by emotion. He'd made that mistake before.

He shrugged away the concerns and set his mind on what he needed to accomplish today. Judging by his silver timepiece tucked into his pocket, he had just enough time to grab his underground conductor's uniform, or rather his commoner's rags, to meet up with his contacts.

Once upstairs, he splashed water on his face and glared at his reflection. A fortnight of whiskers and curling locks nearly six inches long. Holden was right. He did look like a ruffian.

With a laugh, he tucked the brown paper package containing a clean cotton smock under his arm. The old wool trousers would have to do with the upscale jacket he wore. For he had to traverse into two worlds. Both of which he was quite familiar. Excitement shot down his spine as he slipped from the room.

Rhapsody sat perched on her bed, hugging the bed post to her face. She hadn't even bothered to fetch Lissy to tend the putrid-colored dress lying in a heap on the floor. Her eyes closed over hot, teary eyes. Her mother was right on some respects. She wasn't getting out enough. She'd become a recluse. In her own bedroom. Of her own accord.

And was it any wonder after the roasting at Mrs. Grafton's tea? She'd gladly add iron bars to her room if it meant she could avoid such an affair again. Though Mother had done her best to turn the tide of conversation, it had all cycled back to her. Time and time again. The pure quantity of questions was enough to bury a weaker woman. But these piercing, demanding, intrusive queries? All carefully cloaked in false decorum. They had nearly sent her racing from the room.

She'd never been snubbed so when Devlin was alive. Her eyes darted to the desk drawer containing the photo of her and Devlin. When he'd been healthy and full of promises to fulfill her every dream. Her every demand. She rose and pulled the offending daguerreotype out and studied it. Even here, weariness echoed from his eyes while a flair of stubborn determination glinted from hers.

If ever she should have been banished from society, it should have been at his death. How could she have pushed him past the brink of health? A cold that had terminated in the "inflammation of lungs and pleura," as the doctor had announced at death. And she'd recognized his weariness, yet the construction of the house had been her utmost concern. Not his health.

How could she have been so selfish?

Once he'd begun hacking, she'd insisted the servants move him into another room. And he'd continued working to fund her expensive demands. Inside of twelve weeks, pneumonia had taken him and the servant who'd cared for him in the end.

She pressed a finger to his image. Entirely her fault. The house had been completed three weeks before his funeral. His final deed on this earth.

A shiver of self-revulsion rippled through her, and she slammed the photo back into the drawer. She glanced around the beautiful room, décor of the finest, steeped in expense and fashion. The intricate wallpaper, the ceiling designed in circular patterns extending beyond the scrolled medallion in the center of the room. A glass chandelier hung there, shooting millions of tiny rectangles of prism lights around the four walls. A stunning sight that was only one more reminder of her negligence of her own ill husband. A husband she had never truly loved.

She deserved a social roasting and more. Yes, it was a just penance that she was now married to a hooligan stranger. Perhaps she, too, would die under his hand of pure indifference. She shuddered and yanked the bed jacket off and then the bed clothes. The room was stifling. She needed a quick breath of air, despite the late hour. With quick steps she approached the armoire and threw open the doors. Never had she dressed without Lizzy. Tonight would be the first.

She sorted and pulled out an old black ensemble that had enough wear to be thrown out. Rhapsody whipped the chemise over her head. Wiggling into a tight corset nearly spent her, but then she spun the cursed piece of clothing to put the laces to the back. Once that was accomplished, she flung on the under petticoat followed by the dress over her head.

Without a crinoline or hoop, the dress hung flat and a bit too long. Much like a working class girl. And all the better. She snatched her black bonnet and moved to the door. Where she was going she hadn't a clue. Just away from here. Somewhere to breathe.

She eased the door to the master bedroom closed, not wishing to alert any of the four servant girls that now wandered the house. Affixing her bonnet, a shadow crossed the hallway in front of her. Blackledge creeping about the house once more. Probably on another nightly escapade.

He swept down the stairs in silence and she waited. If he could do it, so could she. What drove a man to risk his life for people he didn't even know? This thought crossed her heart as she touched the stairway banister. Was he, too, working on penance for some past misdeeds?

She tiptoed down the stairway. There was only one way to find out.

Chapter Nine

Rhapsody hid behind the rose arbor as she watched Cavanaugh Blackledge talk with Barton in the open door of the carriage house. Beside him stood his black stallion, swinging his head in anticipation of the ride. Then Barton disappeared and the carriage house grew dark. Through the filtering light of a cloud-blocked moon, she saw him mount and head for the road.

She licked her dry lips, her breaths coming in huffs. The best method to follow him dozed in the stable. But Barton resided there and had not quite settled for the night. Therefore, she would be afoot. How base. At least that is what her mother would be inclined to think, for a woman on foot to spy through the neighborhood, trailing a man at night.

No time to waste on the recklessness of her actions now. She scrambled through the yard and stole through the back garden, keeping him in sight. He trailed to the north at the intersection, which she'd anticipated, and Rhapsody cut through a neighbor's fine lawn, watching for unanticipated obstacles like the low-set planter full of flowers. Daisies maybe? Rhapsody didn't care what, but rubbed her shin as she hurried through to get another glance at him.

As fortune would have it, a horse stood saddled at a rear hitching post. Taking this as providence, Rhapsody untied the horse, and swung aboard. All the times she'd snuck out to ride straddle in her country house had paid off. Although, her mother would rant otherwise.

The horse was well-mannered and took her direction without a fight, and Rhapsody steered the gentle accomplice toward Blackledge's trail. She stayed well behind, lurking in the roadside shadows to keep him from realizing he was being trailed.

He took to the same road of her unfortunate wheel mishap, and she leaned over her mount, feeling confident in the way. Then, without warning, he steered to the right, directly into the woods. She caught her breath and pulled up her mount. Dare she follow him into unfamiliar territory? In the dark? She hesitated only a second before she pulled her horse to the right, entering the darkened unknown.

Cav grinned. Whoever tailed him was either a child or completely stupid. Despite the fact they'd kept to the edge of the road, they were much too close and entirely too noisy. He continued into the darkness, acquainted with this stretch of woods. Circling right, he could easily backtrack to his pursuer. He pulled his horse to a stop and dismounted. With one quiet command, his well-trained horse continued to walk and would do so until he whistled.

With stealth, he trod through the undergrowth until he was sure he was behind the one who trailed him. He crept closer and spotted the shadow of a person hunched low to the horse's neck. Small enough to be a child, but surely an informant for the fugitive slave catchers. When the pursuer paused, he latched onto the moment and rushed the horse, yanking the form to the ground.

Cav landed with a grunt atop the petite form and clutched wrists, pinning them to the ground above his captive's head. At the feminine cry, he froze. His quarry whimpered and he peered at the face, bonnet skewed beneath her head.

"You!"

The word came much louder than he'd intended. But seeing his wife sprawled beneath him had been quite a shock. The spitfire had followed him from the house.

"Get off me, you brute." Her whispered demand did not hide the alarm or mask the pain in her voice.

He scrambled up, grabbed her waist, and tugged her from the ground. Another cry of panic tore from her. Then, a resounding slap met his cheek. Round one to the darkness. He gripped her wrists once more and wrenched her tight against him while his face burned from her blow.

"You little minx," he breathed into her ear as she struggled against him. "Stop wiggling. You've got plenty of explaining to do."

She continued to writhe until she lost strength and sagged against him, breathing hard. He gave a shrill whistle to beckon his horse before he addressed her. "What in the blazes are you doing out here?"

Her sniff made him ease his hold, but not let go. He wouldn't take another blindside smack to the face. "Answer me."

"Following you."

"Why?"

A silence stretched and then he felt a shrug. Curse the gloom that hid her face from him. "I'm not letting go until you talk. Are you an informant?"

"Informant for what?" Her shaking voice told him for all her bravado, she was frightened.

He pressed his lips to her ear. "Slave catchers."

Her head shook in denial.

"You better be telling me the truth, Rhapsody," he muttered lowly in her ear.

"I…swear on my grandmother's grave."

He released her. She stumbled back, rubbing her wrists. Shame washed over him. He'd hurt her. But he couldn't take a chance. What he did could cost lives.

"Are you wounded?"

"No."

"I apologize." Was he really in the middle of the wood apologizing to a high society lady? "You may swat me again if you'll forgive me."

Her head came up then. He braced for the stinging contact that never came.

"I doubt that will erase any offense," she whispered at last.

"Perhaps you're right. So why are you following me?"

Again her delicate shoulder arched in a shrug. Most unbecoming for most upper-crust, genteel women. And he liked it. High society and its rules and wiles repelled him. Perhaps one of the reasons he'd become invested in his current hobby.

"Nonetheless, I have places to go." He captured the reins of her horse. "This one of ours?"

Her stillness gave the answer. Good heavens, the woman had no trepidation at all. He stepped toward her and she shrank away.

"Rhapsody. I don't have time to play games. I've a stolen horse and an injured wife in the middle of a dark woods. And I have a rendezvous in the next hour. You made your choice the moment you decided to follow me."

Blackledge tied off the borrowed horse onto a low branch and grasped his wife's hand as he strode forward. He met his horse a few steps more, grasped his wife by the waist, and situated her on the saddle. Then he swung up behind her. He wrapped his arms about her trembling form to grasp the reins.

He let out a sigh. "I'm not going to hurt you. Anymore."

"I know."

As much as the night had gone off the rails, he rather enjoyed her curvy body against his. With her bonnet trailed down her back, her soft blonde hair brushed his whiskered chin. Stuffing down the desire to nuzzle the side of her face and inhale her sweet scent, he urged the black forward. He gritted his teeth. He would finish his intended purpose and then deal with the aftermath. Rhapsody, like it or not, had just become his partner in crime.

Rhapsody could no more stop her unsteady nerves from quivering than she could stop a runaway carriage. Her ribs still ached and her wrists throbbed. To her benefit, he'd landed more to the side of her than straight on. Otherwise, she doubted she'd be moving about now. As Blackledge guided the stallion through the trees, the man's powerful body enfolded around her, her face warmed. His nearness made her forget to question their route. But perhaps she'd sacrificed that right when she'd trailed him through the night.

His lips pressed to her ear. "It's imperative that you are quiet. Understood?"

She nodded.

A small, dilapidated barn came into view and a shed that seemed familiar. The door hung open, and Blackledge steered their mount through the black door opening. He pressed her down against the mount to avoid banging their heads on the door lintel. Rhapsody shivered as he dismounted. They paused in near darkness. Then, the door closed, shutting off any and all rays of moonlight. A matched scraped to life and her husband's profile lighting a lantern appeared.

"You have me all out of sorts tonight." He freed the package from the saddle pack behind her leg and stripped the jacket and shirt from his body. Her small gasp drew his eyes.

"Like what you see?"

Arrogant lunkhead. Her face burned, realizing she did indeed like what she saw. Blackledge fairly bulged with muscle down to a slim waist. Not an extra bit of flesh anywhere. She tugged her gaze away with a quick snap of her neck. Devlin had never been a brawny sort of fellow. Perhaps that explained her attraction and courtship of the farmer she'd cast away before him.

He dragged a cotton smock over his head and tucked the tails into his wool trousers. He combed his fingers through his over-long hair, tousling it, making him look more like the commoner he impersonated.

"Don't worry, your virtue is safe tonight." Then that wicked grin. "At least for now."

He approached her with his eyes full of mystery and swung her from the horse before she could put a thought into her head. What an idiot she was. Frozen in awe of the male physique. Her mother was right. She was ruined.

Then his hands dipped behind her shoulders and righted her bonnet. "Lass, as much as I regret that you are here, you are the perfect foil." He tied the ribbons beneath her chin as if she were a child. Then he held out his hand. "Are you willing?"

A challenge rested in his gaze. She knew what this would entail or at least she thought she did. This was certainly no society tea party, wallpapered with the city's most influential matrons and their daughters. No silly fluttering fans or fires blazing in the summer heat simply to satisfy a mere whim.

No, this went much lower than that. Illegal and dangerous, risking her life. A deed that would disgrace her family name forever should it come to light.

She swallowed and stared at his big hand. The only way to find out what drove Cavanaugh Blackledge beyond his circumstances into liberating strangers as his way of life was to…jump into the fray. Jeopardizing everything she held dear.

"Rhapsody?"

With a nod she laid her hand in his. If she had no life, perhaps she could aid in giving others one.

Rhapsody could barely snatch a breath of air as he tugged her behind him toward the dilapidated shack. Surely they were not going in…there. Her husband rapped a rhythm of knocks upon the worn door and a few moments later, it eased open. Dark eyes peered out before it swung open and her husband hurried her through the doorway. The smell of a baked sweet met her nose.

With all her restraint, Rhapsody kept from gasping at the clean but dingy kitchen. Mostly what garnered her attention was the dirt floor. Then her eyes had no time to search the scant furniture, for the room had gone silent.

Blackledge inclined his head to the old man she'd seen before. "This is Preacher Dubber. His wife, Adalia. And this good man is Lazarus."

She clutched both hands around her husband's as she managed a brief nod at the dark-skinned occupants. The older man called Preacher stood a bit hunched, cotton white threading his black froth of hair. The woman appeared the same age but very petite, wrinkles of care around her puckered mouth. Lazarus, big and muscled, had to be slightly older than herself, but a scar tore down the right side of his face. All of them stared at her with not only censure, but distrust. Then they looked to Blackledge.

The big man spoke first. "What's da meanin' of dis, Mista Cav?"

"This is Rhapsody, my wife. She's already been in on one operation. She's here to help."

A grunt commenced from the older man, his body shifting toward the pine board table laden with crockware and a couple of pies.

The woman followed him, wiping her hands on a cotton cloth hanging from her shoulder. Lazarus, however, squared up to Rhapsody's husband.

"That ain't wise, Mista Cav. The more involve wit it, da harder it be to keep quiet."

Blackledge set his hand on the man's shoulder and squeezed. Rhapsody felt the trembling in her body. The men were close to the same size, yet the black man slightly taller.

"I guess you'll have to get Preacher to pray us up, then."

Lazarus studied her husband for a moment before he switched his intense gaze to Rhapsody. The audacity of his stare set a burn of offense and fear searing through her belly. Instinctively she stepped closer to Blackledge's back and lifted her chin.

"She ain't one of us," Lazarus declared and stalked off to the bench on the far side of the table but didn't seat himself.

"I speak for her character." Her husband's voice rumbled low.

Lazarus snorted. "You think dem catchers done care 'bout dat? Dey get their hands on dat fine lady—"

"Laz, sit." The preacher man interrupted and gestured with a fork to the bench seat. Then he shifted his whole upper body to motion to them. "Come, we get ta business."

They were staying? And eating? Rhapsody glanced around as Blackledge guided her to the empty bench across from them. Under the window stood a long rickety table of rough boards topped with a large enameled pan and a flat, wooden tray. Bins along the next wall indicated some sort of storage as well as the tins on the shelf overhead. That only left the table where they perched with barely room to scoot around it. The room itself was smaller than her master bedroom's water closet.

"Pie, Mista Cav?" The older woman's screechy voice sounded like the back gate in need of oiling.

"Always, Miss Adalia." He nudged her with his leg. "And I'm sure Rhapsody wants a piece, too."

Swallowing at both the nudge of his muscular leg and the thought of trying to eat in such a place, she dipped her head in acknowledgement.

“Peach or buttermilk?”

“P…peach.” Between tremors, she managed but one word.

The older woman sliced the pies and handed out three chipped pottery plates heaped with the dessert with a spoon stuck into the crust.

Their mumbled conversation began as she assessed the strange sight before her. No napkins, china, silverware arranged in perfect rows on either side of the plate. She brushed her boots against the grain of the dirt beneath the table. She might as well be dining in a cattle stall.

Wrinkled Miss Adalia moved about the room, poured water into enamelware cups, and plopped them near the three with plates. Lazarus gulped his dessert down and handed his plate to Mrs. Adalia who promptly washed it in a metal tub, reloaded a slice of pie on it, and set it before Preacher Dubber. Then she hovered near his elbow, eyes alight with frightened curiosity and tenacity.

Wrestling proprieties and boorishness in her soul, Rhapsody at last gripped the metal spoon and scraped away a small bit. Her eyes met the woman’s whose gaze narrowed as Rhapsody touched the morsel to her tongue. Surprisingly, the familiar taste stymied a gag reflex. Her brows rose. The pie was delicious.

“Here they’ve been spotted.” Blackledge pointed to squiggles on a scrap of paper. “So I will locate myself further down the river. Near the Falling Run Creek outlet.”

Lazarus nodded. “Still you watch yer back.”

The sweet taste disappeared as fear spiraled down Rhapsody’s torso. What had she gotten herself into?

Chapter Ten

As Rhapsody studied the old woman, Lissy filled her mind. And Barton. And Mabel. What did they think of this activity, for surely they knew of it? Did they, too have dreams of escaping? Finding freedom at any cost? Did they desire to live their life in a dirt-floor shack filled with tattered handoffs? Lissy's eyes were always full of compliance and yes, a touch fear.

Never before had Rhapsody ever stopped to analyze such things. It merely was and that was that. Lissy had been with her since she was a child. Rhapsody had simply inherited her when she'd married.

She gritted her teeth. Helping others find their life might be an unpleasant eye-opening task. One she was not fully prepared for. Her eyes darted to her husband, conversing quite naturally with these people. Like friends. Like colleagues.

Lazarus studied the chicken scratches on the rumpled hand-drawn map and nodded. Then the big man picked up the scrap of paper and touched it to the candle. The paper curled and blackened as if suffering a painful, uninvited mutation until the paper shrank into glowing embers. Lazarus dropped the remnant to the floor and stomped it. Rhapsody shivered.

Then the big dark man dipped his chin at Blackledge.

Her husband scraped the last of the pie into his mouth and handed the sorry excuse for a dish back to Miss Adalia. After a quick wash, she loaded a small piece of pie on it, and spooned a bite in her mouth, avoiding Rhapsody's furtive glances.

While half of her was repelled at the notion of utilizing these primitive plates, the other half of Rhapsody feared this might be the sum total of their dinnerware collection. The hutch at her home contained nearly a boundless supply of expensive china. She'd badgered Devlin for weeks on end to get the place setting up to forty. An odd discomfort needled her as she forced herself to eat another bite in the uneasy atmosphere of this social paradox.

Abruptly Lazarus rose, staring at the door. Rhapsody's spoon clattered to the dish, but her eyes did not swing to the door. Rather to the dish that had given such a heart rendering snap. The force of the spoon had broken the plate nearly in half.

"Shhh." Her husband pressed his hand upon her arm.

Miss Adalia's eyes raked her. But not with hate. With sorrow. Rhapsody's breath caught. Lazarus motioned to Cav, and he grasped her arm to pull her through the low doorway into another room. If it could be called that by the indication of the moonlight and candle glimmer, for it might have fit beneath her stairwell at home.

Cav pulled her to the space between a straw tick and the wall and hunkered down. The thought of sleeping on a rough mattress lying on a dirt floor caused Rhapsody to wrinkle her nose. These people lived in a hovel.

A coon dog howled in the distance, and suddenly the candle snuffed out.

"What's happening?" she whispered, digging her fingers into the cloth of his sleeve.

"Shhh."

A slight creak indicated the door opened. Running feet could be heard alongside the thin walls of the cabin. Rhapsody pressed her face to Blackledge's arm and squeezed her eyes shut. What was she doing here? What a fool she'd been. They could all be caught and accused of aiding escaping slaves. She'd be publically shamed, fined, or worse yet, jailed.

No, that wasn't the worst scenario. The authorities could be bypassed entirely and they'd be left in the hands of vile henchmen known for their cruel streak. Men with no scruples who wouldn't hesitate to exact their own kind of justice. Trembling quivered through her body.

A hand pressed to her cheek and her husband inclined his head. "Don't be afraid. I'll protect you. It's probably just another delivery."

Far-off squeaks indicated an arrival of a wagon. Then all was silent for much too long. Then a match scrape, the glow growing ever brighter until Preacher Dubber poked his head around the worn wood of the door facing.

"All's clear, Mista Cav."

Blackledge rose and drew her up, thankfully, as her toes had gone to sleep. The big preacher whispered in her husband's ear as they aimed for the door. He nodded at the big man as Blackledge disappeared through, tugging Rhapsody right behind. How could she not stumble after him? Her fingers seemed welded to his arm.

Once inside the dark barn, Blackledge made quick work of lifting Rhapsody to the horse's saddle. Then the door opened, and he wrapped his arms around her, urging the horse to exit with a squeeze of his legs. She couldn't help but cast a glance behind her as she gripped the pommel, wondering at the earlier disturbance.

Only Lazarus's shadow stood there, sweeping straw to the middle of the barn, just as a trap door slid shut in the floor.

Cavanaugh drummed his fingers on the library desk. He pitched the invitation down on the gleaming surface. Mother's flowery cursive chided him. A dinner, grand style. It irked him, yet was entirely expected. He'd witnessed the invitations from the foyer table disappear without once being informed that his presence was required, evening jacket not an option. His new wife's reticence for all things social worked right into his plans and definitely his preference.

But this one could not be declined with a mere excuse. Otherwise, his father's associate would be pounding on the door or, worse yet, his mother, escorted by her maid, would arrive, with imploring eyes and prying questions. He wouldn't have even known of this particular invite had he not caught sight of it on the side table, along with numerous others. The meticulous script had identified the sender immediately.

He would need to address it. But first he would have to lay eyes on his wife, who'd holed up once more in the vast recesses of this extravagant mansion. Visiting Preacher Dubber's house nearly two weeks ago had been the last he'd seen of her. Occasionally he'd asked offhand questions of the servants, but they were just as elusive in their answers.

Strange a wife that rarely left her bedchamber. Indicative of a woman clearly not happy with her world. Whether within or without, he couldn't rightly tell. But the puzzle stayed at the back of his mind and he pondered it.

Dismissing his thoughts, he rose. Nothing like shooting straight for the bullseye. He meandered through hallways and trod up the steps. Down the middle wing, he stopped at the last door on the left and rapped sharply. A long moment passed, and he tipped his head to the door. No one seemed about.

He glanced down the hallway. How the woman could be about and not be visible was quite curious. Cav stepped toward the hall where the three wings met and scanned down each. A clink led him to believe someone might inhabit a room down the opposite hall of his bedroom. Walking slowly, listening for further noises, he finally settled on the last bedroom door.

He eased closer and listened. Indeed, shuffling came from inside. His wife was missing and now an intruder into his house? He grasped the doorknob and turned, pouncing through to catch the perpetrator.

"Oh!" Something breakable dropped to the floor and landed with a clatter. Rhapsody's face transformed from terror to fury. She stomped her foot and thrust her fists down to her side. "What in heaven's name are you doing, Blackledge?"

He glanced about the bedroom that was devoid of the usual trappings of a guest room. Instead, stacks of dishes stood in piles everywhere. "I might ask you the same?"

Her head shook and her mouth pursed as she paced to the door and shut it without a sound. Then she spun, making her skirt bell totter. Her voice came in a hiss. "None of your business, sir."

Well, that certainly put him in an interesting situation. A lazy smile stretched his mouth as he assessed her lovely form outlined by a light blue dress. The comely color made her even lovelier. "Is that so?"

She lifted her chin, eyeing him with what had to be disdain. Why that seemed to both tantalize and annoy him at the same time, he had no idea. Two weeks ago she'd had her fingers firmly planted into the skin on his arm and now, she spat fire. "So, what goes on in the confines of my house is not my business. Is this what you are telling me, Rhapsody?"

The fire in her eyes made him want to kiss her to extinguish it, but that would solve nothing. That would be the last thing on her mind. He'd merely be darting another flying hand. But, he couldn't resist calling the house his. It amused him to vex her.

Her fingers appeared relaxed at the sides of her skirt, yet he knew by the whitened skin over her knuckles that she was anything but relaxed.

"I hardly think you, of all people, should be concerned with my coming and going. I'm sure you've had your share of misadventures in the last few weeks."

Why, that almost sounded like jealousy. He stepped closer. Her eyes registered surprise and then shot a glance to the door. He wanted to grin. Quite the faux pas shutting them behind a closed door. Good thing they were married.

"Oh, but I am concerned. Greatly. I've hardly seen you in the past weeks. It appears you've some sort of endeavor developing here." He tapped the delicate stack of the cobalt and gold edged bone china at his feet. His wife flinched.

"Have you no shame? Those dinner plates are worth a fortune. And as you should clearly know, one small tap can slice the most valuable china."

Now this had taken an unexpected turn. He lowered his voice. "You mean like at Miss Adalia's?"

Her nostrils flared and the prettiest of pink tainted her cheeks, making those sapphire eyes blaze. Cav found himself more fascinated with the high color on his wife's finely featured face than the plates at his feet. Then a discomfiting thought rose. "What are the plates for, Rhapsody?"

He stepped even closer, avoiding the porcelain dainties on the floor. She twisted her face from him, but he latched onto her chin, gently guiding it toward him. Her eyes opened in startling clarity. Their unusual hue claimed his attention, the darker navy outer rim bursting into a lighter sky blue in the center.

Rhapsody spun away and retreated to the far wall where she stood in her best society pose, face silhouetted against the light through the window. My, the woman was dazzling. No doubt she'd melted lesser men.

"I feel it is my duty to replace that which was damaged. Therefore I am sending the dinnerware to Miss…Adalia."

Cav's captivated trance fell away into a snort, which drew arrogant blades shooting from Rhapsody's luminous eyes. He turned and paced, kicking the poor teacup she'd dropped at his entry. Without a handle, it rolled to the far wall. "Have you lost your mind?"

"I assure you, sir, I have not." Her tone slashed at his jugular to match the blue flame of her eyes.

"So, you intend to insult her. Or worse, sentence her to death."

A gasp accentuated her vehement denial. "Never."

He shoved his hands in his pockets. Dishes. He was dealing in dishes. "What do you think is going to happen when the authorities find Mr. and Mrs. Cavanaugh Blackledge's bone china lining Preacher Dubber's pantry walls?"

She swept her hands over the floor. "I'll deny they're ours."

"So you'll lie?"

That rosy tongue appeared and scrubbed at her upper lip. For a high society lady schooled in the niceties of social proprieties, she gave away her insecurities quite baldly. Best he keep her from the gaming tables.

"I'll…say they were a gift."

"And of Miss Adalia's pride?"

"Those dishes of hers, if I could call them that, are atrocious."

"But paid for by their own funds. Money they earned free and equal. And for a woman used to having nothing, they are everything."

"But these are so much better."

"To you. Everyone has an innate dignity, however poor they may be. Even Miss Adalia, former slave." He took a deep breath. Time to dive deeper. "Have you never experienced the humiliation of not measuring up?"

Her lashes swept down and her chin lowered a fraction. Indeed, she had. His beautiful, self-sufficient wife, who lived in the most elegant house in the city, had most definitely experienced not being enough.

Rhapsody tugged the curtain aside and glanced out the window. The perfect view of the driveway, not that she cared. Merely a distraction to gather her thoughts. Blast the man for having the ability to touch on the most sensitive of subjects. She raised her head. "Fine. I see your point. Nevertheless, something must be done to help."

He inclined his dark head, curly mop falling forward. "And it is."

"How?"

"Money."

She studied Cav's chiseled face. So confident in everything. From the wildness of the dark woods to the investments that saved this house. And despite this inconvenient marriage, she admired his devil-may-care approach. With some reservations. Perhaps she would just have to content herself with being the disguise for her husband's covert affairs. That would have to suffice for the sum total of her aid. "Very well. I'll not send the dishes."

A sly smile snuck across his face and a bit of veneration for his self-assurance evaporated. "But somehow, I'd like to replace the broken dish."

"Done."

Quite strange how he just agreed. It startled her still.

"Now let's get to my reason for barging in. First of all, I am Cavanaugh to you. Or Cav, though less formal."

She'd done it again. Addressed him by his last name.

"I'd appreciate it if you would address your husband in such a way. Any other name will draw attention."

She nodded.

"Also," he tugged his mother's invitation from his pocket and slapped it against his empty palm. "We have a little problem."

Chapter Eleven

Just the picture perfect day. Ensconced in Judge Blackledge's Greek Revival estate on outer Prather Street, she assessed the perfect dining arrangement in front of her. Mrs. Blackledge seemed to have a floral obsession judging by the gold trimmed plates. Foley, if she remembered the china company correctly. They had been much too delicate and reserved for her. Even the grand home boasted mostly white with dashes of color in paintings of blossoms.

Three dishes, five forks, four knives, three spoons, and two goblets graced the intricate lace tablecloth over a pale green linen. Her name, written in gilded calligraphy, graced the silk paper place card resting in a silver holder. Tiny personal salt and pepper shakers as well as an individual lidded butter dish surrounded her place setting. No fault could be found in the arrangement. Only extreme extravagance and the uttermost attention to detail.

Perhaps Cavanaugh was correct. Surely her mind bordered on being unstable, for she couldn't help but compare the elegant place setting, screaming the care of the utmost details, to the simple plate of peach pie impaled with a tarnished spoon on a pine board table.

She didn't want to center on Cavanaugh's opinion at the moment. Or the man himself. For he presented well in his black evening wear and roguish horizontal tie , his long unruly hair pulled back in a leather cord, his beard oiled down in obedience. Ordinarily, she'd have scoffed at such a barbarian, long hair, untrimmed facial hair. Yet the way he bore it, with such confidence, he oozed masculinity. Unbidden came the knowledge of how that coarse beard felt against her face. It hadn't been objectionable in the least.

But her mother spoke with her society voice. Rhapsody tugged her attention to her mother's rigid face, servants in starched uniforms cycling in and out in the background, quiet and unseen.

"You'll have to escort us on the grand tour of your lovely home. Being in Louisville is quite the treat for us. And, of course, the countryside is charming."

Mother had spent the journey deriding the distance from New Albany, even though it hadn't been much more than a half hour drive from the ferry. But it had been long enough for Rhapsody to regret having agreed to share the ride with her mother and father. Cavanaugh had merely pointed out points of interest to shush her mother's self-absorbed backhanded compliments of the city. But by the time they'd arrived, the twitch had set up home under Rhapsody's left eye.

Mrs. Blackledge, although part of the same social circle as her parents, appeared to have a genuine love for her son and a welcoming bearing when greeting him. A dark hand appeared from the right and set a bowl of clear soup in the charger in front of her from the left. Thankfully, the oyster entrée had been removed. The mere smell had tightened her throat.

Once the host sipped his first mouthful of soup, Rhapsody removed the fruit fork from the bowl of her bouillon spoon and dipped the utensil away from her into the clear liquid. Cavanaugh, or Cav, disgusted with herself that she favored the nickname, at her right did the same.

"Thank you so much, Mrs. Lennox. We adore it here. The large tidy yards, room for gardens in the back away from the bustle of the city."

Small talk continued, the judge speaking to her father in the fine arts of shipbuilding, her mother pretending to enjoy the meal. The soup was removed, and a fish plate replaced it. She flaked a corner of the tiny square of white catfish garnished a swath of a white dill sauce.

"What a special type of fish."

And by "special" Mother's tone and word choice insinuated she may as well be eating cow pies. She certainly had a knack for negating positivity with her tone yet using innocent words. But Mrs. Blackledge, dressed in ivory, cast a pleased smile in her direction. "Yes, our servants obtain the fish fresh from the Ohio docks early in the morning. Quite delicious."

If you like fish. For which Rhapsody had never accumulated a taste. No matter. She was well versed in pretending to eat. She'd gotten quite good at it especially of late.

"I'm sure your office sees a great deal of reprobate traffic?" Her father engaged the judge.

Mr. Blackledge's salt and pepper brows elevated over his long face for a moment before launching into an escapade in his courtroom sans names, of course. Meanwhile, Rhapsody touched the fork to her tongue, hoping no one would notice she had yet to eat even a bite.

She raised her eyes in an attempt to stay in the conversation. A small fork appeared in her side vision and stabbed the square of fish on her plate. Her mouth dropped open, and she swung her head in time to see Cavanaugh pop it into his mouth. Then he grinned and winked. She all but gasped. A refined gentleman would never wink. At least at a lady. And he'd never steal food from a woman's plate. Sensing the perusal of others, she schooled her features.

Everyone laughed at the judge's tale, and Rhapsody pasted a small smile to her lips and tried to force a laugh from her chest even though she had no idea what had amused them so, thanks to Cav's little caper. Yet all she could focus on was Cavanaugh leaning so close his lips brushed her ear.

"You might be able to eat if you'd loosen your corset."

She sucked in an audible gasp and felt her face flame. The man had no manners at all. To discuss a woman's undergarments at a formal meal? Miss Bickle's scold on table manners threatened to repeat in her mind.

Mrs. Blackledge's sharp eyes had not missed the exchange. "Oh, Cavanaugh. Are you whispering outrageous secrets to your bride? You'll have to forgive me, Rhapsody. I tried to raise a gentleman with all my heart. But I will admit, he can be a rascal."

"I have no idea what you're talking about, Mother." A wicked glint in Cav's eyes told everyone at the table that he spoke a lie.

Friendly laughter tittered around the table.

"I'm afraid with that length of hair and scruffy beard, one only needs to run their eyes over you to agree with me." His mother gave a soft laugh, but softness abode in her eyes. "Oh, Cav, you've always been a handful. Even as a boy he used to torment his brother with outlandish maxims."

Her companion stiffened at her elbow. His next words came with a bit more truth. "My brother never appreciated wittiness."

The judge joined in the conversation from down the table. "Oh, Shafer had, and still has, plenty of wit, my boy. I believe the word you're searching for is uncouthness."

The room slipped into a moment of uneasy silence until the judge gestured with his fork and spoke again. "Finishing your degree would have helped round out those ungentlemanly traits."

"Or it might have finished me," Cav returned in a low tone.

Mrs. Blackledge cut in as the judge started to speak again. "But now Shafer and Eunice are married, and you and Rhapsody are, as well. I've so looked forward to this day. Why, I'd begun to imagine your little infatuation for Eunice might divert you from marriage for good. So I can't tell you how pleased I was to hear of your wedding arrangements, Cavanaugh. And Rhapsody, maybe you can tame him, dear, although I think he's quite lovely as he is."

"Still you can't say enough for a college degree. More opportunities, more prestige." Rhapsody's father chimed in.

And thank you, Father, for revisiting an obviously unpleasant subject.. The servants took the fish plate and replaced it with a serving of chicken smothered in gravy. At least the food had improved even if the conversation had taken a dive.

"Yes. At least his brother earned a degree. He's quite the success story in New York. Putting in his bid to run for Senator," the judge said, tearing into his chicken.

Mrs. Blackledge patted her mouth with the pale green napkin. "Nevertheless, I'm beside myself with anticipation both for his nomination and for another reason. Shafer's making a trip home next month. Well, they'll both be coming, I should say, Shafer and Eunice. I hadn't had the opportunity to tell you before now."

Cav's fork and knife stilled for a fraction of a second. "Shafer's coming home?"

"Isn't that wonderful?" Mrs. Blackledge turned a somewhat artificial smile to him.

"Delightful."

Rhapsody focused on her meal rather than her husband's sarcastic reply.

"Now, son. This whole incident should be beyond us by now." She graced Rhapsody with an indulgent nod. "Especially now that you're married."

"Of course."

"I suppose you know that Cavanaugh endeavored to court the same woman that Shafer eventually married. Eunice Foley. Delightful young woman. Skilled in the gentlest of graces." Mrs. Blackledge smiled at her parents at the other end of the table. "But I think it all turned out as it should. And now it's merely water under the bridge."

Splish, splash. Despite the airiness of Mrs. Blackledge's words, Rhapsody sensed ominous undertones. She had to give Cav credit for his restraint. If Mother had brought up Devlin, or worse, Miles, she surely would have fainted dead away under the table. But then, her mother had experienced enough social scandal of late.

But perhaps this Eunice woman had meant nothing to him at all. And while she couldn't have agreed that things had turned out for the best, since she knew nothing of this previous flame, she did feel a strange kinship with Cav. He, too, had grown up where his all was never enough. And that is perhaps what drove her to finally speak.

"I'm inclined to agree with you, Mrs. Blackledge. I believe things did turn out as it should." Rhapsody paused a moment to layer in some false intimacy and embellish a few lies. "My husband has done quite well for himself and possesses a great deal of compassion and generosity. Perchance he may have a bent to be rather…outspoken in a charming sort of way. He may not have acquired a degree of higher education, but he's incredibly intelligent, kindhearted, and as gallant as Sir Galahad. I assure you, Mr. and Mrs. Blackledge, you've done a fine job raising him."

My, she may have overshot just a bit. The whole Sir Galahad reference had seemed like a good idea in the moment. Endeavoring to carve the casques of parental callousness and expectation or some sort of thing. Perhaps lashing back from her own pain? That's what she got for staying up through the night to read Lord Tennyson.

Nevertheless, he'd stood beside her in that cabin, when all could have gone south. His big soothing body blocking her from whatever danger would explode through the doorway. And hadn't he paid the house debts she'd run up in her extravagance? Hired new maids? Personally guided people to garner freedom? Brought her into the deciding equation about the household when he had no duty to do so? Even married her to save her reputation?

Yes, she had to admit. He had. All of it. Except those around the table would never know the half of such things. Perhaps she hadn't exaggerated the truth as much as she'd originally thought.

The lump in her throat made it difficult to swallow the bite of meat from her fork. To cover, Rhapsody shot an indulgent smile at the man with disbelief clearly screaming from his eyes. But he obscured it well with a quick grin.

"Could I find a better wife?" He reached his arm around her and gave a squeeze.

Mrs. Blackledge crooned a soft laugh. "You two are just precious. Don't you think so, Mrs. Lennox?"

Mother merely inclined her head, busy collecting shards of information she could use to inflict harm later. Rhapsody filled her mouth with chicken as the conversation drifted to other subjects.

She couldn't help but cast a stealthy glance in her husband's direction. Another wink nearly had her spouting water from her mouth. One moment an unsullied knight, the next a bawdy scoundrel.

❧

Cavanaugh smoothed the saddle blanket across the back of his black mount. He had no official assignment tonight. Merely a desire to ride through the night. Clear his brain. Dinner tonight had turned out much as he expected. Except for Rhapsody. She had pluck. Basically backed his father off his usual trail of disappointment with actual praise. Not sure he really deserved any of it. Yet the fact was, she'd defended him. His inconvenient/convenient bride had come to his defense.

Thoughts of Rhapsody's mother chiding the travel time and the evening's veiled compliments which were anything but, filled his thoughts. Growing up under such confines would be strangling. He knew first hand. However, there was more. Just as he had Eunice, she had Devlin. More so, as they had married.

He threw a leg over his mount and directed the thoroughbred toward the road. Sure, Rhapsody's defense might have been offered to save face of their odd marriage arrangement. Or a joining of demoralized souls. Still, he'd take it. He circled the block and the huge mansion drew his eyes. A dim light gleamed through the master window's curtain lace. Even this late, she appeared awake.

What was his new wife doing up past midnight? He'd grown so used to being awake, it had become a habit. But her?

And Sir Galahad? A grin danced across his face. He'd gained new heights of purity to be likened with such a character. It was almost laughable.

His gaze was drawn by the shadow that briefly darkened the window. She'd be in that white bed jacket and bed clothes. An ethereal vision at evening tide. Face soft in a darkening room. Perhaps cradling Lord Tennyson's book of poems? Reclining against her pillows, encased in silken sheets. Her fetching eyes would glance up, only this time, in authentic adoration with a trace of sensuality.

He tugged his thoughts away from their racy direction and urged the horse down the road. More practical difficulties needed his attention. He patted the pocket with the pouch of money he would leave in Preacher Dubber's barn. He seldom left a note with his drop-offs, but tonight he'd included a short one. *Buy dishes.* Short, simple, to the point. With it he'd honor his promise to Rhapsody.

Speaking of whom, his wife would be a great foil next month when his brother and Eunice arrived. Just thinking of Eunice's corkscrew curls and dimpled cheeks made his heart squeeze. She'd knocked him out the first time he'd met her. So small and dainty. Personality as sweet as fresh maple syrup on a warm plate. Never had he seen her flustered, angry, or out of sorts. Quite contrary to his current wife. Just the thought of the comparison made him shake his head.

But Eunice was Shafer's wife. She'd always intended to marry a man who could go places, for she'd endeavored to trail right along. She'd shared that from the very beginning of their relationship. His years at Princeton University had impressed her to no end. His sentiments to an oppressed people crying for freedom had not. Once his elder brother had obtained that gold-plated Princeton University degree, and Cav had made that life-changing about-face into the underground to contribute to the freedom movement, Eunice had also chosen. And it hadn't been him.

He'd desired the petite brunette like no other woman. And surely he'd loved her. And still did, deep down, if he were honest. It would cut him to see her again on the arm of his brother, casting coy glances at her husband. If Shafer allowed her to do so in public. Most likely not.

Nevertheless, a dinner party would ensue, and having gorgeous, leggy Rhapsody on his arm wouldn't be a bad way to avert discomfort of being around and seeing Eunice once again. And it would definitely deflect his brother's condescending attitude toward him. He might smooch his new bride in front of old Shafer, just to watch the outrage swell on his pompous face at such lewd behavior.

Kissing Rhapsody? He almost laughed outright in the dark. He'd dodge a slap to feel it again. Those soft lips, her mesmerizing gaze. He should kiss her in the daylight. That way he'd get the full effect of her flashing blue eyes.

Strange how shocking his brother had suddenly tumbled to second place behind experiencing Rhapsody's kiss. He growled just under his breath. My, but what a kiss it would be.

Chapter Twelve

Rhapsody sat up in bed, feeling incredibly refreshed and invigorated. She hadn't felt this good since before Devlin had passed. Maybe since before she'd married him. For afterwards she'd been consumed with the construction of the house and selection of its interior furnishings.

As a matter of fact, the last several weeks had worked some kind of miracle over the melancholy delirium she'd started to experience long before Devlin's death. Getting out of bed, even exiting the room had become almost an impossible task.

She'd tried her best to shield herself from being suspect of such gloomy vapors. But shunning so many social engagements might have been perceived as if she suffered from some such malady. She shivered. Hadn't Mrs. Coglin down the street been sent to the county asylum for melancholia insanity?

The poor farm. Imagine being confined in such a place. Hopefully, her marriage to Cav might have also helped to dispel any rumors of suspicious malaise she may have developed. Who could have foretold she'd be thankful for this inopportune marriage? That it had been fortuitous when Cav had wrapped her in an indecorous embrace on a dark empty road.

Her face flushed even as the memory deluged her thoughts. Thinking back on it, it hadn't been unpleasant except for her outrage, which had been quite significant if she remembered correctly. She'd even managed to get a slap in later. She let a small laugh escape from her lips. The poor man.

Yes, the blight seemed to be lifting. Last night, she could hardly sleep a wink. She'd paced with an energy and conviction she hadn't felt since taking on the building of this cursed house. And she'd come up with quite a scheme.

So Cavanaugh had vetoed the dish brigade. She had to admit, he'd been right. And in the end, she'd concurred. Eventually. Crating up a plethora of expensive dishes would have been quite foolish in the light of her new resolve to help others find freedom. Instead, her mind had bubbled with what could be done to assist the freedom endeavor. And what she had discovered had been brilliant.

Dishes were the least of these people's problems. Still, a fine mess after all those late-night trips up the stairs to squirrel away almost ten place settings. A predicament she'd think on later.

As she had paced, she'd realized she had to dig deeper into the basic needs of human flesh. Yes, yes, money solved an abundance of issues, sure. But there were more immediate needs. Clothing to be exact. Those escaping enslavement at the drop of a hat needed to shed their outer appearance of what had held them prisoner. Their uniforms, clothing, poor tattered ragged skirts, pants, shirts, the lack of blankets, even food. These were the things of utmost importance. And she would deliver them.

Instead of asking Cav for currency, she would raise the money herself. Right here, in this very mansion. She'd conceal it all under the cover of the church's charitable fund. She had the perfect residence to hold such a function. Put out invitations to the richest citizens for an elegant meal, music, even dancing. Then, of course, she'd give away a portion she collected to the church's charitable fund and save back a share to support her clothing philanthropy.

Why, they could supply shoes, socks, small dolls and keepsakes for the children. *Children.* She really hadn't considered the dark, soul-eyed moppets following the same dangerous trail as their parents. How frightened they must be. Rhapsody bounced from her bed. Yes, this was her calling.

She pranced toward the tassel to ring for Lissy and then froze. Lissy. Some of the elation of her new venture faded. The aid was intended for people like Lissy who'd grown up beside her, serving her and her family for years without home or family to call her own. Her hand fluttered to her throat. This double life would not be as easy as she had once conceived.

Rhapsody spun and hurried to her armoire to fling it open. She could care for herself, couldn't she? She'd dressed herself before. She ran her hand across the profusion of gowns. So many. Lace and beads, silk and brocade. Designs that had taken weeks to prepare.

Suddenly it all smacked rather...egotistical to own so many expensive garments. It caused her to pause a few moments before she pulled a navy silk from the selection.

No need to ponder all of this excess now. She had work to do. With a flash of excitement at her independence, she whipped the bed jacket from her shoulders and actually giggled when she swiped the night gown over her own head. Although she'd dressed herself before on the night she'd followed Cav, this seemed different somehow. Like she was finally maturing. Or becoming someone new. A sympathizer. An...*abolitionist.*

She pulled on her cotton drawers and chemise and was just about to try her hand at tightening her corset when a soft knock sounded at the door. Oh, it must be late if Lissy were trying to stir her from bed. Yes, indeed. The clock indicated just before noon.

"Enter."

Lissy's eyes grew wide when she popped around the door. She scurried forward to help tighten the laces with eyes full of questions and dread. The woman gave a mighty tug on the strings and Rhapsody saw darkness fuzz in the outer recesses of her vision. It couldn't help but bring to mind Cav's bold comment at the Blackledge dinner.

"No, Lissy." She murmured. "Looser."

As Rhapsody braced herself against the bed post at the foot of the bed, she could sense the maid's hesitation.

"Mum?"

Rhapsody turned and saw more worry mount in the woman's face. "I want to breathe, Lissy. Breathe, eat. Live."

Lissy dropped her eyes with a nod and Rhapsody turned to let her finish her task. It did feel monumentally better. She took a deep breath. And then another. Gracious. It did feel freeing.

Her maid finished the small buttons in back and assisted Rhapsody with the petticoats, though not as many as she normally wore, which also drew a puzzled frown from her servant's face.

Once the task complete, Rhapsody brushed her skirt front down. Her next words came with a moments' hesitation. "Thank you…Lissy."

The large-boned woman's mouth dropped. Rhapsody doubted she'd ever said those two words aloud to the one person who had seen to her every need.

Lissy nodded. "You's welcome, Mum."

"Well, I have a lot to accomplish today. I'll need to eat a bite and then I'll require a carriage."

Again the nod. But the woman didn't scurry to do her bidding as she always did. Instead Lissy stood grasping her rough work hands together, dread growing ever present in her eyes.

"Is there something else?"

"Yes, Mum. We be missing some…dishes," the last word rushed out in a whisper.

Somehow it struck Rhapsody as humorous and a smile eased across her face. "Don't worry. Follow me, Lissy."

Rhapsody brushed through the doorway and turned right down the third wing to the bedroom at the end. She swept the door open and let the maid creep in behind her, trepidation in her wide eyes.

"A bit of a misunderstanding. I intended to shed some of our excess dishes. But I've changed my mind." She ran her eyes over the array of dish stacks and caught sight of the poor teacup that hadn't escaped unscathed in her face-off with Cavanaugh.

The corner of her mouth creased in amusement. Lissy caught sight of the nomadic cup too, and scrambled over to pick it up. The maid's breath caught in her throat.

"The handle done broke off, Mum."

With a nod, Rhapsody crossed the floor, took the wounded vessel, and turned it in her hands. "Indeed. It shall never be the same."

The words flowed from her with such warmth that Lissy looked her over, hands worrying at her middle.

"No matter. I'll find some use for it." Rhapsody strolled to the door. "Don't be in a hurry to have the servants return the dinnerware. Only when there's time. There's no hurry."

Then Rhapsody faltered a step and stopped. "Wait, well, it might be important to return the dishes in the next week or so. For the mansion will be filled with people soon."

She returned to her master bedroom, caressing the dainty teacup in her hand. With a sigh on her lips, she shut the door and placed the navy and gold cup with a floral centerpiece on the table near her bed. No longer a cup, but rather now a…vase.

The piece of china, through its brokenness, had exchanged its lowly purpose for a higher one. Now it would embrace the beauty of flowers to cheer her day. To inspire her and the others around her. Such a revelation was surely the muse of Lord Tennyson.

Her eyes glanced toward the window. Not with thoughts of a famous poet, but of one man much less well-known. And much closer. One who resided just a few bedrooms away.

Cav tapped the ledger before him. It would please him to no end to shove the neat column of numbers under his father's nose, verifying his success as an investor. But that would prove Cav held a jealous grudge against his brother, and honestly, did he really care? He dropped the leather bound volume onto the gleaming desk and recalled his father's prideful reference to his brother's bid for the Senate. Being in government spelled success in his father's eyes.

But his returns this quarter had far exceeded any he'd had previously. He strolled to the back of the library where the previous owner's painting hung. He assessed the man, Devlin Hastings. Thin, tall, but good-looking enough, Cav supposed, with long bangs flipped to the right and eyes the color of tea. Had Rhapsody been in love with the dashing young man in the gray dinner jacket, white silk cravat at this throat? Or had she married for money and influence?

He supposed he should store the relic. He was, after all, the new owner of the estate. But, as was his inclination to include Rhapsody in decisions, he wanted to check on his wife's preference. She may have some reason to continue leaving the painting hanging. Perhaps she came into the library in his absence and gazed upon it, grief thick with adoration and longing. Odd how that bothered him more than a little.

His thoughts were interrupted with a tap on the door. Ah, just on time. For more than one reason. He strode back to his desk.

"Enter."

In filed his six uniformed servants who lined up in front of his desk, heads bowed. Some dared to shoot him wide eyes, fear evident by their countenance.

"Good morning, staff."

They greeted him in return with a group utterance.

He passed a bit behind the desk, looking them over. The grey uniforms of the women were new and overlaid with starched, white aprons. Barton and his carriage assistant wore darker gray working suits, clean and pressed. The carriage driver clutched a top hat in his hands. Cav circled the desk and checked their shoes. The black leather boots gleamed in the morning sunlight. Excellent. Rhapsody had seen to keeping them well dressed. The woman was a wonder.

"I'm very pleased with all of your work, and I'm proud to have you taking care of the details of this house." They seemed to stand a little taller, eyes a little clearer.

"Thank you, sir." The women bobbed a small curtsy and the men nodded.

"Mr. Wadell, Mr. Barton, Miss Mabel, Miss Betty, Miss Sena, and Miss Lissy." Knowing his staff like the back of his hand, he pointed down the row, including his new maid Miss Betty, and the new scullery maid, Miss Sena. "First of all, I don't consider any of you property. You're men and women who work to take care of my home, grounds, and carriage house. I appreciate that. And I'm a man who believes a man or woman is worth their wages. Which up to now, you have received nothing but room and board. That's about to change."

A few quiet gasps from a couple of the females brought Cav's head up. He declined commanding Miss Betty to close the door. Instead Cav strode across the room and shut it himself. Then he spun, clasped his hands behind his back, and paced forward. He lowered his voice. "I'll force no one to work here who has dreams of other…ventures. Therefore, you only have to speak with Barton, and he will inform me of the changes. We here at the Blackledge Estate will carry on without you."

Several faces lifted, mouths agape. Good. They'd caught his meaning. Would any of them be heading to Preacher Dubber's in the next few weeks? Only time would tell.

He stepped behind the desk and pulled out six envelopes and tapped them on the desktop. "Meanwhile, I wish to extend to each of you, a current wage with back pay depending on your years of service here and to my wife. And from now on, you will receive a monthly stipend as our appreciation for a work well done."

Confusion etched lines on a few of their faces. But Barton would bring them up to speed if they didn't understand. "However. This is a delicate matter, as I'm sure you will understand quite fully. One that is of no business to our neighbors, acquaintances, or friends. Therefore, silence is of the greatest importance. At times, a matter of life and death. As far as to the safety of your savings, I'd be glad to store your currency in the house safe or invest it for you should you choose to do so. Are there any questions?"

The group had been struck dumb. A smile tipped his mouth and Cav stepped to Wadell and held his hand out. The big man's head came up and, at first, he stared at Cav's proffered hand. Then his gaze dashed up to lock with his. The black man's jaw worked a moment before he extended his hand, much like touching a viper. Wadell placed his palm in Cav's and shook. Then the stable hand took the envelope.

Cav continued down the line, giving a small bow to the ladies as they curtsied back. Envelopes in hand, stunned expressions upon their faces, his servants stood frozen. Cav paced to the door and opened it. "Thank you all, and have a pleasant day."

At last they blinked and filed solemnly out the door.

Cav grinned as he shut the door. That had almost been as gratifying as driving Number Two to Preacher Dubber's place.

Chapter Thirteen

Mother leaned back against the cushions of the Blackledge carriage seat. She always grew nervous when the carriage wandered into the dirt tracks. Rhapsody found the country scenery quite relaxing.

"Seems a bit too rushed for such an affair."

"Not at all." Rhapsody returned. "The invitations have been sent, the quartet engaged, and the servants are working on the menu. Everything is right on time."

"I mean for decorum's sake. Two weeks is hardly time enough to expect influential people to arrange their schedules to accommodate your…soiree."

The tone of the last word fairly sliced Rhapsody's wrists. "It's a charity event, Mother. People will understand. I've already received a few acknowledgements, and the pastor is thrilled."

“That doesn’t excuse poor timing, Rhapsody. It’s boorish to assume people will flock to a mishmash gathering for the sake of aiding the less fortunate.”

Rhapsody glanced out the window. She refused to apologize. The Blackledge Philanthropic Charity Gala would commence in two weeks whether her mother endorsed it or not.

“At least you’re returning to the social scene. Quite mortifying how you declined so many opportunities to call on the ladies of our circle.”

Again, Rhapsody set her teeth on edge to halt yet another apology that popped to her mouth. Instead she changed the subject. “So, you said Mrs. Graves would be joining us today. I can’t recall our association with her, although I’m sure she must be of a prominent family.”

“Dear heavens, Rhapsody. The Graves are quite invested in lumber to supply the plethora of businesses at the docks. Your father has a standing contract with them for our steamship building enterprise. Surely, you remember your grandmother visiting with her years ago?”

She didn’t, but what did it matter? What did interest her was the opportunity of extending an invitation to the gala. The more that attended, the better. Or rather, the higher the fund collection.

“She has the large mansion on Main with the twin spires.”

“Ah, I see. And her family?”

“Oh, it’s dreadful. Their only daughter married beneath her years ago and moved to Kentucky to live on a mule farm. Can you even imagine? And now, she’s passed. Quite the expectant consequence for allowing some proletariat to take your only daughter. I understand she has several grandchildren from that union, but they are estranged as far as I know. Nauseating business. The Graves name dragged through such disgrace."

Scandal, scandal, scandal. How her mother loved to savor such stories. Rather than ask more questions, Rhapsody chose to be silent than hear more of the lament. The carriage slowed as they approached the Broussard Estate, and turned up the lane. Beautiful grounds. Cattle grazed in a field nearby.

"I detest the country. Why anyone would so choose to live out here rather than in the city is beyond me. The roads, the smells. It's repulsive." Her mother huffed with a flip of her folded fan as she exited the phaeton, clutching Barton's hand. "The usual group will be here, plus Mrs. Graves and of course, the O'Sullivans."

Her mother nearly vomited the last name out. Ah, yes. Mrs. O'Sullivan came from the hills of eastern Kentucky and was quite a bumpkin in both outspokenness and casual ways. My, it would be humorous to watch her mother's face today.

Rhapsody nodded and thanked Barton for his help. A new light shone in the older man's eyes.

Mother continued. "She has five plump daughters. Why they have no restraint is a reflection of their ignoble patronage. All five offspring look exactly alike and have names so similar they escape me at present. Plus Mrs. O'Sullivan's sashayed around pregnant for five solid years, walking barefoot. Shameful. And rumor has it, they tried to have even more children but failed. Thank God for small favors." Her mother completed her whispered soliloquy in time to paste a smile to her face at the door.

A servant with the skin tone of honey nodded, shut the door, and guided them to a large parlor. My, the room practically swam in ladies, standing and chatting. Giggles came from near the fireplace where the infants stood huddled.

Rhapsody had no trouble picking out the chubby O'Sullivan girls. Like stair steps to the second floor, they each resembled one another in slightly smaller versions. Mrs. Broussard introduced the O'Sullivan matriarch, who in turn, with a genuine smile and a great deal of pride shining from her voice, named off her children one by one as they curtsied. Saralynn, Loralynn, Taneylynn, Barbaralynn, Adelynn.

"I know I got a bit carried away with the Lynns, but it was my dear mother's name," Mrs. O'Sullivan recounted in a sharp southern twang. "And after the first two, I just couldn't stop."

Imagine wanting to name your children after your mother. Fancy that.

After introductions, the women seated themselves on the furniture and extra chairs. Across the way a distinguished elderly woman dressed to the nines, hair in a low bun, sat upon a wing chair. That must be Mrs. Graves. The woman leaned over to speak to the young blonde woman next to her.

Rhapsody stiffened and her breath halted. Cora Taggart. Miles's sister. Miles—the Miles she'd rudely spurned to marry Devlin Hastings, his best friend. A mortified blush rose up Rhapsody's neck.

The heat of the room couldn't stop the cold chills that broke across her skin. Why was Cora here? She didn't circulate in their social circles. The object of her horror raised her eyes to collide with hers. Reservation rested there in the slight narrowing of Cora's eyes.

Rhapsody had to get out of the room. Her mother seemed engaged, talking to Mrs. Broussard next to her, so she rose and marched determinedly toward the foyer. The maid there opened the door, and Rhapsody rushed through. The slight breeze swept over her and tiny goosebumps dotted her skin. She avoided the windows in the front and breezed around the side. There the splotched black and white cows munched in oblivion, in peacefulness. No social stigmas to avoid or endure. How nice it would be to be a cow.

Surely Mother had known Cora would be in attendance. Of all the dirty, dastardly things to do. Fail to prepare her for coming face to face with her old suitor's sister. The man she had jilted shamelessly. The door opened behind her. Her mother, following her more than likely. She turned. Cora stood behind her.

"Hello, Rhapsody."

She'd forgotten how tall Cora was. She swallowed, looked up, and lied. "Cora, how nice to see you."

"I brought my daguerreotype of my marriage picture and forgot it in the carriage." Cora blessed her with a newlywed smile. "Want to see?"

Rhapsody's hand fluttered to her throat and continued the falseness. "Of course."

She trailed Cora to the fancy phaeton near the front of the drive. Cora pulled the photo from a brown paper wrap. "See, this is my husband, Trigg Gentry. And me, of course."

The metal plate displayed a fine picture of the couple, both tall and handsome. They stood between two white porch posts, evergreen flouncing the railing. Both very happy. "It's…lovely."

"We were married just before Christmas. It was sort of a whirlwind. But I guess when you find that special one, you just know."

Rhapsody blanched. How could she follow such a revelation? She'd scorned Cora's brother with a mere letter. The only thing she could think to do is spew the whole wretched truth. "Listen, Cora. I owe your brother and family a huge apology. I…spurned your brother's courtship, and you can't know how much I regret hurting him."

Cora's brows rose. "That's quite unexpected, Rhapsody. Forgive me, but I never pegged you as a person given to regrets."

A burning started in the back of her throat. "If you only knew…"

"I'll pass along your sentiments. But I assure you, he's wonderfully happy. His wife's a sweet woman. They have two little ones now."

An ache started low and seemed to radiate. She knew Miles had married. Petite little thing, if she remembered when she'd spat out some scathing remark or two to her. She handed back the daguerreotype. "I'm so glad."

"I hear you are remarried." Cora turned to walk back to the house, and Rhapsody fell in step beside her.

"Yes. To Cavanaugh Blackledge."

"Yes, Trigg's grandmother mentioned seeing it in the papers."

"And she is…"

"Mrs. Graves. I married her grandson, Trigg. We live down south of Henderson, Kentucky. He breeds mules."

My, Cora didn't seem to bat an eye to be part of the working-class life. The woman seemed to glow. Mother's scathing attacks of consequences when joined to commoners didn't seem to be affecting Cora and Trigg Gentry any.

"And—" she leaned forward eyes sparkling, "I'm expecting."

Oh, Rhapsody recovered nicely from what seemed like a blow to her middle section and clasped Cora's outstretched hands. "Congratulations. When will the little one arrive?"

Her smile lit the shade beneath the huge poplar tree as they approached the porch. "Around Christmas. I think Grandmother will announce it today, so keep it to yourself for a few more minutes."

Cora preceded her when they returned to the house, waved, and joined Mrs. Graves on the other side of the room. Rhapsody's mother widened her eyes, chastising her for leaving the gathering. She sank into her chair. Seeing Cora so in love dampened the relief Rhapsody had felt after confessing her regret in doing Miles wrong.

What must it be like to be so in love that life was like spring year round? To feel the product of your love grow deep in your belly and feel the joy of expectation of a new life? Cora's blushing face and shining eyes as she passed her wedding photo made Rhapsody cringe with envy and sour disappointment.

She hadn't loved Miles. That had been obvious. She'd only loved controlling him. Giving Miles up only became a regret because the match with Devlin had been so disillusioningly dull. And now, guilt ran deep in her soul for letting Devlin go so long without medical care. Her eye had been on the completion of the mansion. Nothing else had mattered.

Scorned sorrow took scandal's hand. In a loveless marriage. Much like she dwelt in a sad Tennyson poem. Yearning for something she could never have. Rhapsody feared a relapse of the brooding malaise that had dogged her every step in recent years.

For when bliss stared you in the face, it became glaringly obvious that Rhapsody's loveless life had no hope of redemption.

Cav glanced up from his book as he heard the back door open. From his seat on the parlor Chesterfield, his wife, head bowed, came scurrying through the room, Lissy at her heels. She was on the third step of the stairs before she registered his presence with a start.

"Oh, forgive me. I didn't realize you were here, I mean…home."

Rhapsody, usually immaculate to a tee, appeared flustered, locks of hair escaping the upswept style, her hand white from gripping the rail.

"Perhaps we could dine together tonight?"

She glanced up the stairway. "I'm not sure…"

"I'd like to discuss a few things with you if possible."

Her body wilted slightly then stiffened. "Of course."

With Lissy on her trail, Rhapsody treaded the stairway in a more sedate manner. He elevated one brow. Had she taken on too much with this rumored charity gala? One of the many things he wished to discuss with her.

He shrugged it off and went back to Hawthorne's *Scarlet Letter*. He wouldn't be mentioning his choice of literature to her parents, however, at the next get-together. He'd already been branded uncouth without the subject matter of his choice of novels coming to light.

Nearly an hour later he sat at the more intimate dining cove, located in front of the bay window at the back of the house. If it had been earlier, they might have enjoyed the garden scenery. His wife appeared at the door, changed and hair tucked deftly into properness again.

He rose and pulled out a chair to his left. She, a vision in an ivory gown, came forward and allowed him to seat her. Cav returned to his chair.

"So, you went calling today, I assume?"

"Yes. With Mother."

Oh, the delights of spending the day with Mrs. Lennox. No wonder she'd come in with such a flurry.

"Quite a late gathering." He leaned back as Miss Betty set the onion soup bowl before him.

Rhapsody squirmed. "Actually, I went for a drive after I dropped Mother off."

"I see. Anywhere in particular?"

Her eyes darted his way. "Not exactly."

Enough small talk. She was being evasive, and he would eventually find out why. "I have a few things of discussion. First of all, the painting in the library. Is it of use to you?"

Her spoon froze.

"Of Mr. Hastings," he continued when she didn't answer.

She dabbed her upper lip with the beige napkin. "Yes, I know the one."

"Are you terribly fond of it? I mean, I know he was your late husband, but the estate has since passed to me. And I'm afraid I've set up my business there in the library. Perhaps we could hang it in some upstairs guestroom."

"You may do whatever you wish with it."

He would have to get more direct. Catching her hand as she reached for the goblet, he leaned closer. "Rhapsody. What do you wish to be done with your first husband's portrait?"

She snatched her hand away and stood, backing away from the table. "It doesn't matter, Cavanaugh. He's haunted me all I can bear. You can burn it for all I care."

She spun and fled through the door as he sat there in shock. Had the woman lost her senses? Burn her dead husband's painting? After a moment, he stood too, Miss Betty's face scrunching in bewilderment as she hovered near the kitchen door.

He strode to the stairway and took them two at a time. He caught up with her as Rhapsody's hand alighted on the doorknob.

"Stop right there. We're going to discuss this."

Her face, alight with fury, turned toward his. "No, we're not."

She wrenched open the door and went to slam it in his face. He deftly set his boot against the base, bouncing the door wide open. Her eyes flared in surprise and she backed away.

Cav entered and quietly shut the door behind him. "Now, where were we?"

Chapter Fourteen

"Get out of my room," she seethed, clutching her fisted hands in a faux repose. How ill fit she was most of the time with proper decorum.

"Ah, Rhapsody. Sadly, I now own the home. That makes this room mine as well. In more than one respect."

To his astonishment, tears sparkled in the depths of those blue eyes. Perhaps he'd gone too far. But the little tigress had been such a charming challenge before, taking him on toe to toe the night they'd sealed their futures together.

However, Rhapsody had fled into the next room, through a double set of doors. He stepped through to a small sitting room he hadn't even known existed. She stood near a piano, back against the far wall, her back to him. A gust of remorse washed over him.

He moved beside her and spoke in a gentle timbre. "I apologize if I came on too strong. I merely endeavor to gain your opinion."

Only her nod answered him.

Her uncharacteristic brokenness touched him, and he turned her toward him, wiping tears with a lace hanky. "Ah, Rhapsody."

He gathered her into his arms, and she didn't resist. If anything, she leaned closer, pressing her forehead against his chest. He snugged her against him, feeling the silent sobs rock her body. What had her so distressed? Having been in the presence of her mother, a personality so full of emotional poison, it could be anything. Yet perhaps it had nothing to do with the woman at all. She'd been in a room packed with women. Any one of them could have caused her suffering.

Or was she yearning for Devlin?

Cav's hands touched the curling tendrils of her sunshine hair. Soft and inviting. How he'd love to erase Devlin Hastings from her mind right now. But, that would hardly solve the real issue. Whatever it happened to be.

He sensed her pulling back, and he let his hands slide to her arms. Head still bowed, he lifted her chin. "What is it? Something happen at the tea? Or do you truly hurt from wanting to burn the portrait?"

Her voice came, defeated and flat. "It is I who should burn."

His face puckered. "Nonsense. Nothing needs to be destroyed. I understand your unwillingness to part with the—"

"No." She thrust her arms down, eyes teeming with agony. "He was sick. And I pushed him. I was always pushing him. He should have seen a doctor, and I just kept ordering more rugs, more tables, more dishes. It was too late when I found out how deep in debt we were."

She whirled from him and wandered over to perch on the fainting couch. "By the time I came to my senses, he was at death's door. And there was nothing they could do. Pneumonia. Pneumonia took him in three weeks." Rhapsody raised her tormented eyes. "I killed him. My own greed took my husband's life."

Cav knelt in front of his wife and gathered her limp hands in his. He studied the tear-stained face in front of him. "Pneumonia is a very dangerous disease. Even if he'd had the best care, he might not have made it. You can't blame yourself."

She hung her head.

"You must have loved him very much."

Her head shook, then lifted. She glowered at him. "I didn't love him at all. The only person I loved was— myself. And I will forever pay for it."

He massaged her hands, the scent of rosewater drifting from her hair. "I don't see that person at all. The woman I know outfits her staff in clean, new uniforms. She carries plates upstairs in the obscurity of night, stacking, and planning to crate and donate them to those less fortunate. She sequesters vital secrets, knowing lives depend upon her discretion, even at the expense of her own reputation."

He searched her face, felt her trembling. His eyes feasted on the loveliness of her forlorn expression, her uncertain eyes. Desire swelled between them, and his voice dropped to a low rumble.

"And then she married a corrupt, vile, immoral being who thinks she's quite generous and…beautiful."

She seemed suspended there, her mouth softly parted, wet with her tears. "I'm so sorry I said those things about you. They're…untrue."

Suddenly he regretted promising her first move. For in this moment, it shook him to realize he had never wanted to kiss a woman more than he wanted to kiss Rhapsody. Ever. Being the baser human in all his masculine need, he couldn't dare initiate…he wouldn't.

Her hands tugged free of his, their eyes locked in fervid ardor. Then her hands threaded his hair, stroked his beard, caressed the hot skin of his face. He squeezed his eyes shut and hung on to his restraint with all his might.

"Cav?" she whispered.

He lifted his eyelids. Blue desire leapt from her eyes.

She exhaled between swollen lips. "Kiss me."

Cav rolled over, delighting in the feel of the silk sheets. He couldn't stem the smile that curled across his face. Without opening his eyes, he felt the mattress next to him, desiring only to bury his face in Rhapsody's fragrant softness. She'd begged for his kiss, and she received it. Many times over and so much more.

He rose up on his elbow in the midst of the master bedroom's huge four-poster bed and found her side of the bed empty. Disappointment sank like a stone in his gut. Starting the day tangled up with his exquisite wife would have sent him off whistling for the day. Maybe the rest of the week.

He slid from the mattress and slapped his bare feet against the Persian rug to the water closet. She wasn't in there. Perhaps the sitting room? He ignored his pants and shirt strewn across the floor and pushed open the double doors. Empty as well.

Cav strolled to the window, covered in a lace panel, shadows and sunlight protecting his buck-naked body from being seen from anyone below. He stretched his arms toward the ceiling and settled his hands interwoven behind his head.

For some strange reason, he had a bad feeling about the absence of his wife.

Rhapsody paced the library, measuring even steps, stopping every five paces to be sure to press the crown of her head toward the ceiling. Proper posture. Then repeated the same. Over and over, pinky and ring finger digging into the flesh of her hand.

What had she done? She'd freed some kind of beast. Not Cav. *Her.* Women were not supposed to entreat a man for a kiss. Nor enjoy what ensued. She sucked in a gasp. She'd done exactly what he'd demanded. That she beg. And heaven help her, she had done just that.

Hadn't her mother schooled her to acquiesce to her husband the night before her marriage to Devlin? Close her eyes and bear the onslaught for the sacrifice of heirs? That she would find her joy in household duties and social gatherings? Oh, glory, it had been nothing like that.

She had not only elicited Cav's attentions, she'd…seduced him. A choking sound caught in her throat. How could any proper lady behave in such a manner? Her face flamed in memory, making her pause her posture drills.

How would she ever face him? Here she'd been accusing him of his lewd, barbaric behavior from the moment of the first stolen kiss, and she was nothing but a wanton woman in disguise of a society lady. Humiliation burned from the roots of her hair to the tips of her toes.

Somehow, some way, she had to get him out of her…bedroom. None of this could be repeated again. Ever. Proper genteel ladies did not behave in such a manner.

She pinched her eyes close and tightened her fists. What she had to do was keep him at arm's length. The man had the ability to provoke her with just a glance.

Rhapsody counted off the next five steps and caught sight of Devlin's stiff portrait. She tramped to it and ripped it from the wall. And the fate of this painting had been the ignitor. She'd known before somehow, how drawn she'd been to the strength of Cav's magnetism. Felt its pull that night in the hallway. Why had she let herself succumb?

One of her hands clutched the canvas and the other covered her mouth. She'd bared her soul to him. Her face crimped into a grimace. How he must be laughing at her now. Pleased he'd conquered the snappish widow. She would certainly be of use to him now since he'd tamed her. Whom did she hate more? Him or herself? Honestly, it was a toss-up.

The scandal of the forbidden tryst in the woods paled in comparison to her degradation now. He had the upper hand. Using her and tossing her aside when the mood struck him. The marriage insured she could never be rid of him. She'd be his simple amusement. A feminine trinket. Checkmate.

With a groan she whirled and strutted to the kitchen. Miss Mabel stood at the stove, frying up fragrant bacon while the two new servants, Miss Betty and—for the life of her, she couldn't recall the woman's name—were hard at work with their tasks, scouring and cracking eggs. But all movement ceased when she burst through the door.

Rhapsody plopped the painting facedown on the long table near the door. "Miss Mabel, I want this wrapped and stored in a safe place. But I don't want to see it hung, or come across it in my wanderings in this house. Is that clear?" She swung to leave, paused, and cleared her throat. "Thank you."

She thrust through the door, sped toward the stairs, and slowed as she climbed, trying to think of a way to extricate that man from her room. Short of charging at him with a shovel or a rifle musket, she had no clue. Knowing his strength first hand, she groaned. Both of those ideas smacked senseless anyway.

Once at the top of the stairway, she paused. Perhaps it might be easier to lock herself in some other bedroom. But eventually she would need her clothing and other possessions.

No. She gritted her teeth. It was time to clean house. And, oh, would she scour this pot. He would know he couldn't toy with Rhapsody Marie. She slowed. And stopped. She shook her head. That wasn't her name. She was Rhapsody Redemption, and she would set her world right once more. She *would* be delivered.

She swung the heavy door open and strode in just as Cav waltzed in from the sitting room. Stark naked.

"Cav!" With a spin, she hid behind the door. She hissed through the crack, "Put some pants on."

Her command must have set him in motion for she heard the swish of garments. When she peeked in, he stood at the foot of the bed, chest bare, a look of pure confusion on his face.

"Shirt."

Peeping around the hardwood door, she watched him slide his arms into the sleeves. She took a couple of fortifying breaths, wishing he'd buttoned up. Her hand pushed the door open a smidgeon more. "I want you out of my room."

Oh, how she wanted to take that back. Commands of such sort were always met with his reminder he owned the entire estate, and that he would go where he pleased. Yet pleading was too close to begging. Begging had started this trouble from the beginning.

"Rhapsody, I was wondering—"

"Stop right there." She held up her hand. "You may wonder no more. I know you own the mansion, but this is my space, my personal space. I built this manor from the ground up. I deserve my own area where I will not be…invaded. And as to what happened last night, it was a mistake, not to be misconstrued as an activity that would be…repeated."

"Ah-ah-ah," she interrupted when he began to speak, flickers of anger in his stance, the clenching fists. "I have no desire to make such a miscalculation in judgment again. You will stay over there, and I will stay here. Are you comprehending what I am telling you?"

His dark eyes sparked with glitters of fury and something else. Pain? Had she misjudged his intentions? His reactions? No, surely not. Surely he esteemed her no higher than his own personal scarlet woman, if his reading material were any indicator.

"Clear as a bell."

He brushed past her barefooted and turned left at the end of the hall, heading toward his wing. With a sigh, she shrank into the room and pressed the door closed. She let her back rest against the wood as she took short gasps, rolling her eyes at his socks and boots at the edge of the rug. With a sniff, she straightened and smoothed the dress front down and examined the lock on the door. Never had she used it. But tonight she would begin. While her resolve proved strong now, he would eventually catch her in a moment of weakness. And she couldn't risk that.

She plucked up the huge boots, shoved the socks inside and plopped them outside the door. With a flick of her wrist, she turned the golden skeleton key in the lock. It made a scraping, ominous sound. She shook the door. Tight and secure. Ha. She…had won.

Somehow, instead of feeling vindicated, she felt like a Shakespearean shrew. The crush of sorrow that draped her heart all but soaked away the pleasurable night. But that was exactly what she wanted. From now on, she'd avoid him as before. Aid his abolitionist efforts just as she'd planned. But his high-handedness would not usurp her soul.

She'd be a fool no more.

Chapter Fifteen

Rhapsody spun for the third time to inspect the bone china gracing the three long dining tables and straightened a fork nearest her. Two extra tables, unearthed from the attic, mirrored her more expensive original one having been swathed in blue linen and lace to match. The huge room appeared slightly cramped, but with the removal of some of the additional dining salon furniture, there had been space.

She had to admit, with the help of a couple of temporary servants, the house gleamed, the tableware sparkled, and all was in its place. Mother may tip her chin in haughty disapproval, but she'd pulled the charity gala together in a whirlwind. Forty people would begin arriving in approximately an hour.

Her gaze flicked to the trio setting up near the grand piano in the music room between the dining salon and the drawing room. The top-hatted tall man tuned his violin, while the mustached cellist positioned his chair next to the large instrument. The third man, a compact red-head, ran chords up and down the keys with limber fingers. Excellent. She patted the white donation box near the entry, checked the parchment donation cards, envelopes, and the fountain pen.

Once the ballet troupe arrived, she would be free to change into her dress. A knock sounded at the door. That had to be them. Miss Betty padded through and opened the door to the traveling group, thin and lithe, and they followed the servant upstairs to the rooms where they would prepare for the exhibition scenes of *La Esmerelda*.

Seating so many people in the dining area had altered Rhapsody's initial plans of holding a ball. Plus, the absence of a ballroom made waltzing difficult although not impossible. Besides the ballet excerpt would keep everyone entertained and corralled. And hopefully center the guests' minds on being generous.

Since the room had emptied and all seemed ready, Rhapsody skipped up the stairs, forgoing her usual step and pause charm-school stair etiquette. She swished through the master bedroom door and gazed upon her gala dress. The lightest of blue satin, it shone with an iridescent radiance.

The bodice dipped a bit too much for her liking. An ancient gown reworked. Why she hadn't altered the neckline was obvious. Money. And time. Her mind had been more focused on the charity festivity. If she had been wise, she'd have selected a gown from her short time with Devlin, who'd frowned upon displaying too much skin. And at one time, she'd have considered him a fuddy-duddy for his prudishness.

Yet, she had feared many would have recognized anything she'd worn in the last few years. Before marriage, she used to revel in being slightly revealed. My, the attention she'd garnered. But now, life had altered. The hard lessons of loss, pain, and guilt had taken a toll. Yet, maybe she was the better for it.

More than likely, only Mother would recognize her choice of costume. And she wouldn't dare announce to the guests her only daughter's dress was a throwback from many years ago. She couldn't deny the old garment had stood up well to the test of time. Lissy's hard work had revived the fabric to like-new.

Rhapsody stroked the gown. Having grown thinner over the last year, the frock fit perfectly. The modified sleeves now hung off-the-shoulder and were lined with ruffles and lace. The long skirt flowed to the floor, new added ruffles tumbling like a waterfall rushing over rocks. Her jewelry lay in a velvet box on her dressing table, multiple strands of the whitest pearls with matching earrings and bracelets joined by a gold medallion. A delicate white shawl rested across the back of the chair. Both the jewelry and shawl, newer additions, updated the look.

A knock at the door and her bid to enter brought Lissy into the room. Without a word, they outfitted Rhapsody, decked her with pearls, and braided her hair into a topknot bun. She swept to the mirror and whirled. With a spritz of magnolia toilette to her hair, she lifted her chin. Nothing could stop her now.

Now to wait for Cav who had been nothing but a dark shadow around the house, arriving late and leaving early. But she left a communiqué on his library desk where he often did his work. He'd had Lissy deliver his reply, in silted tones, that he'd come for her at a quarter of the hour.

She tapped her foot and glanced to the clock. If he thought she'd wait until the gala was in full swing he had anoth—a soft tap indicated he'd followed through on his promise. Lissy scurried to open the door.

Rhapsody clenched her jaw to keep her mouth from falling open like some dimwit. The velvet-lapelled frock coat set off his body like a Greek statue. His long legs were encased in pleated linen trousers. The silk vest he wore in a bold pattern of navy and white matched the white silk cravat at his throat. Had she ever seen the man with anything more elegant but a brash horizontal tie?

But his striking figure is not what stole her voice. His locks had been shorn into a short style and the beard was gone. *Gone.* A slight dimple accented his strong chin.

She worked away the moisture gathering in her mouth. If the man had been drop-dead handsome before, he was three days dead as a doornail now.

"I assume I pass muster?"

She blinked and pulled her ears back. The swishing sound ensued. Yes. Block out anything that hindered the progress of the mission. And she didn't dare contemplate how fetching her husband looked at this very moment. His dark hair and eyes. His sleek cheeks. The oddly cocked head, his stance imbued with a swagger that drew her like a light-hungry moth to a candle flicker. His manly charisma weakened her defenses before she could even be aware of where she was. And she had to keep the strings of this party gathered tonight.

Remember what happens to the insect when it gets too close.

She inhaled and pulled her posture upright, realizing he was still waiting for her to leave the sanctuary of her room. With a sniff, Rhapsody fibbed. "You'll do."

He gave a slight bow, sweeping his hand into the hallway, and she swept past him. Then he stepped to her side and she had no choice but to clutch his elbow. The muscles there bunched, sending a thrill whistling down her spine. Glory, he smelled of a woodsy cologne which seemed to dominate her senses. Just what she needed. More elements that tossed unwanted notions of the man into her thoughts. *Focus on the task.*

They descended the stairs to stand sentry near the doorway to greet the guests. A few moments of silence grew into unease. She peered at anything to avoid openly staring at him. The fireplace, the wall hangings, the trio sawing away at a Mozart selection.

Yet, her gaze kept returning to Cav to assess whether she preferred the rogue look he usually wore or this finely-cultured gentleman style. She dug her pinky and ring fingers into the flesh of her hands as an unladylike grunt stalled in the back of her throat. Why would no one arrive? She dearly needed the distraction. Anything to keep her mind occupied. Finally, Miss Betty let in the first of the guests.

⁂

Cav stretched his neck to one side and then the other. How he wished this were a few weeks back, when he could have possibly changed the course of his intimate encounter with Rhapsody. It stung the way she'd thrown him out of her room. He'd brooded about it for several days afterward. Then pondered for days why he felt the need to brood.

And now he stood pretty much in the dark about this whole shindig tonight. Clearly it was to raise funds for the church's charity fund. But somehow that didn't ring quite one hundred percent true with him. Rhapsody was up to something. He just hadn't figured it out yet.

And he hadn't even had a chance. That had been on his list to discuss with her after putting the whole Devlin portrait thing to rest. Only, he'd never had the opportunity. She'd blurted the whole mess with Devlin, and things had spiraled out of control. And now, she barely spoke to him.

Buck up, man. Was it even important what she did? This marriage was a sham, the result of three slavecatchers getting too close. But when he glanced at her, greeting another benefactor, decked in the shining gown, it was like looking at the sun. Yes, exactly that. And he'd gotten too close. He leaned forward to greet another filthy rich humanitarian, dressed to the hilt to tour the mansion, watch some dancers, and donate big money. "So glad you could attend."

"The Judge is well?"

Cav nodded. "He'll be here directly, sir, so you'll see him yourself."

The gray-headed man with sharp eyes nodded, his double chin jostling. "Very good, very good."

The line continued out the door. The September weather had cooperated, bringing in a mild break from the August heat. Still, it was going to be one long night. Smile and chat. Dine and chat. Sit and chat. Way too much chatting. Way too many people. Nevertheless, he would do his part. And his part had been carefully scripted by his beautiful wife.

The attendees gathered around the table, and Rhapsody tugged his arm to start him toward their seats. This was his cue. Just as his wife, the stranger, had outlined in her note. He saw her to her chair, tapped the wine glass with a spoon, and cleared his throat.

"Welcome one and all. Mrs. Blackledge and I are so pleased you've chosen to spend your evening with us to benefit those less fortunate. May God bless you all for your noble hearts." He bowed slightly. "As you know, we covet your prayers, but also your money."

Chuckles went around, and Cav gestured to all three tables and to his right, where Rhapsody stood like a vision in a dream sequence. "And if you so desire to donate to the cause my beautiful wife has coordinated tonight," he tipped his head to her, trying not to fixate on the strange light in Rhapsody's eyes, "you may write your name on a donation card with the amount you wish to contribute, insert it into an envelope, and slip it into the donation box. Now, with no further ado," he raised his glass and the others took up theirs in a toast. “To good food, good friends, and good intentions.”

“Here, here,” several chorused.

He took a sip, pleased to see his contained tinted water to appear the same as the guests’ wine. He would need his head about him tonight.

The trio began their soft music, the finest classical favorites. The gentlemen seated the ladies and the covered trays appeared from the kitchen door. First the grapefruit, then the Soupe à la Reine, cucumber salad, Cav noted the absence of fish, and then came sorbet, roast, vegetables… the list went on.

The forty guests chatted and laughed through twelve courses. Silverware and glassware tinkled. The room smelled of cologne, meat, and yeast. Rhapsody had outdone herself. Even his mother only served seven, her favorite number.

The trifle at the end pulled everything together, and Cav wondered if he could remove his suffocating cravat or rip the buttons off the waist of his trousers. His cheek dented at the thought, lips dancing to stem the smile. That would stop the donating on a dime. He felt his wife’s eyes on him.

She leaned in. “What’s so humorous?”

Her stiff tones made him realize she’d taken offense to his short display of wit or rather, in his father’s word, uncouthness. Oh, how he wanted to press his lips to Rhapsody’s ear and mumble some nonsense about the lovely valley resting below her chin. But a slap would be less likely to impress Cav’s generous constituents than him whipping off squeezing clothing accessories.

"Nothing. Merely a tickle in my throat." He set his face in neutral and spooned in another bite of trifle topped with strawberries. This would be the only sweet he'd enjoy tonight.

Rhapsody fluttered her lashes as she studied her now stoic husband. So he could lie, too. No surprise. It often came in quite handy in high socialite circles. She'd caught his gaze trained just south of her face. Several times. His hidden cleverness probably centered around that area if she were guessing. She flopped her shawl over her far shoulder, hiding that point of interest from his view.

What she hadn't bargained for was missing his slightly off-color humor. He didn't seem quite like Cav without the thrill of the unexpected kiss, or a bawdy joke whispered in her ear, often centered around her tight corset. While most women would be outraged, and maybe she'd been that way somewhat as well, secretly, it shot a zing through her to know he'd noticed such intimate things or dared claim her lips with his. It screamed intimacy. Something she'd so rarely enjoyed.

She gritted her teeth and reminded herself of her pledge to stay detached. They were here to raise money. Then she could hire out seamstresses from remote places to piece together her clothing brigade. Helping others find a new life because she couldn't.

Cav rose and nodded to her, extending his hand. She clasped his rough fingers in hers but avoided his eyes. He knew the routine.

The servants had set up the seating in the front drawing room, and the ballet selection would soon begin. Everyone quieted as they hesitated.

"Please don't forget to record your endowment on the donation cards and slip them into the donation box. My wife and I will now retire to the drawing room as the ballet will soon begin. Please, take your time and join us when you are ready."

Oh, yes. He was good. Quite the young philanthropic gentleman, well-versed in social propriety. Her gaze flicked to her mother down the table next to the judge and her mother-in-law. Even she had a grudging admiration in her eyes.

He kept her hand held high, the shawl slipping back to the crook of her elbows. Had he done that on purpose? Probably. She let it lie. She needed something to raise her advantage. Though using her feminine curves wasn't the best choice with a man like Cav. He'd probably only enjoy it all the more.

But he disregarded her, seated her in the front, and disappeared. So much for gaining the upper hand. Focus on the task. It wasn't to exasperate him and certainly not to kindle any heat between them. It was already there. No, just to use her feminine wiles to…manipulate him.

The food in her stomach threatened to reappear. Had she really just let that word circulate through her brain? She'd manipulated Miles and then tossed him aside. She'd manipulated Devlin until the poor man perished. These instances had capped years of manipulating people to get her way. Regardless of their feelings, regardless of pain.

Tears pricked the back of her eyes. Dear God. Why was she such a dragon? Rhapsody blinked away moisture before anyone noticed. Father approached and sat next to Rhapsody with mother on his other side, thankfully setting up a barrier to her mother's inevitable disparaging remarks. Yes, evolving into a scheming snob had begun with Mother, but it ended or continued with Rhapsody's own choices.

She yanked the shawl across the front of her dress. All she wanted to do was live her life. Not maneuver people for a living. Well, beyond this festivity. But personally. Seemed she constantly butted face to face with one epiphany after another.

A deep breath later, Cav seated himself and the room filled to capacity. So he hadn't abandoned her even though she deserved to be.

The ballet troupe came out and the dance began. The music swayed the figures, twirling, tiptoeing. Catching, sliding, holding, hugging. The beauty of the movement rocked her. Such fluidity of movement. Cav was right. Life shouldn't be so orchestrated. Rather, boiled down to a passion of fluid beauty. One person helping another. Lifting, hugging, helping. Rescuing. And all she could do was think of ploys to satisfy her selfish wishes.

Ugh. Cav would be the death of her yet.

Chapter Sixteen

Rhapsody counted the stacks of paper-covered dresses against the wall. Instead of dishes covering the extra room's floor, there were now not only ladies' clothing making tall piles, but men's shirts and trousers, children's clothing, a few dolls, small cloth balls, and blankets. Along the windowed wall, pairs of shoes lined up like suitors at a debutante ball. The underthings lay in the armoire.

A smile danced on her face. The gala had done its job, pulling in a good chunk of change. She'd donated the checks and draft notes to the church and kept the cash money for the clothing brigade. Each organization had received nearly half the collected money. Well, the church's charity fund had ended up with slightly more than half, but still, the funds she'd hoarded would make sure garments could be supplied for at least a year.

She pulled the skeleton key from her pocket. Always, she'd lock herself in and secure it when she left. No one knew but her what was contained in this room. And that's the way she intended to keep it. Garnering these supplies had sent her far and wide from New Albany to Louisville to avoid her activity being traced. Well, perhaps Barton had an inkling of what was occurring. After all, she'd exited garment shop after seamstress's shop to collect the clothing.

The plainness of the garments did smite her, yet she knew things had to be kept simple. Which led to filtering the supplies to the need. She frowned. That would either include partnering up with Cav or possibly Preacher Dubber. Or others? For there surely were other conductors guiding these folks north. But how to connect with them proved quite a puzzle.

Plus, trusting a stranger with her project, with her life, seemed unwise. No matter how she tossed it, the best course of action was to couple with Cav. She growled and stamped her foot. Not couple, dear heavens, poor choice of words. Ally. Yes, that was better. She would avoid any thoughts of being a couple with Cav. She would instead ally herself for mutual interests and for the good of the freedom movement.

The key twisted in the lock and she stepped out into the hallway, quickly shutting the door. One more twist had her secret concealed once again. She clutched the key then slipped it into her pocket. With a twirl and a gasp, she froze. Cav stood before her.

"Good morning." His face appeared deceptively impassive. "Busy already?"

Drat. It was terribly early. And she'd stamped her foot. What a fool she could be. Cav's eyes studied the door and then flicked back to hers.

"Is this an encore of preparing dishes to transport, or something new?"

Well, he didn't waste any time. "No dishes. Sorry to disappoint you."

She tried to duck around him, but he deftly stepped in her way. "I think that room would be an excellent place to discuss some further household issues. Wouldn't you agree?"

"I tend to think the library as our space for business. Why don't we head downstairs?" She tucked her shoulders down and raised her brows in forced compliance. But he was having none of her restrained emotions. His hand gripped her upper arm.

"Give me the key."

She hesitated, considering spouting and defending her right to do as she pleased or wrestling out of his grip, which would bring on more of his embrace to hold her. That would not do at all. With a whoosh of exhalation, she pulled the key from her pocket. Yet he didn't' release his firm grip on her arm.

"Excellent. So it's decided. We'll discuss business in here."

Scoundrel. He made quick work at the door and soon they were inside, he assessing the piles with a wrinkled brow. Except for the rows of shoes, the brown paper packages gave no indication as to what lay within. Her mind boggled over what she could say. Some fabrication to shield him from the knowledge staring him in the face.

“What’s all this?” he gestured.

Rhapsody tugged her top lip into her mouth to scrape her teeth against it. What to say? He stepped closer.

“Where exactly did the money go from the gala?”

Oh, dear. The questions would pile up until he got his answers. He stepped closer.

“Rhapsody, I’m waiting.”

Her arms wadded up across her chest. “I split the proceeds from the gala so I could fund a clothing brigade for Preacher Dubber’s people. This is clothing. Dresses, shirts, trousers, you name it. I figured it was easier to appear free if you had decent clothing. A small token of…comfort for people who have very little hope to grasp.”

Cav’s stiff posture relaxed. “You did all that in the last couple of weeks?”

She nodded.

Something akin to pride crossed his face. “You’re an incredible woman.”

Those flutters in her stomach made her wish he wasn’t in the room. Or anywhere near. Yet, she stood immobile as he approached, the look in his eyes feeding the eager butterflies in her middle.

“That’s an outstanding idea. Adalia is usually busy trying to help out in some small way, but this is perfect. Readymade clothing for the taking. And no one the wiser.”

Her cheeks burned at his praise. “I was going to tell you eventually. You were my most likely contact.”

His eyes shuttered. "I would have thought I was your only contact."

She shrugged.

"We must keep this as quiet as possible. The less people know, the better."

"Hence the key."

Cav's eyes narrowed. "Not just in this house. The community as well."

"You have no worries concerning my caution."

With a gaze that raked her, he nodded. "I have one other concern. My mother's dinner party."

Inclining her head, she held out her hand. "I'll need the key, and I've already RSVP'd your mother for this Friday night. Was there anything else?"

For a moment Rhapsody thought he'd say more, but he merely handed off the key and strode to the door. "I'll leave you to it then."

The absence of his presence made her shoulders and stomach relax. While she hated the tension between them and the barrier that kept them as strangers, it was vital to keep building that wall. Too much was at stake. He'd duped her into revealing her closest secrets, and taken advantage of her vulnerable state, but he would not succeed again. She would not be his bauble to lob about.

Still, that not so quiet whisper reminded her that he hadn't compromised her virtue alone. One could not waltz without a partner in crime.

The place boiled over with noise. The jumble of musicians on the worn elevated platform kept up a steady beat to the singer's low husky tones. People filled the dilapidated tavern perched on the bank of the river and everyone seemed to talk at once. Smoke stung Cav's eyes and burned the hairs in his nostrils. Even with a big hat, his commoner smock and wool britches, he felt out of place. What he really wanted was to drown his sorrows in the amber liquid, but he'd sworn off it years ago the night Eunice had switched ponies to his brother.

He wasn't here to drink anyway. He wanted to speak to Lazarus, and he always hung out behind the scenes, seeing to the band and sometimes participating in it. The only black faces in the crowd consisted of the boys in the music band. Drums, violin, cello, an ancient harpsicord.

Shoving away from the counter, he decided to head around back. He meandered through the jostling crowd until he found the back door. With relief, he slipped through. Being outside muted the sharpness of the roar, and he cleared his lungs with a fresh breath of air.

His eyes flicked to his farm wagon. Number two dozed in the moonlight. He wound around the back of the smoke house pouring out a tangy fragrance of smoking meat. His stomach lurched. Not his brightest idea to skip supper. But he couldn't put eyes to Rhapsody.

What was he going to do with her? One minute she stomped and spit, arguing, slapping at him and the next she garnered money, amassing supplies to help oppressed fleeing slaves. He remembered when he'd probed Eunice on her feeling of the abolitionists. In her genteel way she shrugged it aside, preferring not to discuss such an unpalatable subject. Rhapsody, however, had battled in like a child who poked a hornet's nest.

He crept around the back and planted himself on a cord of chopped wood. A noise caught his attention to his left. Lazarus, by the large shadow. When he sat next to him, he recognized his features.

"You cooking tonight, Mista Cav?"

The big man's low laugh made him smile. "Not tonight. At least not food."

"You smoking something else?"

Cav wanted to snort. Right now, there wasn't even a flame. "Not a thing."

"Then watcha doin' back here? Contemplatin the world's troubles?"

"Mine, anyway."

"Mmmm. That cain't be good."

A harrumph popped from him. "You got that right, old friend."

"The packages giving you trouble? Or the good wife?" Lazarus crossed his arms and eased back against the rough building.

"Does it matter?"

"Yep it does. Been stompin' round Preacher's place. Lots o' traffic going through. Oughten not be so much."

An alarm rang in Cav's ears. "Who do you think?"

"Catchers most likely."

"Hound prints?"

"Plenty."

Cav went still. If the slave catchers were picking up a scent around Dubber's cabin, maybe he'd have to find a new safe house. At least for a while. "You got a new place?"

"Not yet. But I'd be leavin' that wife of yours at home. Jist in case."

He nodded. Not that he'd be teaming up with Rhapsody anytime soon. Other than utilizing her mountain of clothing. "We need a new contact."

"Workin' on it."

Cav stood and rubbed the start of his next beard. "I best be getting a move on. I got wood to haul."

Lazarus nodded and Cav climbed the slight slope to his wagon. He didn't lift a hand in goodbye. The less people saw, the better. And it sounded like things were getting dicey.

Extra dicey. Cav decided later, with his three packages loaded from his Boiling Springs Creek pickup point. Either Lazarus had him overly suspicious, or the night felt unnerving. Everything caught his attention. From the flipping of the leaves in the late September breeze to the sounds of the insects buzzing in the woods. Something felt…off.

He studied the gloomy road around him and then reached down to feel for his basket of flowers. He'd forgotten it. The basket was empty and his pockets depleted of cayenne as well. His soul beat out a prayer of invisibility. Meeting those catchers on the road would be a sure way to get his three charges discovered.

He heard it before he saw it. Crackles. Fire devouring wood. When he drew closer, orange light in the direction of the Dubbers' place had him bringing the reins down on Number Two for more speed. When the trees parted, the blaze devouring the cabin soared high, smoke filling the air, rushing at him on the wind. Hot floating ash stung his face. The cabin, the rickety barn, all just kindling to the hungry flames.

He had no business stopping. If they were in there, they were gone already. Heartache wrapped in anger boiled up his throat. He drove past and pulled to the side of the road. Cav leaped from the wagon and ran for cover in the woods. He'd nearly circled around when he caught sight of a lump of huddled figures.

Pastor Dubber lay sprawled on his back, rasping breaths coming from his throat. Adalia knelt beside him, crying and clinging to his chest. She rose up when she saw Cav approach, fear live in her dark eyes.

"What happened?"

"Theys came. Lookin' for runaways. Theys shot Dubber and burned us out." Her voice broke. "Dis is all da farther he could go."

"I'll get the wagon."

At this point, Cav thundered back, caring not who might be looking on from the darkness of the trees surrounding the horrid scene. Blast, it seemed it took forever to wheel the horse and vehicle around. He could only imagine what his wagon's occupants were thinking, with the smoke washing through the back and the sounds of crackling fire engulfing the two nearby buildings.

Back with the Dubbers, Cav all but dragged the preacher to the wagon. Between the scrappy Adalia and himself, they managed to yank him atop the pile of firewood. Adalia insisted on staying with Preacher instead of the bench beside him. Cav didn't know what was worse. The sobbing woman covered in burnt clothing cradling a man stretched out on the wood pile, or the fearful wails and pounding fists of the three hidden packages.

Either way, he was in dire straits. Lazarus had not found an alternative safe house for him. And now he had five packages needing refuge. And Preacher Dubber needed care. Immediately. His breath came in great gasps as he slapped the reins to the old nag's back. Somewhere safe. Somewhere disguised. A place no one would think of. A place he knew well.

Dread coursed through his veins as the possibilities drummed through his brain one by one. Each location he dismissed for a myriad of reasons. He clenched the leather straps. He had to keep his circle tight. Discretion was everything.

There was only one place he knew to go. Only one place big enough to lose five people.

He'd have to take them to the mansion.

Chapter Seventeen

Rhapsody inhaled a sharp breath and ran a hand across her face. She blinked. No light filtered through the master bedroom window. She rolled over and buried her cheek in the soft silk. A thump brought her eyes open again. What was that?

She sat up stiff when the rumble of whispered voices hit her ears. Men's voices. More thumping. Footsteps. Fear sliced through her heart. Burglars. She jumped from the bed, threw the bedclothes from her, and slipped on her clothing as quickly as possible.

By the time she monkeyed her arms behind her to finish the buttons, she'd calmed some. Whoever it was moved too slowly to be thieves. She grabbed up the fireplace poker and crept to the door. With a slow hand, she turned the key in the lock and cracked the door enough to see the shadow of legs encased in boots sliding across the floor and disappearing down the clothing brigade wing.

A woman's soft whimpers echoed down the hallway. Then a door closed and all was quiet.

It had to be Cav. What in the world was that man up to now? She clutched the poker to her chest and crept from her room. Just as she crested the master bedroom's hallway, the door opened again. She froze. Lifting the poker, she waited.

A shadow hurried past her but instead of bringing her weapon down, she gasped. The figure spun. Oh, she knew that shape.

"Cavanaugh Blackledge," she hissed, "what are you up to now?"

Then she was in his arms. The poker slid to the floor with a clang. For a moment he didn't speak. He smelled of smoke and dirt. And of blood. His hand came up to cup her ear to his lips.

"It's Preacher Dubber. He's shot. Burned out," His throaty voice carried the impact of his emotions.

Then, he just held her for a few moments. She wanted to beat him. Slap him. Anything to get him to tell her this was some poor excuse for a joke. But she knew by the tightness of his hold, that he'd been rocked. She knew she should demand he take Dubber away, but she couldn't summon up enough strength to bludgeon him anymore given what he'd already faced.

Instead, she circled her arms around him and held him close. His breathing came in sucking gasps.

"I'm sorry, I'm probably getting you filthy."

"Not to worry. I have plenty of dresses stored up."

Something like a quick chuckle came as fast as it left. Then he pushed her to arm's length. "I'm going to get Barton. He has some experience in doctoring horses. He's the closest thing to a physician we can afford to have."

She nodded. "I'll arouse the staff. I'll get bandages, water, food. Whatever we need."

He ran his fingers down her cheek. "Thank you."

Then he pulled from her and rumbled down the stairway. Trembling made it difficult to lean over and retrieve the long cast iron poker. She steadied herself and rushed back to her room. Lighting a candle, she gathered her thoughts, paying no mind to the blood and grime smeared across the bodice of her dress. Her eyes darted to the fringed pull next to the door, but she ignored it and headed for the service stairway. Miss Bickle's step-climbing posture flew from her mind as she scurried up the narrow staircase.

The house became a tomb of hushed work. Water boiled, bandages ripped from linens, food delivered. By the time Rhapsody had a glance into the room where Cav had stowed his escapees, she found Pastor Dubber in her guest bed gasping for every breath, Adalia, quiet tears dripping as she perched beside him, and three others, two men and a woman, hovering in the corner, sheer terror in their eyes.

Dear Lord, why had Cav brought them here? But even as she thought it, she chided her cowardice. They had nowhere to go. She studied the four windows. Of all the rooms to take them to, he had to choose one with the most access to the outside world.

She whirled, pulled the key from her pocket, and accessed her private storage room. They had to hang blankets and now. Even as she hurried to gather supplies, candle flickers announced to passersby an occupant in the guest quarters. She stepped through and pulled the door shut, loaded with several packages of blankets.

As Barton tended the preacher, Mr. Wadell teetered on a stool, nailing the wool coverings to conceal any light through the windows while allowing the lace curtains to hang undisturbed.

"Lissy, gather those three and follow me," she whispered to her maid, the water having been delivered. With some coaxing, she led all of them to the next room and laid out clothing for them. She showed them the water closet for privacy and left Lissy to calm and direct them to a room separate from the Dubbers.

Rhapsody slipped down the stairs with a careful tread, the events making her shake. She turned into the library at the base of the steps and pushed the door closed. Unable to seat herself upon the padded chairs due to the filth on her dress, she instead sank into the wooden desk chair and cradled her head in her propped arms.

Prayer had always been that vague thing off in the distance. Something she so rarely utilized, having been quite capable to handle any and all difficulties that dared come her way. A sob broke from her lips. The last two years had made it painfully clear how wrong she'd been. And if it were just for her benefit, she would carry on. Or at least that is what she told herself.

But now it involved others. Preacher Dubber's life hung in the balance. Adalia, burnt out and beaten. The three runaways. Her staff. Cav. She was in deeper than she could ever extricate herself, let alone rescue the others.

Hot tears burned her eyes and scaled down her hot cheeks. There was no turning back. *God.* No one to help. What would she do if Preacher died? What if the secret of the whole operation leaked out? She and Cav hung and quartered, jailed, or run out of town. Her mother would disown her. The marriage would be for naught.

She sniffed. Yet it was hard to imagine life without Cav. And how silly to worry about herself. People would die. That's what really mattered. As important as her reputation was, getting these people to a safe place up north presented a much more urgent task.

Had she truly considered the toll of involving herself in this operation? And now it was too late. Tonight she had just invested everything in the freedom fighter's cause. Everything but her soul. She caught her breath, knowing there were now two things.

Her soul…and her love of a man named Cavanaugh Blackledge.

Cav hovered near the guestroom door. Locked to keep anyone out who happened to end up in this hall. But inside he knew Dubber struggled for his very life. Lazarus rocked in the chair beside the bed while Adalia cuddled close to her husband, dabbing his head with cool rags and keeping him covered.

The locked bedroom across the hall housed the three he'd thought would be on their way farther north by now. They begged not to be separated—a wife, her husband and a brother. At least they'd been cared for, water for bathing, new clothes, food. For now, he would have to leave it and carry on with a normal day.

Alerting his neighbors to the turmoil that lay within the mansion walls would sink them for sure. Light began to peek through the window in the hall and he paced toward the master bedroom. He hated to wake Rhapsody, but she'd disappeared shortly after seeing to the needs of the extra people in her house. *Their* house.

Who was he fooling? He still thought of the place as hers. Every wise crack that he'd issued forth about it all belonging to him had merely been a play to stir her up. And it always worked. He tapped on the door. Nothing moved so he tapped again. Could she possibly be up so early?

He directed himself to the stairs, stepped lightly down, and searched the lower floor. When he got to the library, he discovered his wife, head nestled in her arms, asleep at his desk. Locks of stray hair hid her face, but her soiled dress told of the long night. He shouldn't have hugged her. But he'd been beyond direction. Finding Dubber shot, both he and Adalia burnt and beaten, had rattled him.

And she'd hugged him back. Comforted him. Woke the staff and gathered medical supplies, food, and clothing. The word of old hammered in his brain, nearly knocking him from his feet. She'd been a helpmeet. Fiery Rhapsody, who'd fought him tooth and nail or seared him with her indifference, had stepped up and stood beside him in a time of great need.

He brushed back a tendril of hair. A longing so strong rose up in his chest, but he tamped it down. For some reason, she'd sent him away after the night they'd become one. So he'd keep his distance. But right now the woman needed care herself.

She stirred, eyes popping wide, and then shot up to her feet. She swayed and he gathered her in his arms.

"Put me down. I'm capable of walking."

He let a small laugh escape. "You're not even awake, woman. And you need to get to bed."

Cav carried her toward the stairs.

"Don't be silly, it's light. There is so much to do."

"Mmm-huh." He reached her bedroom and swung through the door. Her eyes drifted closed as he laid her on the bed. On impulse he leaned forward and pressed his lips to her sleep-limp ones. It only took a moment before her mouth responded to his. He pulled away, her eyes now open, deep and seeking. Cav stepped back. He couldn't get involved with exploring her soft underbelly now, though he was tempted.

"You shouldn't have done that," she whispered.

He let a sad grin curl his mouth. "Sorry. It's my modus operandi. You've been ensnared by a knave of uncouth misdeeds."

She sat up on the bed, hands splayed on the white silk sheets. "I think the man doth protest too much."

The unfathomable blue in her eyes made him want to stay and find out the meaning behind her scrambled Shakespeare. But he knew he had to get out. Now. "Rest."

He shut the door behind him. When this mess ironed out, if it did, perhaps he'd delve back into her doubting he was such a scallywag. For there had been something there in her eyes. Something warm. Something inviting. Something that looked like hope.

It was late morning by the time Lissy helped Rhapsody dress in a muted burgundy gown. The color of mixed red and black seemed so appropriate for the blood of Preacher Dubber and the black threatening pall of death that hovered in the house. She left with Barton driving, just as she had on the days before, putting on the appearance of the same routine to friends and neighbors. After all, there were the dresses she had to pick up on the other side of New Albany.

But her heart weighed heavy in her chest. Cav and Lazarus were scrambling around to find an alternate route for the runaways and the Dubbers, but so far, hadn't managed to secure safety. The burnout had spurned gossip among the townspeople, creating a delicate, dangerous atmosphere.

Rhapsody paid the seamstress for the three dresses and was soon on her way. She would be glad to be back, yet loathed to be back between the mansion's walls. However, more surprises awaited when they turned into the drive. Her mother's parked carriage forced Rhapsody's legs into a sedate pace as she tread the brick walk. Miss Betty opened the door and a relieved light flared in the woman's dark eyes.

"Is that my mother's conveyance in the drive, Miss Bet—"

"You know full well it is."

Her mother stood in the archway between the music room and the drawing room. For a woman who insisted those around her follow the strict code of decorum, she hardly afforded the same decency as to not interrupt her daughter. A lump formed in Rhapsody's chest. Had her mother been exploring the house?

"I apologize profusely, Mother dear. I had a fitting downtown." Not quite exact, may the Lord forgive her slight alteration of the truth.

Her mother sniffed and glided into the room, motioning to Miss Betty to help adjust her full skirt in order to recline upon the fainting couch. "Really, Rhapsody. A genteel lady has her driver fetch the required help and bring them to her home. Stepping out into the common businesses of town is such a dirty business."

Then her mother had no idea how filthy she'd become collecting finished garments from nearly all the local seamstresses in the area. Nevertheless, the less she knew the better.

"I will certainly keep that in mind." Now, how to get her off that couch and on her way home? "No teas today?"

Her mother dabbed her mouth with her lace hanky. "Unfortunately, no. Therefore, I thought it prudent to call on my only daughter and perhaps spend the noon hour dining."

"Here?"

Her mother's brows descended on her powdered pale face ever so slightly. "Of course. Where else?"

"Perhaps out? They have a marvelous café near the river that serves such a wonder—"

"Did you not attend to the subject of which I just spoke? I have no desire to dirty myself by going to some hole in the wall near the river. Surely, you can attend one more person in your lunch plans."

Rhapsody parked herself on a stiff brocade-covered chair near her mother. "Oh, of course you're welcome to stay. But I…" she cleared her throat, hoping to cover the gaffe, "Cav and I eat very lightly during the day."

The cock of her mother's head told Rhapsody she hadn't missed the error. Rhapsody stood before she commented on it. "Let me alert the staff. And, perhaps they can bring some lemonade to the porch. There's so little good weather left, we might as well enjoy it."

Her mother harrumphed as Rhapsody paced through the dining hall to the kitchen. Miss Mabel's eyes flashed wide at her entry. Rhapsody set a finger to her lips and shook her head. Then she approached the big black woman and had a quick whispered conversation of lunch, lemonade, and the crucial importance of complete stillness of the occupants on the second floor.

Rhapsody managed to get her mother escorted to the large covered veranda to sip lemonade in the bright late September day. But Mother expressed her disapproval in the overly bright location. Trying to keep the conversation going to cover any possible sounds, Rhapsody felt bound to answer her mother's plethora of nosey questions. Mostly about Cav, of course, for Rhapsody recognized her mother's reconnaissance mission in her innocent social call.

A door slammed. Feet thundered across the back lawn.

"Whatever could that be?" her mother intoned, setting her lemonade on the wrought iron table. The woman stood and strolled to the far railing.

Rhapsody jumped up. Everyone should have been alerted of the dangerous infiltration of her mother's presence. Pounding horse hooves started out somewhat distant until they swelled louder. Cav, aboard his black, raced up the driveway and slid into a curve to gallop down the street.

Chapter Eighteen

"What in glory's name is your husband doing? Quite uncouth."

That word had started to annoy her. The displeasure with such a term had birthed at almost the exact time the Judge bandied it about, describing her husband. The husband, who most likely at this very moment, was trying to save a life. But she had other things to attend to than dwell on either matter. "Mother, I fear my husband has some sort of emergency, for this is totally out of his gentlemanly character. Perhaps we could postpone our lunch until—"

"Certainly not. You may need my assistance."

And her mother was the antithesis of that definition. Especially now. "Very well. Let's see if lunch is ready."

"Surely your servants know to announce the readiness of a simple luncheon." Her mother tilted her chin.

"Nevertheless, I'll check." Rhapsody managed a sedate pace until she was within. Then she scurried to the kitchen. The servants stilled as she entered. She set her eyes upon the faithful cook. "Serve us in the breakfast room. And please hurry."

Mabel nodded.

Rhapsody moved closer and whispered. "Is it Preacher Dubber?"

Sadness threaded through the woman's eyes, and Rhapsody knew before her head dipped in acknowledgement. Had Cav gone to get a doctor? Since the effort earlier had been too big a risk, Dubber must be on the brink of death. She pulled in a shaky breath. While Preacher Dubber could be dying, she'd be entertaining her mother as if nothing heart-rending transpired over their very heads. Yet her main concern was to keep her mother from being privy to Cav's hurried return.

"Serve lunch now, Mabel. Please."

Rhapsody rushed to the porch. Minutes ticked by until she managed to coerce her mother inside, the very person who'd been so reluctant to relax outdoors in the first place. Then another disagreement erupted over dining in the small breakfast room instead of the dining hall. By the time they had their seats, her mother's mood had exponentially soured.

"How insulting to dine on lunch in the breakfast room. It defies the mere name."

Apparently the discord had not settled. Rhapsody nodded, sipping the cucumber soup. "Yes, Mother. But it's just you and I so I felt it would create—"

“Just you and I?” the older woman’s voice hardened. “How dare you insinuate that I’m nothing but an encumbrance in your day?”

“Not an encumbrance at all. It’s just more intimate here. More homey.”

Her mother exhaled. “Homey or homely?”

Rhapsody forced the congealed milky mush down her throat. Even in the basest of rooms, her home could never be considered homely. “Please, I really—”

The rush of a carriage pulling up the drive met her ears. Blast those open windows. Her mother turned a bewildered look her way.

“It’s probably just Cav. Excuse me. Please, continue to enjoy your meal.”

Rhapsody shuffled away, praying her mother, for once, would heed her voice. She whisked through the hallway and dining salon to enter the drawing room. The front door flew open and Cav, accompanied by an older white man, rushed through the door. Another person had entered the sacred trust of secrets. The look Cav shot her danced fear down her spine.

She followed, creeping up the stairs and slinking down the hall, to peek in at the sickroom doorway. Cav paused, shook his head, eyes dark with sorrow, and closed the door. A shuddering breath shook her. Somehow she had to return downstairs to her mother. She straightened and brushed her hands down the front of her gown, the red and black mixed colors very much haunting her mind.

Once she arrived downstairs, her mother stood poised in the drawing room, Miss Betty waiting at the door. “I see you have no time for your only mother. I'll not be treated in such a rude manner. Leaving your guest to dine alone is in very poor taste. I'll bid good day to you." The woman spun and whipped her wide skirt through the door.

Rhapsody sagged against the stair rail post. Thank God she'd left. She spun and made her way back up the stairs, yanking her skirt from under her boots. At the top she turned left, down the hallway that had become her underground railroad. Doors were shut, and she loathed to open any of them, so she paced the floor.

A few minutes later, Cav eased through the last one, and she paused. Unaware of her at the end of the hall, he stood, head hung, fists pumping. She hurried toward him and he lifted his head.

"Cav?"

His Adam's apple bobbed a few times, and then he shook his head. "He's gone."

"What?" Trembling took hold of her body and her skin doubled up into goosebumps. "How?"

The helplessness of his shrug, the lost-boy look on his face propelled her forward into his arms. He buried his face in the curve of her neck, and she squeezed him tight.

"I'll make arrangements immediately," she whispered, "I'll order the casket—"

He stepped back and stared into her face with a shake of his head. "We can do nothing to call attention to ourselves. No funeral. No memorial service. We'll bury him at dark. Tonight."

"But..." She pressed the back of her wrist against her lips. He was right. They couldn't even gather over his grave to mourn. A man who'd been close to Cav would be buried like an outlaw with a contagious disease.

The door opened behind them. The bespeckled older doctor clenched the black bag in his hand. He merely nodded to them and stepped into the hall, sympathy live in his eyes. Miss Adalia's raw sobs echoed behind him.

"What is going on up here?"

Pivoting in a rush, Rhapsody met the gaze of her mother standing at the end of the hallway. The matron strode forward. "I came to fetch my cape, and I find a doctor. And wailing. Who's here? Who's ill?"

Rhapsody broke away. "Now is not a good—"

But the woman dodged to the open door, taking in the dead man in the bed, the dark-skinned woman sobbing, splayed across his chest in grief. The three fugitives, who'd whisked across the hall to comfort Adalia, huddled against each other in the corner, horror mingled with misery engraved on their faces.

Her mother revolved in sickening slowness and fixed her hard eyes on Rhapsody. "Aiding and abetting runaways. You've desecrated the Lennox name. I knew this day would come. A bad seed from the moment you were brought to me. And now we've come full circle. There'll be the devil to pay for your betrayal, Rhapsody Redemption."

Her mother's spittle landed on Rhapsody's chin. Then her mother strutted down the stairs and the front door slammed shut.

She felt, rather than saw, Cav's hanky against her cheek, wiping her mother's hate from her face. But to move seemed impossible for the moment, so she stood trembling, her mouth parted, lip quivering. Then arms both supported and urged her down the hallway.

Once she'd blinked and realized she stood in her bedroom with Cav's arms around her, she gripped his shirt while the sobs poured out.

Once Rhapsody dozed in her room, Cav worked the rest of the afternoon to rid the mansion of the temporary people housed there. Who knew when the authorities would show up? Lazarus made arrangements for the coffin and the late night burial. Cav readied the wagon, quickly throwing up an arched canvas to hide the many passengers. They'd leave at sundown and search for a distant place to bury Preacher Dubber. Then Lazarus would continue with the wagon, and Cav would have to return.

A day and a half later, deep in the Hoosier forests, he and Lazarus dug the grave by night and whispered scripture over the man. Then Lazarus and Cav prepared the passengers for a long trek. It would be a dangerous journey.

Cav shoved freedom papers in Lazarus's hands and then peered into the back of the wagon. Six souls plus Lazarus bumping through the countryside in an old wagon, three on one side bench and three on the other.

The amount had grown since he'd promised Miss Betty and Miss Sena freedom some weeks back. Poor Miss Adalia, frozen in her grief, Miss Betty's arm about her. The three runaways who'd he'd stashed at his house stared at him, their doubt mingled with fear written in bold letters across their faces. He couldn't blame them for their distrust, given the circumstances of the last few days.

"If the catchers stop you, Lazarus has papers. But you'll have to use those cuffs to make it look like he's transporting you. Lock them on until danger is past. He has the keys in his pocket."

A couple of them gave short fearful nods.

He lifted his hand. "Godspeed."

Lazarus brought the reins down. Cav could do nothing more. He swung up on Black, set his feet in the stirrups, and waited until the wagon disappeared through the gloom of the night forest. He whispered a prayer to a God he'd hardly known.

His gaze returned to the earth they'd smoothed and covered with leaves and debris to hide the spot. Preacher Dubber deserved so much more than being hidden amongst the leaves. And he'd spoken to Cav of eternal things. Perhaps Preacher was right. For surely he'd earned a heavenly rest.

The hidden grave and the runaways represented more evidence of Cav's involvement in the freedom movement. As if he needed more. Many things could implicate him. Including the forged document with his father's name on the freedom papers Lazarus carried. His father would be livid at the use of his office. But he couldn't think of that now. He had to get back and protect what was his. Most of all Rhapsody.

Rhapsody stared at her father seated on the Chesterfield. It certainly hadn't taken long for her parents to return to the scene of the crime. Cav had barely crested the driveway at dusk before they'd pounded on her door. To her surprise, they were alone, just the two of them. An unofficial visit.

"Your mother is quite ill with the events."

She shifted her gaze to her mother's stiff figure beside her father. Not so ill that she'd miss the opportunity to witness the bludgeoning of her only daughter with words and threats.

God help her. Rhapsody refused to feel remorseful for helping those poor souls. "And?"

Her father's jaw worked and his lips tightened. "And you will sell the mansion and leave New Albany. That is your penance."

"Dead to you."

The words Rhapsody murmured made her father hesitate, but her mother jumped in. "Yes."

Rhapsody pulled a calming breath through her nostrils. "And if we don't?"

"We will alert the authorities. According to the Fugitive Slave Act, they will scour every inch of this place, seize your financial records, and talk to witnesses. You'll be fined and jailed. Cavanaugh will most likely be hanged by rioters."

She sucked in a swift breath. "You would do that? Turn us in?"

Not once had Father looked her eye to eye, but now he turned his head and fastened her with his gaze. "When I heard your name that woeful day, I thought you'd redeem us back to society. I believed accepting you in as a replacement would protect your mother's dignity. Heal her grief. Shield the family name from being tarnished. But it remains clear your blood is not ours. I rue the day I brought you home to replace our—"

Her mother jumped to her feet and shrieked, "Stop."

Rhapsody rose, blinking. "What are you saying?"

"No more, Milton. Not one more word," Mother shouted. A woman who'd always disciplined with quiet menace, dissected people's character with the care of a solemn surgeon, suddenly appeared in the middle of a mental seizure.

Her father stood and collected his top hat. He put his arm around Mother and strode toward the door. Then he turned. "You have one week to decide."

And the door clicked shut.

The following morning, after tossing most of the night, Rhapsody sat in the carriage. She blinked her eyes, rough and sandy from tears and little sleep. Curse her promise to stay detached from her husband. When would Cav return? Just thinking of him made her breathing convulse. She needed his strength. His presence. She needed...him.

But instead the carriage pulled in front of Mrs. Grafton's elegant home. The only woman she knew old enough to know the circumstances of her birth. For she had to know. Her parents had obviously hidden something. If Cav were here, his companionship would help gird her for what she may uncover.

Barton helped her from the carriage, sadness cloaked on his erect shoulders. Her hand lingered in his merely to mirror grief in her gaze. Then she stepped with purpose toward Mrs. Grafton's front door.

The usual servant ushered her through the opulent home and showed her to the parlor. The same as always. Not as big as hers, the parlor's walls were covered in swirling gold wallpaper matching the black and gold rug at her feet. That floral couch glared at her, as out of place as she herself. The white fireplace stretched massive against one wall, the room crowded with collected foreign objects, indicative of her travels.

She rose when the woman stepped into the room. After chatting in a low tone to the servants, she shut the door and bustled forward.

"Ah, Mrs. Blackledge. Rhapsody. To what do I owe this pleasure?" She gestured to the chair. "Please, sit."

"I'm not sure I'll be a pleasure today, Mrs. Grafton." Rhapsody settled into the gold-patterned chair.

An eyebrow stretched Mrs. Grafton's wrinkled forehead. "I see." Her eyes were sharp. Even knowing?

"I need to speak to someone who might have been privy to the circumstances of my…birth." Rhapsody had feared a servant may interrupt them. But apparently Mrs. Grafton had foregone such polite niceties as the door remained shut. She took a breath to fortify her courage.

"And you thought I would be such a person?"

"Yes."

Mrs. Grafton's fingers tapped while folded in her lap. "Why so? Has your mother said something to indicate I would know such matters?"

Rhapsody shook her head.

Mrs. Grafton leaned back against the sofa back. "So what brings you to this conclusion?"

"I'm…not sure." Rhapsody forced her hands in her lap and refused to shrug. Not polite among the elite. "Perhaps I feel you harbor some animosity toward me. And Mother. I may be mistaken. But you are someone who's graced this neighborhood for a reasonable amount of time."

"In other words, I'm old?"

To Rhapsody's surprise, the older woman laughed, though not a cheerful sound.

Then the matron continued, flicking at the front of her black dress. "I've dressed appropriately for today, I see. Well, I suppose twenty-seven years was longer than I'd hoped. Still, if it had never surfaced, I'd have been quite happy."

"Twenty-seven? I'm…twenty-seven."

"So you are. Born January tenth in the middle of the night."

"Actually, the third," Rhapsody corrected.

The elderly woman's mouth hardened into a button. "You can rest in my knowledge, dear girl. You were born on the tenth."

How could that be true? And how could she know that? "So, you're saying my mother is not my mother?"

A wry smile ghosted across her face. "That's between you and her."

Rhapsody shook her head and leaned. "No. She will never speak it. Please, Mrs. Grafton. I need to know. I beg you."

The older woman tapped some more, her gaze on the fireplace. “The rumors have been buried. I prefer they stay there.”

Seconds ticked by on the Parisian clock hanging over the mantel. Rhapsody tightened her jaw. “I’m not leaving until I know the truth.”

The woman turned to her. “You have his tenacity, I see.”

“Whose?”

Mrs. Grafton’s tightened lips trembled. “My husband’s.”

Chapter Nineteen

Rhapsody's mouth dropped open. She shook her head and pressed her fingers to her hairline. Thoughts refused to line up in her head. "Are you saying your husband is my father?"

"Clever girl." The woman's voice strangled the words.

"How can that be? You can't be my…"

The refined woman snorted. "Heavens no."

"Then?"

Mrs. Grafton inhaled a deep breath then fastened her intense gaze to hers. Her face had gone as pale as buttermilk. "Very well. The worst is out, so to speak. I knew I couldn't guard it forever. My husband keeps an…exotic in downtown Louisville."

Breath snagged in Rhapsody's throat. What it must cost Mrs. Grafton to confess her husband had his own private concubine. A fancy. She'd heard the whispered rumors of wealthy gentlemen keeping courtesan slaves for pleasure. But never had she known for sure that it occurred. She swallowed a lump.

The woman flung her hand. "I long ago learned to accept it. Embrace it even. To have someone else tend to his base desires freed me to do other things. And I have the girls. And that was enough for me. After all, what else could I do? Unfortunately, there are consequences for my husband's indiscretions. Living consequences."

Like her. An illegitimate birth. Spots rose up to block Rhapsody's vision for a moment. But Mrs. Grafton continued to speak.

"At the time, I had a servant named Miss Pinny. She was a midwife of sorts. Knew how to deliver a child. Lessened the embarrassment of engaging a gentleman doctor. I lent her to your mother in hope she would make that distressing time of delivery a little easier. So I was quite privy to the whole sordid affair."

Mrs. Grafton rose and paced to the shelf displaying her large assortment of decanters of varying sizes. The ones she so glowingly boasted about at her teas. She selected a green glass vase and lifted it, stroking the painted floral design. "I believe I picked this up in Austria shortly before it happened."

She replaced the delicate bottle back among the collection, a muffled clink the only indicator of Mrs. Grafton's state of unrest. "Anyway, your mother had given birth to a live child a week before. But rumors circulated that the child was infirm, weak, and misshapen. Miss Pinny confirmed it. When I visited her, your mother was quite beyond herself. Not necessarily with grief, but with disgrace. Your mother couldn't abide with an imbecile as her only offspring. She refused to hold or care for the child. Refused to even look upon it. And who could blame her? The child passed within a couple of days. Shortly after, my husband's paramour spewed out yet another result of their shared passion."

She spun, her dress swirled about her ankles. "You."

As Mrs. Grafton strode closer, hate threaded with weariness radiated from the woman's eyes. As if exhausted from years of keeping the whole liaison quiet. The twitch below Rhapsody's eye tugged.

The older woman perched back on the sofa. "My husband needed to dispose of you and found a willing party in Mr. and Mrs. Lennox. The addled child would have smeared their standing in the community. So, to appear as if they'd never lost a baby, they… bought you. For quite a sum. With your white skin and blond hair, they reasoned they could pass you off as the child your mother had birthed."

Rhapsody gripped the bodice of her dress and trembled. "Oh, dear heavens."

Mrs. Grafton stood, tottered a moment, and exited the room. Rhapsody focused on breathing through her shudders, letting tears run down her cheeks. An oft-repeated Miss Bickle precept dredged up from the past.

You are highborn gentry, ladies. Superior. Noble. Meant to rule the inferior, lowborn servants. And rule, you shall.

Yet, she had servant's blood flowing through her veins. Slave's blood. A few puffs of air rushed from her mouth. A baseborn child of a rich man's passion. An illegitimate daughter swaddled in the Lennox name.

...Lowborn.

The words pounded like hooves of twenty horses running rag-tag over her skull. A desire to rise and pace struck her, but her legs had turned to cream. The door opened again and a servant entered and laid a tray of dishes on the low table before her. She poured two glasses of water and then hurried from the room. Rhapsody couldn't take her eyes from the woman's movements. But for the grace of God, she'd be pouring refreshments and working in the kitchen of a great home. Or worse.

Mrs. Grafton entered, clicked the door shut, and returned to her seat.

"Quite the tarnished exposé, hmmm?" The matron lifted a glass of water, ice clinking against the sides. "Your mother sold her servants. I released Miss Pinny. And we buried the matter."

Rhapsody couldn't speak.

"Come now. This can be quite a useful tool for you. Whatever circumstance you've gotten yourself into with that wild husband of yours can be fixed immediately." Mrs. Grafton leaned forward and held out the other glass to her.

With a swab of her tongue around her dry lips, Rhapsody accepted the glass. How to get liquid past the ball of horror lodged in her throat remained a mystery. Pressing her lips to the rim, she let the cool liquid wet her lips. Mrs. Grafton's eyes bore into hers once more.

"Did you hear me, Rhapsody?" At her nod the old woman continued. "You have within your grasp, a powerful weapon. Should you choose to use it against my family, I suppose I shall have you killed."

A raw tinkling of Mrs. Grafton's laugh lit the parlor walls. "But that may already be arranged for me. You see, word gets around of underground activities. Therefore, I personally have some…munitions, if you will, stored back. However, I think a better choice for you would be to save your own hide. If…you catch my meaning?"

Rhapsody's swimming mind cleared a fraction. Her mother's threats. Their exposure. Rhapsody choked down a mouthful of water and slammed the glass to the wooden table. "I think I do."

"Then we understand my need of the vital privacy of the Graftons'…dirty linens?"

Rhapsody stood, took a quivering breath, and swiped the tears from her cheeks. "Mum's the word."

~

Dusk had descended on Cav before he crested the driveway to slip down into the carriage house. He'd pushed Black to exhaustion to get back so soon. At the stable, Mr. Wadell scurried to see to the horse, and Cav caught Barton descending the carriage house's back stairway from the rooms overhead.

"Anything?"

Barton approached and whispered, “Her parents came yesterday evening. Mrs. Blackledge visited with Mrs. Grafton today. She seemed quite…distressed.”

Cav nodded and sprinted across the lawn, avoiding the cast iron fencing, and slipped into the back door. The entire house seemed shrouded in dark silence. He navigated the dim interior and shot up the stairs. At the master bedroom door, he knocked and it cracked open.

Her hand latched onto his arm and pulled him inside. Only the moon cast shadows across the room, her face just a shadow. “Rhapsody, what is it?”

“Just…just, hold me.”

The hoarseness in her tones wrenched his heart, and he gathered the trembling woman against him and nestled her hair. For a long time, they stood, arms locked around each other, Rhapsody weeping silently against him. Then he led her to the bed and settled them both on the side, she still clinging to him.

“Whatever this is, let’s light a lamp and hash it out.”

“No. I can’t face you in the light.” She gripped the front of his shirt.

“What are you talking about? Nothing you could say could ever—”

“I’m lowborn chattel. An illegitimate child of an exotic paramour.”

He stilled. “That’s nonsense, Rhapsody. You’re the blond, blue-eyed Lennox daughter. How could you—”

She jumped to her feet, a shadowy figure in the moonlight spilling through the window pane. "It's the truth."

He rose, struck a match, and laid it to the gas lamp. Rhapsody paced to the far dark corner, dressed still in her day clothes, her hair a muss. Cav turned up the light and followed her. She stood with her back to him and poured out the tale. Then she mumbled through her own parents' threats, and punishments they faced.

Still talking to the corner, head bowed, she whispered, "Everything I thought I was, I am not."

He placed his hands on her shoulders and rotated her to face him. Tears tracked down her face. That beautiful face. "You're right. You're even more." He cupped her cheek and pressed the softest kiss to her swollen lips.

"I'm not worthy of you." Her bottom lip trembled. "I carry slave blood."

He dipped his head and lifted her chin. "Are you saying the tone of people's skin makes them not worthy? Because we've just given practically everything to prove that concept is wrong. To free those victimized by that idea."

"You know what I mean." She sniffed.

He let a sad smile curve his lips. "You are my wife, Mrs. Blackledge. And that won't change because of the circumstances of your birth."

Rhapsody gripped her hands, her eyes entreating in a blue puddle. "You can put me aside. No one would blame you. Not even me."

Cav rubbed her upper arms, wanting nothing but to console her brokenness. "We've become partners in both crime and pleasure. I have no intention of renouncing our marriage."

She blinked and reached up to trail a finger down his shirt. "I…thank you. I'm not sure I can do this alone. We only have a week to decide what to do."

He nodded. "And in three days, my mother's dinner party."

She caught her breath. "How will we ever manage to get through it?"

"Together." He said. "You, me and…. God Almighty."

Rhapsody pressed her head against his chest. This woman was becoming as needful as air. Her scent drove away the mounting concerns. He gathered her into his arms and pressed a kiss to her forehead. Her soft cooing sound made him continue the light kisses down the side of her face.

She splayed her hands against his chest and turned her face toward him. "Please don't leave me tonight."

"Oh, Mrs. Blackledge, I wasn't planning to." He cradled her into his arms.

Eunice's gentle humming chuckle grated across Cav's nerves. How could he have ever fancied himself in love with the milksop? Sure, she was still beautiful. The petite brunette's genteel demeanor and soft feminine ways were eye-catching. She defined gracefulness. Even now he could feel its tug. But his gaze drew to

Rhapsody. The nights they'd spent together had solidified their dependence on each other.

Dependence. Not a word he'd use to describe the exhilarating relationship with his fiery wife, so full of passion and not afraid to display it. Unlike the woman who sat across from him this moment. Perhaps addiction would better describe their bond. Or at least his. He craved her in every respect.

The tepid conversations flowing about the table of his brother's bid for the senate, the usual woes of society from his father, Eunice's cotillions, and high-class hobnobbing had begun to turn the seven course meal into a sour mash in his stomach.

Didn't his family comprehend the bigger problem? Slavery had to be eliminated. To own a human being defied the basis of what made the United States an independent country. Thomas Jefferson's own words in the Declaration had clearly spelled out all men as equals with freedom endowed by their Creator. How could Shafer, a Princeton graduate, a man well-versed in politics not see how slavery contradicted America's basic principle of freedom? The heated issue had driven a wedge between the north and the south for years. And Cav feared it would only continue to escalate.

How could Shafer not address the inequality of it? The cruelty, the inhumanity of it all. Preacher Dubber's death would not be in vain. His brother would hear more on the subject. If Shafer were elected, he would have a direct influence to stop the injustice. But he could hardly blurt his demands. Cav gritted his teeth and nodded as Eunice described the music ensemble at the last Governor's Ball.

"Quite charming to have so many tones of violins. They were well practiced, too. Practically perfection. One of the best instrumental groups I've ever had the privilege to witness, I believe. Although Princeton's graduate ceremony troupe had been quite impressive. Your brother gave the address this year. Could you pass the cream, darling?" Eunice batted her green eyes at her husband at the end of the table.

"Of course, my sweet."

Perhaps Shafer poured on the endearments to drive a stake to his heart, but it meant nothing. Cav saw now the shallowness of his former attraction. Imagining his brother's wife aiding in the abolitionist movement, offering to be an accomplice in ferrying fugitives to safe houses or stockpiling necessities for the runaways, was almost like imagining a sow decked in a cotillion gown. Jewelry included. No, Eunice was much more suited to his brother and his brother's way of life. Now, Cav thanked the Almighty's wisdom in orchestrating Eunice into his brother's arms.

"Not for me, of course, but I think your father is ready for his coffee." Eunice leaned back to shoot a glance toward the waiting staff in the background.

As if on cue, the maid arrived with the hot pot and went about the table to serve it. Ah, a lull. He thrust straight to the heart. "So, Shafer. Where do you think we're going on the slavery issue?"

"Cavanaugh Blackledge. We'll not speak of such subjects at the dinner table," his mother cut in.

He stared at her in her pale pink dress, hair carefully coiffed, skin flawless. Still a beauty at her age, even with an elegant pinch to her lips. His mother had been spared years of backbreaking toil and had lived in the lap of luxury from a small infant.

Shafer lifted a placating palm to his mother but turned a tolerant smile on Cav. "I believe we've reached a suitable concession with popular sovereignty, dear brother. The Compromise of 1850 clearly set the tone. Not only does it work in the territories, I believe it will work in the established states as well. Compromise is our only course of action."

Compromise? On slavery? Cav stiffened and felt a hand on his arm. Rhapsody, reminding him to tread lightly. Yet, how did Shafer think the country would ever shed the horrible scourge of bondage if every new territory had the power to vote it in? Or if federal and state man hunters could invade free states with deadly force to capture escapees? A political seat was worthless if not used to right the wrongs of society.

This wasn't merely a new state simply deciding a…flag design or ratifying a new state constitution. This was about people. Living people with hopes and dreams.

Why, the country would end up compromising themselves into being a slave-holding nation indefinitely. The resolution the government sought with the Compromise of 1850, and more importantly the Fugitive Act of 1850, was no resolution at all.

It was a powder keg.

If only President Taylor hadn't died before rejecting the Compromise of 1850 and thus ushering in the Fugitive Act under its umbrella. If only Vice President Fillmore, President just two years later, courtesy of Taylor's death, hadn't quickly ratified the bill package. If only President Pierce hadn't signed the Kansas-Nebraska Act…if only… If only his brother had a moral bone in his body. So many if onlys.

All it added up to was making Cav's job more difficult. Even free blacks like Lazarus were susceptible to re-capture and passed off as slaves, sold for a profit by vicious slave catchers. Or worse, being killed and burnt out like the Dubbers.

And the most immediate problem? Anyone helping slaves escape would be swiftly and severely punished. Cav doubted his father's high standing in the Kentucky court system would stop a lynching mob. Which was why he, himself, could possibly be facing the gallows in two days. He stymied the facts in the back of his throat and merely nodded. Rhapsody was right. He would not reveal his hand now. Death breathed down his neck.

Shafer, his clean-shaven jaw haughty above his silken cravat, shot him a dour face. "And Mother is indeed correct. Politics are best isolated to the gentleman's rooms. Quite an indelicate subject for the womenfolk."

Beside him, Rhapsody raised a napkin and pressed it to her face. It was her turn to stifle a retort. For surely his hot-blooded wife, who kept his operations from being discovered, raised funds for clothing and feeding fugitives, and who most recently housed transient runaways—even caring for a dying black preacher—would have plenty to say on the subject. Especially in the face of the sternest opposition. Her parents. As a woman of high society, Rhapsody had not turned her face away from the truth because of its unseemly side. She had plunged right in.

"Let's move this conversation into pleasanter subjects, although it may be somewhat improper in polite society, not here among family. It's grand news." His brother cast an indulgent smile toward his blushing wife. "We'll be expecting our little family to be a family of three soon."

A cry burst from his mother and his father raised a glass with a chuckle. Eunice carrying his brother's child. No jealousy mounted. None at all. If anything, a quip about passing on their debased beliefs of allowing slavery mounted his lips. But he pressed it down. Instead he smiled and pounded his brother on the back and shook his hand. He would silence his tongue for now.

With Rhapsody's parents ready to squeal on them, he had no choice.

Chapter Twenty

Dim morning light filtered through the lace curtain, lighting the master sitting room. Rhapsody sat perched on the fainting couch while Cav had the wing chair snugged close to her. They sat, her knees framed by his, foreheads almost touching.

"But, Mrs. Grafton knows. Isn't that proof enough?" Cav whispered, his eyes live coals into hers.

She shook her head and breathed her words back to him. "If Mrs. Grafton's dirty laundry is hung for all to see, she will expose us. I promised not to involve her family."

Cav pulled from her to rub his rough jaw. He hadn't shaved yet today, and his hair stuck up in places on his head. Both adorable and appealing. Although to her surprise, she missed his long mussed locks.

Dressed in only his commoner smock, untucked, with long underwear covering his legs, the moment screamed intimacy. Especially with her still in her night clothes. If it weren't for the urgent gravity of their discussion, she might have smiled and shot him a coquettish glance. But she couldn't. They wouldn't be talking long if she did that.

How crude she'd become, longing for her husband's touch. She'd been taught the ways of a man with a woman were to be tolerated, not embraced. Yet she'd relished her time with him. If she were a fool, she'd embrace it. Love for Cav pounded through her veins, and she wouldn't push him away any longer.

Sure, he may not return the emotion, but he desired her. That was better than wrestling and exhausting herself day and night to remain detached. She could no longer do that. Rhapsody needed strength to battle elsewhere. Accepting him into her arms and bedchamber had been a compromise she couldn't turn down.

She shook herself free and focused. "I know my mother, Cav. Using my illegitimacy as a blackmail to block her from exposing us will not work. She will deny, deny, deny. Mother will do anything to save face. Then we will be left without a leg to stand on. And Mrs. Grafton will not endorse my story. She wants nothing to do with this muddle. Name is everything in high society. Besides, the less people who know, the better."

He stood and strolled to the window and glanced through the lace and she couldn't help but admire him. He turned. "Didn't she say something about paying a large sum of money?"

Rhapsody rested her hands on her cheeks. So many emotions had rolled tide over tide during that exchange, it was difficult to recall. "I…believe she did."

He nodded and stepped closer, her eyes sweeping his fine form again, settling on his feet. His bare feet. A warmth migrated to her face as she lifted her eyes. A cocked eyebrow met her gaze.

"While I appreciate your awareness of me in my semi-undressed state, we must gather a plan." He saddled her knees and plopped back in his chair. "I have a feeling your father is an astute businessman. And shrewd businessmen keep meticulous records."

She straightened, her voice rising in volume. "Yes, oh, yes. Cav, you're a genius. Any type of record of transaction is carefully recorded in his books."

He grinned, but held his fingers over her mouth. Then he pressed his forehead to hers and whispered, "And where would he keep such confidential records?"

Her eyes widened, and she pulled his hand down to clutch it. "His safe. His downstairs study has an iron safe fitted into the wall."

"Combination?"

She nodded.

His countenance fell. "That might pose a problem."

Rhapsody shook her head. "My father has a hard time remembering the combination. So he's always kept a record of it."

Cav's eyes grew hopeful. "And do you know where that might be?"

"Unless he's moved it, top right shelf, third book, page one hundred. It will be written on the inner margin."

"Ha-ha!" he exclaimed, threw his arms around her, and planted a peck on her nose. "That's it, then. We'll sneak in, take the record of adoption, and then your parents can't deny the transaction. Nor will anyone else."

Joy radiated from her very soul. "Of course. I know every inch of that house. I know the comings and goings. With a little bribe money filtered through Barton, the servants would be more than happy to turn a blind eye. It's perfect."

"Well, not perfect, but it will do." He pressed a hard kiss to her lips before he pulled away. "It must be tonight. For we have little time before your parents arrive to carry through with their threat."

With a deep breath and a shuddered exhale, she nodded. "Yes. Tonight."

Dressed in a black skirt and matching shirtwaist borrowed from her fugitives' clothing collection, Rhapsody pressed against Cav's side. He, also dressed in basic black clothing, reached out a hand and turned the doorknob. Around them the sounds of the insects' songs were the only noise at nearly three in the morning. The back door opened soundlessly thanks to the servant's oil. Rhapsody hurried in first.

Dread cloaked her. Not only did she feel scandalous from the lack of petticoats beneath her skirt, it felt wrong to be here, without invitation, in her childhood home. Oh, so very wrong. But the fear of jail or worse for Cav, possibly execution at the hands of outraged rioters, made her slink through the kitchen, her husband close on her heels. She tiptoed through the dark interior until she made it to the back hallway of the house. With a twist of her wrist, they were in the study, jet black from the hidden moon that had aided their stealthy arrival.

The scraping of a match made her catch her breath, even though she'd expected it. Had waited for it. Yet the noise seemed as loud as a ringing gong. Cav touched the flame to the candle he held and eased the door closed. Losing no time, Cav reached up to the top right shelf of the enormous built-in bookcase and pulled down the third book. He handed it to her, and she flipped through the pages with unsteady fingers. On page one hundred, her father's scratches met her eyes and a small smile creased her cheek.

Cav shook his head, his face scrunched, hands splayed in question. Perhaps he sought the safe. Yes, Father and his cleverness. Rhapsody moved behind her father's desk and he followed. With a quick touch in the right spot, a section of the wainscoting popped open. There rested the black front of the safe and the combination lock. She plucked the candle from Cav's fingers. He'd have a cooler head for dialing the combination. Holding the candle to the book, Cav glanced over the numbers and then knelt at the face of the iron safe.

In no time he clutched the handle and a loud clunk lit the room. Rhapsody froze from the unaccustomed sound, but Cav grabbed the candle and stuck his head in. He knew what to look for. Within, her father had piles of ledgers carefully filed for each year.

But when he emerged, he held not only a ledger inscribed with the year of her birth, but an envelope with 'Rhapsody Redemption' written across the front. Her mouth opened in surprise. Footsteps sounded above their heads. Cav coolly pressed the safe door closed, repositioned the wainscoting, and motioning her behind the large desk. She slid underneath in front of the chair. Fear spiraled down her spine when Cav disappeared and the room snuffed pitch black.

Mumbles came from upstairs. Then silence. Rhapsody took breaths in small quiet gasps. Where was Cav?

Heavy footfalls approached. Her father. It had to be. She could hear doors open and close quietly. A few squeaked. Her father moved closer. If there were burglars, they had no worries of avoiding him. She could easily follow Father's bumbling pathway through the house and when he reached the study door. A light started dim and then grew brighter. Not only was he loud, but he carried a lantern as well.

Then the room went dark, the door closing with a click. Retreating footsteps thumped toward the stairwell.

"No one, Minerva. Just as I said." His words, though faint, came to her clearly. From that point, more mumbles met her ears. For the next hour, she waited, her joints growing stiffer by the minute. They had to get out of here. Servants would begin their morning tasks before too much more time passed.

She pressed her sore body from under the desk. The candle. Cav had it, and she wasn't even sure if he were still in the room.

In her softest whisper she uttered. "Cav?"

A blaze lit up his face. He stood behind the doorway. So he'd hidden behind the door as her father searched. Relief sluiced through her. He slid the book that bore the combination back into its place and beckoned her toward the door while the matchstick still glowed . She set her hand on the door and hesitated until the light fizzled into total darkness.

Like a raccoon stealing eggs from a hen's nest, they slithered out the door and down the hall. Rhapsody wanted to shout with glee when they slid out the back door. Instead, Cav grabbed her hand and tugged her through the darkness down the block where he'd hidden his horse behind a neighbor's stand of bushes. With quick hands, he deposited her aboard and swung up behind.

Rhapsody let out a soft laugh. Never would she have thought she'd be joyful to have the proof of her illegitimate birth. Or proof that she, too, possessed slave's blood. But she knew in her heart, it was the only thing that could save them.

Cav breathed in the scent of his wife's hair. He hated to wake her, but he couldn't draw her close enough to suit him. The master bed's silk sheets, as cool as spring water, made him want to snuggle closer to her for warmth. They'd forgotten to seal the window once they'd returned from their escapade, and a cool October wind blew through the crevice. A grin creased his cheek.

Fact was, he wanted her nearer for more than warmth. He tugged up the quilt and pulled her closer. Ahhh. Pure heaven.

His little minx had proved to be a skilled thief. Except for the interruption of her father roaming the house, they were in and out. And today, he'd peruse his cache. Hopefully what they needed was contained in one of those items.

Adding breaking and entering to his list of misdeeds didn't deter him much. Jail and lynching already stared him in the face. After all, the intended target had been his own wife's childhood home. And the valuables they'd garnered, only proof, not conventional plunder.

His wife gave a waking coo of sorts, and he grinned, snugging her in even tighter. But she continued to sleep, sighed and burrowed closer. Her chamber had become his chamber as well, even though most of his clothing and possessions still remained in his previous bedroom. Yet, he couldn't help but wonder how long this bliss would last. Right now, she needed him. Facing the consequences of their involvement in the Underground Railroad had her running scared into his arms.

He wouldn't complain, though he dreaded her throwing him out again. A man never welcomed a blow to his pride. He inhaled. No, he had to be honest. The fear of her rejection was more than mere damage to his dignity, it struck closer to his heart. Something he'd only opened to Eunice. Or so he thought.

He pressed a kiss to Rhapsody's forehead, her face relaxed in sleep. Her deep blue eyes, now hidden from him, burned in his memory. They could go from cold and cutting to passionate and sultry quick as a lightning strike. He gathered a handful of her blonde curls and spread it across his chest, stroking its golden beauty, intermixing the locks among his dark chest hairs. My, what a fool he'd become for this woman.

Something powerful and baffling threaded its way through him. Molten and spreading. Unavoidable. Taking over his thoughts, his desires, keeping him thinking about his wife more than he ought. This thing incapacitating his heart could only be described as…what? Desire? Need?

How he'd thought his affection for Eunice had been love. But looking back, he realized how shallow and self-serving he'd been. Eunice was desirable, thus he wanted her. Once they'd begun sharing their hopes and dreams, reality should have smacked him in the face as to the incompatibility of their personalities. However, he'd continued to pursue her, despising his brother when she'd drifted toward Shafer. At the time it had been a great injustice. Now, Cav only felt thankfulness that God had directed her away and brought a fiery blonde instead.

Cav rose on his elbow. Sure, Rhapsody was beautiful. Breathtakingly so. Far more fetching than Eunice on face value, if the two were to be compared. Eunice still possessed that quiet grace that charmed him once. But Rhapsody's zest for life went farther than charm. It enveloped him. A quiet grunt emoted from him. He'd analyzed the two women like a banker comparing investments. Insane, considering Rhapsody held him captive. There were no cold hard decisions, pro or con. This woman had left an indelible mark on his heart.

He stroked her cheek and then froze. Dear Lord in heaven. He'd fallen…in love. His lunatic musings could be described no other way. His wife had intertwined herself into his carefully guarded heart and stolen it right from under him.

A slice of alarm cut through him like no other. Shuffling fugitives in the middle of the night, chancing discovery, loss of reputation, and possible lynching had never brought on such fear. She'd woven herself into his very being. Amongst his expectations, his aspirations. Even his God-given destiny. Rhapsody held his heart in the palm of her hand, free to crush it at will for any whim.

His heart thumped. And what would happen, when danger passed, when fear no longer sent her seeking comfort in his arms? Where would he be? For if she rejected him again, all he'd held dear would surely lie in shattered ruins.

Chapter Twenty-One

Cav tapped the ledger in front of him and cast his gaze out the library window. No actual mention of a "child." Only a "package" costing nearly five hundred dollars. Quite a sum for a package unless it contained gold. And it was listed on January eleventh, the day after Mrs. Grafton had claimed Rhapsody was born. That had to be it.

He reclined in the stiff chair and took up the envelope on his desk. Perhaps there was something in here. Adoption, legally, had only been in force since 1851, a mere two years. So, officially, no paperwork need exist. Yet some type of legal document had to verify her existence. He scanned the document and grinned.

An Act to legitimize a certain female child.

Whereas it appears by petition of Milton Lennox, formerly of New York, now of Floyd County, Indiana, that a certain female child, so referred to as Redemption, born on January 10 of said same year, was bequeathed to him, by an anonymous person for purposes of nourishing and raising, and by petition of Milton Lennox, and from parental affection toward said child, is desirous that she should be legitimized and called Rhapsody Marie Lennox.

Be it enacted by the Senate House of Representatives (of the State of Indiana) in General Assembly met, that from and after the passing of this act the said female child shall be called and known as Rhapsody Marie Lennox; any law to the contrary is not withstanding.

Daniel Medford

Speaker of the House of Representatives

Barron Fozholden

President of the Senate

Assented to, January 31, 1827

W. Hendricks, Governor

"Thank you, Lord for your bounty," Cav mimicked an old table prayer with no truer sentiment.

He was armed and ready.

Rhapsody paced and patted her forehead with her lacey hanky. Even with the evidence that Cav presented, the meeting with her parents stretched ominously before her. They'd given no certain time, only that they'd arrive a week later. Today was that day.

Cav had buried himself in the library, and she, with no compunction to leave her master sitting room, had chosen to whittle away the empty time reading. The book, discarded long ago, now lay upon the small table near the striped settee. Instead she walked from one spot to another, petitioning a God she had little to do with. But never had she been in such a desperate need for deliverance.

"Forgive me, deliver me. Help me," she whispered. If only she had some sign that the Almighty Creator of the universe even heard her pleas, for it seemed quite unlikely. Rhapsody settled at the window, where a light breeze eased through the cracks. At least fall brought cooler weather, although from the unseemly moisture gathering at her brow and neck, one would never believe the temperatures had dropped.

She stood, spun, and paced once more. Jail seemed imminent for both Cav and her. At least, she was just shy of begging the Lord, bargaining even, for only incarceration for Cav. The thought of hanging simply sent her into hives and panic. How would she ever be separate from the man who now filled her life? She'd rather swing from a noose beside him.

Shaking off her thoughts, she continued to barrage the ceiling for clemency from her parents' blackmail. And facts be known, even Mrs. Grafton had hinted she knew of their endeavors in the freedom movement. How many others were aware? Even if Cav managed to reach an agreement of silence with her parents, others may very well know of their activities. She groaned and rubbed her forehead.

The heavy door clicked open in the master bedroom, and Rhapsody treaded from the sitting room. Cav stood near the door, so cavalier in a fine black suit, horizontal tie giving him a jaunty air. He danced his brows at her and a roguish grin crossed his face.

"Ready for the inquisition?"

How could he be so cheerful about it? Trembling started to take hold. "Absolutely not."

He approached and set his hands on her arms, smoothing comfort through her rose-colored sleeves. "I knew you'd be shaking."

"Is your associate, Mr. Albridge, coming?"

"Already here."

"So we're just waiting for my parents."

"Actually, they're in the library."

A choke of breath sucked down her throat. "They're here?"

He nodded.

"Why the library? Shouldn't we house them in the drawing room? My mother will not likely appreciate being installed in a room for business."

"Your mother is not likely to approve any room we put her in. So perhaps we could deposit her in the water closet?"

Despite the impending doom of the meeting, a quip of a laugh burst through Rhapsody's lips.

Cav rumbled a chuckle. "Now, there's my brave, fiery wife."

She shook her head. "I'm not brave. My parents, especially my mother, whom I believe," she lowered her voice to a whisper, "may hold a grudge against me for who I am."

"It would explain her incredible loving behavior." Cav reared his head back and barked another laugh.

Rhapsody stomped her foot. "Cav. Be serious."

The smile, still vined across her handsome husband's face, coaxed a small grin on hers. Then he pulled her into his embrace. She closed her eyes and rested her cheek against his chest with a deep breath. The man's very smell had entwined into her senses until she craved it. How she wished she didn't have to leave this room. Or this particular spot tucked beneath her husband's clean-shaven chin. Far too soon he set her away.

"Come, my dear. Let us know our fate." His face turned somber, determined even, and he lowered his hand to grasp hers. Together they left the room and navigated the stairs. At the library door, he stopped, faced her, and brushed a stray hair behind her ear. Then he winked. Oh, the audacity of the man. How love for him burned in her heart.

Then he swung the door open, letting her enter before him. In front of the imposing desk sat her parents in the two stuffed brown chairs. Both of them were decked in their best funeral clothes, making Rhapsody glad she'd chosen a muted rose gown. Another seat next to the desk held a stranger, Cav's associate and lawyer, she assumed. The men rose as she entered.

"This is Holden Albridge." Cav gestured to the compact man with dark hair and brows, eyes intelligent behind round glasses. "My wife, Rhapsody Blackledge."

Rhapsody Redemption Blackledge. She gritted her teeth, but forced a smile at Cav's associate. Then she dipped her head to her parents. "Mother, Father."

"Good to see you."

Strange greeting from her father, wasn't it? Her mother sniffed. Now, that made sense. A fourth chair sat on the other side of the desk facing the occupants, and Cav escorted her to it. So, her husband had clearly marked their territory. Their side against the Lennoxes. The only problem, she would have to directly face them.

Cav seated himself behind the large desk and organized the papers in front of him.

Her father cleared his throat. "This is highly irregular. I maintain this gentleman," he indicated Mr. Albridge, "has no business in family affairs. We will settle this man to man."

Cav gave a calculated smile. "Since our womenfolk grace the room, I hardly think this a mere discussion between men. Besides, there is more to discuss than your betrayal, there's—"

"Betrayal?" Her father surged to his feet. "How dare you insinuate we are the disloyal ones? I demand you dismiss this outsider and leave us to discuss private matters."

Rhapsody's admiration for Cav rose as he sat back and steepled his fingers, touching them to his chin. Nothing but coolness emitted from him in the face of her father's outrage. "Don't you mean private threats?"

Her father remained standing. "Very well. If you insist on making this a public spectacle, I refuse to discuss this any further unless my lawyer is present as well."

Cav leaned forward and grasped a small bell perched on the corner of the desk. A few tense moments later the door opened, and Father's lawyer, Tavin Lockwood, ducked through. Father sank to his chair, face limp. Barton entered behind him, fetched another chair, and set it beside Father's. Mr. Lockwood took a seat with his leather case.

"Oh, you're very cunning, Blackledge." Her father's face flushed red, eyes hard as granite.

"What my client would like to express," Mr. Lockwood began, his courtroom demeanor falling into place, "is why you've summoned us all here?"

"All in good time. Tavin Lockwood, my associate, Holden Albridge."

The men nodded at one another.

"Perhaps you'd like to start, Mr. Lennox." Cav folded his fingers and leaned forward.

The two men stared at one another, one hot as a stovepipe on a subzero day, the other as icy as a pump handle in January.

"You wish this matter to go public?" Her father's voice barely contained his rage. "You may have no regard for your reputation, Blackledge, but I assure you, I value mine."

"You have no trust in your attorney's discretion?" Cav leveled smoothly.

"Blackledge—"

"Gentlemen. I believe it's in the best interests of all parties to air the grievances," Mr. Albridge cut in.

Rhapsody stood. "Exactly. So I will commence. My father and mother, on hearing our involvement in the freedom movement to help fugitives escape, have threatened to expose us to the authorities if we don't sell the house and leave the area. Given the new strict guidelines of the Fugitive Slave Act, I fear that I may be incarcerated and a worse punishment for Cav. I fear he may hang."

Silence hung in the room like a moldy wet blanket. Without any replies, she continued, "I've no desire to leave this city, given the urgency of our operation. I merely suggest my parents keep mum about our venture. Therefore, they are safe as are we."

"You can't possibly believe that we would be safe," her mother spat. "When you're discovered, it will lead them right to us."

"Then maintain you had no involvement," Cav said.

"That's preposterous," her father exclaimed, pounding the chair arm with his fist. "She's our only daughter. The authorities will never believe us. We'll be accused right along with you. And we are completely innocent. The only recourse is for you to relocate."

Rhapsody wilted into her chair. So her parents would not back down. There was no option except the journal hidden within the desk. Was she ready to oust her parents? She grasped her hands in her lap to still the trembling.

Tavin Lockwood pulled his leather case to his lap. "I'm inclined to agree with my client, despite the thread of extortion I decipher in such a demand. Punishment for aiding and abetting fugitives carries stiff penalties."

Mr. Albridge also spoke. "But as you said, it reeks of coercion. If the Blackledges have no desire to relocate of their own free will, Mr. and Mrs. Lennox have no legal grounds to insist that they do."

"But it is in their best interest," Mr. Lockwood returned.

"I disagree. It is only in the best interest of the Lennoxes." Mr. Albridge looked to Cav. "Are you wishing to utilize my services to make a legal claim of blackmail against them?"

"No." Cav's one-syllable reply stilled the sputters of her parents.

"Then, I see no reason for us to be here." Mr. Lockwood collected his papers. "This appears to be a family dispute."

"It's more than that." Cav opened the right hand drawer and pulled out a ledger. Her father's face blanched at the sight of it.

"You thief."

Cav's brow rose. "Do you consider your daughter trespassing when she comes into your home?"

Her father's mouth flopped open.

"Then she is not a thief. Merely, a borrower of her own father's things. We will be glad to return these items once we divulge the contents." Cav flipped the pages.

"You are nothing but a reprobate. I rue the day I forced this marriage," her father hissed. "You'd stoop to such levels to protect your criminal activities."

"No, Mr. Lennox. I stoop to grant freedom to the oppressed. To save human lives. As does your daughter." Cav stood. "Two can play the game you instigated."

Her husband spun to the two lawyers. "I wish for you both to note this entry in Mr. Lennox's financial journal, from the year of Rhapsody's birth. A large sum of five hundred dollars for a package from a Mr. Hortice Grafton."

Her mother's hand rose and grasped the collar of her black silk dress. "Milton, you must stop this."

Her father shot to his feet. "I demand you cease and desist."

Rhapsody could bear it no longer and stood. "We will not, Father. For we are not the only ones harboring secrets."

A choking sound oozed from her mother's throat. And Rhapsody turned to her, the woman's face white as a freshly washed apron. The pain Rhapsody read there smote her soul. The familiar twitch in her cheek jerked. Rhapsody stepped forward and knelt in front of her mother to rest her hands upon her knees. "Is this why you despised me? Why you always were so concerned of your reputation, fearing scandal at every turn?"

Her mother's watery eyes locked on hers. "We have no secrets."

"Mother—"

Mrs. Lennox stood and tugged her skirt free from Rhapsody's hands. She glided to the window and stood staring out, a statue of stiff formality. And then Cav was there, helping Rhapsody stand on limbs that refused to support her. How could Mother deny the truth even as the evidence lay right before her? How could the woman not confess and embrace her only daughter who wanted nothing more than reconciliation? Reconciliation and…her mother's love. His questioning gaze bore into her eyes.

"Present the letter, Cav."

He nodded, guided her to her chair, and pulled the envelope out of the same drawer. "To verify the identity of the package, I have—"

"Blackledge, I'm warning you," Rhapsody's father stepped forward.

Cav raised his gaze. "Another threat, Sir? Shall I have our attorneys document this one as well?"

Her father whirled and dropped into his seat. Sweat glistened across his brow.

"Here, gentlemen. Documents from the state of Indiana verifying the package was indeed a child." Cav handed the document to Mr. Lockwood and then strode to Rhapsody and placed his hand on her shoulder.

Her mother turned from the window. "So what are you proving? That we acquired a child? So be it. Then, yes, we did. Where is the offense in that?"

Trembling seized Rhapsody. Indeed she had a point. "I believe the main glitch is my birth mother, wouldn't you think?"

A gasp escaped the prim older woman. "You have no proof."

Weariness sloshed through Rhapsody. "Perhaps not, but you and I both know Mr. Grafton's exotic paramour birthed me, and you bought me to replace your blood-born child to preserve the Lennox honor. Therefore, I carry slave's blood. Your daughter. And when that information is released, how honorable will the Lennox name be then?"

Her mother staggered and laid a hand to the window facing. The conferring attorneys, both assessing the contents of the legal document on the desk, froze. Mr. Lockwood's narrowed eyes seared Rhapsody to her soul. Perhaps this was just one more tally of disgrace in her honor rather than her parents. She tipped her chin up. Fine, so be it. She chose to err on the side of truth. And freedom.

Stifling a shudder at what she had to do, Rhapsody knew she had no option but to drive it home. "So, here's the bottom line. You expose us, we expose you."

Her mother's hand dropped to her side and she stiffened back into her aloof Lennox matriarch posture. "As you wish. Our silence for yours."

Mrs Lennox, shawl snugged around her, strode to stand in front of Rhapsody. "With the understanding that no Lennox will ever be involved with fugitives again. Is that understood?"

Rhapsody hesitated and then nodded.

Mrs. Lennox strode past the chairs to the door. "I'm ready to leave."

Mr. Lennox stood and joined her. He cast a glance over his shoulder, locking eyes with Rhapsody. Was there any love in her father's gaze? No, they only seemed soaked with regret, anger. And humiliation. Tears stung and toppled Rhapsody's lashes. *Please...don't turn your backs on me.*

With a deep sigh, her father whirled and trailed her mother out the door.

Chapter Twenty-Two

Rhapsody sniffed and pulled her legs upon the cushion, taking care to wrap her skirt tail around her. Decent ladies didn't sit in such a way. Miss Bickle would say—blast the old bat. Rhapsody wasn't a woman with privilege any more, was she? Besides, all she wanted to do was to make herself as small as she could. She'd chosen to watch the day flit by from the master sitting room chair set close to the lace-covered window. As was yesterday and the day before.

With protection from incarceration came the searing knowledge that her parents no longer cared for her. If they ever had. True, she'd never had an overly close relationship with them, but her father had indulged her in his tepid sort of way. Both her parents' reserved elite traditions coupled with strict boarding school methods had successfully constructed a wall of emotional separation even in her early formative years. Yet, they were her parents, albeit adoptive, and if her heart didn't crave them in terms of overt affection, she felt the void of their withdrawal.

The master bedroom door clicked open. Probably Lissy with another tray. Perhaps she'd put something in her mouth just to satisfy the woman, covert concern in her expressive eyes. If she could keep herself from gagging on the perfectly-prepared food. She had to do something. Her dresses were beginning to hang on her thin frame.

A shadow from her left made her glance up. Cav. He knelt beside her, taking her hand. "Are you going to sit here again today?"

The softness of his low voice made her want to weep. "I don't know."

He bowed his head for a moment and then brought his gaze up to search her face. "I'm concerned for you."

She blinked back moisture. "Did we do the right thing? My mother seemed crushed."

Cav tightened his hold on her hand. "What else could we have done? We had to force silence with a threat of our own. Most parents wouldn't put you in such a position."

"Would yours?"

Her husband lowered his eyes as if thinking through the possible scenarios. "I think most likely not. But, I think my father would be very angry."

Rhapsody nodded and turned to watch the orange leaves flutter against the window and then fall away. "I've been thinking. If we wall over the guest suite bedroom, we could create a secret room which would be much more secure for fugitives to hide. What do you think?"

His brows descended. "I think we need to distance ourselves for a while."

"Whatever for?"

He stood and paced to the far wall and leaned against it. My, he looked handsome today, as always, decked in a brown suit that matched the warm molasses of his eyes, a burnt orange tie spun beneath his chin. His cheeks bore evidence of the beard he'd started and his hair needed a cut in the traditional sense. Personally, she'd rather he let it grow to his shoulder-length waves. .

"You promised your mother that you wouldn't be involved anymore."

Rhapsody shifted her bare feet to the floor, flushing when she caught Cav assessing her ankles. "No, I promised that no Lennox would be involved. I was born an illegitimate Grafton, and now I am a Blackledge. I've never been a Lennox."

He took a deep breath and shoved away from the wall. "But legally, your name was changed to Lennox."

"But—"

With a step he stood in front of her, pressed thick fingers against her mouth, and grinned. "You are an amazing woman, Rhapsody Marie Blackledge."

She shook her head and tugged his hand from her mouth. "I want to change my name."

A pucker tightened his brows.

"I want to be Rhapsody Redemption Blackledge."

A laugh bubbled forward from his kissable lips. "So be it. I'll get Holden on it immediately. In the meantime, I think we need to lie low."

One hand captured hers while the other stroked her face.

"Then we may have to relocate after all. For I feel it's our duty to help the oppressed."

He nodded. "Perhaps."

"Will you keep conducting fugitives to safety?"

With a groan he rose. "Rhapsody, you are too inquisitive for your own good. And the less you know, the better off you'll be."

He tugged on her hands and she rose. "Instead of sitting here, let's go for a drive. It's fairly warm for late October. What do you say?"

Rhapsody nodded. Getting out would help lighten her mind of the troubles that weighed it down. And being on Cav's arm would be lovely, too. She nodded and went to collect her wrap.

Cav loaded the last of the blankets of Rhapsody's clothing brigade into the back of the wagon. The drive a few days back had been chilly, but he'd warmed himself thinking of the woman huddled against his shoulder. She'd smiled, but her eyes still held despondency. And as they'd ridden, he knew he had to cut her out of the operation. That meant clearing out Rhapsody's clothing collection.

Plus, he'd found it harder to leave in the middle of the night, not only because lying next to his beautiful wife was both intoxicating and comforting, but also because of drawing attention to himself and his activities. For he couldn't stop. But this was the next to the last load of the supplies in that room. The last one, ladies' dresses and men's shirts, lay tucked in the carriage house and he would haul it soon. Lissy would put the rooms back together and the guest rooms would appear as they always had. One completely empty, the other outfitted for the next visitor.

Oddly enough, another mansion just seven blocks away, would be the new safe station. And they had agreed to house the emergency clothing. He yawned, and stretched his arms wide. Once he used the wagon, he'd return it to Heaker Thomas, a blacksmith on the northwest corner of the city. Another safe contact he'd established that could help supply items of need.

He climbed aboard the wagon and set Number Three toward the Fulsom home. Not that Heaker Thomas's old nag was actually named that. But he missed his old plodder that now tugged Lazarus on his journey for freedom. Cav grunted. He missed Lazarus much more than that old horse.

He whispered a prayer for Lazarus and the group he led. Cav raised his eyes to the sky. Barton often made references to the care of the Lord. Preacher Dubber—my, the name brought a stab of sorrow to his heart—always claimed the Lord was his protection. *The Lord is my light and my salvation; whom shall I fear? The Lord is the strength of my life; of whom shall I be afraid?* Always the Preacher had muttered the verse. So many times Cav knew it by heart. Yet, it hadn't really played out that way.

"Maybe you needed ole' Preacher in heaven like Miss Adalia said. But I'll admit I have my doubts. If you're up there, prove it by delivering Lazarus and his wagon of freedom seekers, Lord. I ask no other petition than that they be safe."

The night continued to surge around him as he whispered, insects chirruping, the soft plodding of the horses feet. Yet something felt different. A peace fell over him like no other. He leaned back in the seat and rubbed the reins in his fingers. The stars seemed to wink at him.

Another petition nagged his brain. Rhapsody. They'd settled into married life, sharing secrets and a bed. But did the woman care for him like he did her? Would she ever? When everything calmed once more, would she still need him apart from financial support?

"And one more request, Lord. Rhapsody. I know she needs me now. She needs me in many ways, and I'm glad to give her my strength, both emotional and financial. Yet, when this mess is all over, I'll want more. Much more."

He paused and swallowed. "I want it all, Lord. Lock, stock and barrel. I've fallen for her with my whole heart, and I long for hers in return. I want…her love."

For how could he continue living with anything less?

Rhapsody stood in the empty room, key tucked in her pocket. So it was all gone. When she'd awoken in the middle of the night with Cav's side of the bed empty, fear had sliced through her. He'd started again. Knowing that, she'd wanted to check her supplies.

Only there weren't any. He toted them all away. At least he wasn't risking his life to transport fugitives without her. At least, she hoped. After she'd given some thought to Cav's advice to step away from the venture, she'd seen the wisdom in his words. Preacher Dubber had been murdered and burnt out of his own home. Adalia was now alone. What kept them from doing the same here at the mansion?

Yet knowing they needed separation for a while hadn't lessened the disappointment she'd experienced finding the room empty. Hiding from the elevated danger didn't help the waiting runaways get to freedom. With a rush of exhaled breath, she stepped from the room and twisted the key in the lock. On second thought, she turned the key to unlock the door. There was no point in keeping the room secure now. There was no evidence inside.

She turned and walked down the hallway, clenching the key in her pocket. The leftover money she'd collected still laid stored in a box deep inside her armoire. Plenty of cash for more clothing. Perhaps she'd pass it on to fund other safe houses.

Slipping into the master bedroom, her fingers rubbed her forehead at the pain that throbbed there. Headaches had plagued her since the meeting with her parents several weeks back. She shook her head to clear it, but only managed to bring on a painful throb. She swung the door of the armoire open.

A knock sounded on the bedroom door. Was it Cav? Surely not, for he'd all but moved into the master's chamber as his own. With her blessing. Her face grew hotter. She scurried to unlatch the door. Mabel stood outside. Not Lissy? How strange.

"Miss Mabel, what is it?"

The big-boned woman hunched over and glanced behind her. When she swung back to her, the older woman's eyes bugged from her dark face, fear dancing in their depths.

"I's got a message, Mum."

Mabel carried a message? True, they were short on staff by two servants now, but surely Mabel had not started answering doors. The woman had been the chief cook for years.

Fear licked at Rhapsody's insides. "Are my parents here?"

Mabel shook her head and then shot a stare down the hallway.

Rhapsody sighed with both relief and disappointment. "Very well. Come in."

The black woman shuffled just inside the door.

"Now, what's this all about?"

Mabel wet her generous lips, and then whispered, "They's free."

Rhapsody stilled. The woman had surely gone addled. Her age must have caught up with her. "Who?"

The woman kneaded her hands as if she turned the dreamy-smelling yeasty dough in her kitchen. "Lazarus. Da whole group. E'vabody. Free."

Rhapsody sucked in a gasp. Her temporary guests had reached Canada. And freedom. Tears pricked her eyes and slid down her cheeks. On impulse, Rhapsody gave a cry of elation and threw her arms around her old cook. The woman in her arms stiffened for a moment before giving a hesitant hug back. "Are you positive? How do you know?"

Mabel shrugged, swiping moisture near her eyelids. "I gots my ways."

As Rhapsody stood there, the big woman slipped back through the door and disappeared. No better news could have brought Rhapsody from her melancholy. Lazarus, Adalia and the others were safe. With a sigh, she knew the divine calling on her life. She would never be able to stop helping slaves become free.

Never.

So this was Cav's largest bank. Rhapsody let her eyes sweep the white marble floor, the arching foyer, the barred counters where at least fifteen cashiers attended customer business. No wonder the man could sweep in and cancel her debts with the speed of a thoroughbred. A man situated in a mahogany desk to her right rose and approached.

The news of their temporary guests making it to Canada had burned a fervent joy in her heart so hot she ached to share it. Immediately. However, by the time Barton had ferried the carriage across the Ohio River and Rhapsody hunted down where Cav might be, it had grown into late afternoon.

"May I help you, ma'am?" the older gentleman's elongated face stretched even more with the rise of white brows. He smacked of a reticent bank official in his smart gray suit. But his sharp eyes spoke of wisdom as well

"I'm looking for Mr. Cavanaugh Blackledge."

The man leaned back at her answer, eyes taking in her fashionable hat and folded parasol. "Do you have an appointment?"

She shook her head and eased a smile. "No, I'm his wife."

The man's face cleared, and he nodded with a brief blink. "Ah, Mrs. Blackledge. I'm Gilbert Rothsmeyer, head loan officer here of the Louisville First Southern Bank. It is quite a privilege to meet you. I would count it a great honor to guide you. Please, come this way."

She followed the man down a hallway to the right which led to a flight of stairs. They trod down a few more hallways until they came to a door on the left.

"I'll leave you to wait in his office while I alert him of your presence. May I fetch refreshment for you?"

"No, no. I'll be fine, thank you."

He nodded and closed the door behind him. She turned and accessed the room in a muted nutmeg color. The large desk dominated the room in front of a set of floor-to-ceiling curtained windows. Rhapsody stepped around and peered through the sheer weave of the curtains without pulling them aside. She recognized the floor she had just entered and the cashiers below as they moved about waiting on customers. Cav certainly had a bird's eye view of the operations of his bank.

She scanned the walls. Only shelves with many thick volumes and an official framed document, proclaiming the bank's name and official endorsement as a state banking business. She stared at Cav's strong signature slanting across the bottom of the document and started when the door clicked open.

Cav shut the door quietly behind him. "Ah, you've found me."

He didn't seem to be overly glad to see her, which dimmed her enthusiasm a bit. "I hope you don't mind."

Instead of answering, he moved behind his big desk and indicated a chair. "Please sit down. I'm curious how you knew where I'd be."

She slid into the leather chair, wondering at his cool attitude. "Actually, I had to do some sleuthing. I visited Mr. Albridge's office, and he directed me here."

"Hmmm. I see." His brow tightened. "I suppose I need to get with you to discuss my daily agenda. I'm afraid you've interrupted a rather important investment meeting.

That didn't seem forthcoming either. She shifted in her seat. Perhaps she should have waited until he arrived home. "I'm so sorry. It's just I've had some rather good news. Splendid actually. Are we quite alone?"

Cav nodded. "We're secure in here."

Still she glanced about, leaned forward, and whispered. "They're free."

Her husband's face screwed up tighter and then cleared. "Lazarus?"

She couldn't stem the grin and nodded.

"All of them?"

"Yes. I'm not sure how Mabel knows, but she assured me it was true."

A laugh popped from Cav and he smacked the desk. "Well, I'll be. The Lord did it."

Rhapsody giggled and rose. "I shouldn't keep you. I apologize for disturbing your meeting. I just couldn't hold in the good news."

Cav stood, a wicked smile still stretching his lips. "I can always use good news."

He circled the desk and set his hand on her waist, escorting her to the door. "And never think you can't run me down wherever I may be in the city."

"I'd also like to discuss something else with you, concerning the leftover funds I have set aside." She hurriedly spilled her harebrained idea. "I can't help but think it might help them settle wherever they are. If we could find a way to get it to them."

His gaze studied over her face and he sobered. "We…do need to talk, you and I. About that and many other things. Now that our lives seem to be settling, and we begin a routine."

Her breath slowed. His penetrating gaze kicked a quiver of uncertainty. He was right. But exactly what were these "other things?" His distant tone set her nerves on edge. Where exactly were they headed now? As a couple? Without the need to cover for his Underground Railroad activities, he would have little use for her. He owned the mansion. He held all the cards. She could be nothing more than a pawn in his game of big money.

"Of course." She breathed, wondering what she was agreeing to.

He pressed a kiss to her forehead and escorted her from the room.

Chapter Twenty-Three

Cav tugged the wool coat around his shoulders. Number Three plodded obediently in the windy night. Leaves scattered across the road, but the horse, well-seasoned to distractions, continued to hoof it down the cobblestones. Heaker Thomas hadn't shooed his horse despite being a blacksmith. Covert operations needed to be quiet. Especially in the middle of the night.

Not that the noisy night needed help stifling the hoof beats down upper High Street. Other than the cold, it was a perfect night for transporting forbidden materials. Cav blinked and yawned. Dog tired and full of regret for not having made it home after work like he'd promised, the chill in the ghostly wind prodded him awake. November brought a hint of the winter to come, and the runaway traffic would slow. Too dangerous to move folks in the freezing temperatures. Especially to Canada where the temperatures would be much colder.

A wisp of frigid air trickled down the back of his neck and he buttoned the overcoat. If he hadn't cut his hair, he'd have more protection from the weather. Why he hadn't grabbed his scarf he had no clue. All this aggravation put him in a downright grumpy mood. Still, it was the last of Rhapsody's clothing brigade donations, and then, he'd think more about staying in his wife's bed throughout the night, warm and very toasty.

Thoughts of her golden hair, escaping the long braid down her back and wreathed against the pillow as she slept, filled his mind. That's where he should be right now. In the master bedroom, snuggled up to her sleepy face.

He shoved that thought away despite the temptation to dwell there. What he should be concentrating on was how to divulge his love for her, confess he never wanted to utilize their marriage as one of just mutual protection anymore, his for cover and hers merely to avoid scandal. Come to think of it, she needed financial assistance, as well. So there was that. Another reason she might outright snub his revelation of love.

That didn't set well. But he couldn't be misinterpreting her coy glances, her welcome arms, her fiery passion. Surely a woman couldn't pretend all of those things, although he'd admit, he'd seen some fairly manipulative women. Even Eunice had schemed to toggle from him to his brother. Shafer had started out being a third wheel and soon ended up conversing more with her than he. Not that he regretted it now.

Surely Rhapsody, for all they'd gone through, couldn't be just tolerating him for the benefits he brought to the marriage. The idea coughed up a bad taste in his mouth.

He shelved the notion as he pulled into the back of the carriage house of the new benefactor. Quietly, he lit from the wagon seat and hauled the sealed brown packages into the designated spot inside the building. The three horses didn't even acknowledge him, merely kept their shadowed heads tucked down. Probably wondering why a human disturbed them in the middle of the night. He deposited the last of the load and then paused at the door. Always good to be on the lookout. Just in case.

But the wind whipped so ferociously, it wouldn't have mattered if he'd stood with ten lanterns. Nothing could be heard for the swirling air and leaves. He rubbed his rough, cold hands together and hurried back to the old wagon. The sooner he finished up, the sooner he could get back.

He steered Number Three out of the drive and set a good pace to Boiling Springs Road. He just had to pick up Black, race home, and be done with it for the night.

Back to Rhapsody. She'd been so beautiful today when he'd opened the office door, it had robbed not only his breath, but his heart. Dressed in a light blue floating creation, matching those incredible eyes, her face flushed with her good news, it had been all he could do not to sweep her into his arms, press her to the wall, and kiss the breath from her. The depth of his love had stunned him. The fierceness of it. It had entangled his heart to the point he wanted to throw restraint to the wind and lock the office door.

He'd almost been rude, he feared, so in awe of the attraction that woman held over his emotions. A chuckle escaped to the November wind. Yes, he'd been called a ruffian on so many occasions, he couldn't count them. Cavalier, devil-may-care, rakish. It didn't matter that those descriptions in all honesty didn't suit, but he'd shrugged and accepted them. It had benefited his mission and served him well in repelling many a designing woman.

But Rhapsody had unwittingly dissolved all his fortifications to keep affection from weaving through his soul. He'd been wholly satisfied with the freedom operation. Fixated on it, even. Then, bang, there she was in the middle of the road, swatting and insulting him. His first thoughts had been to use her to his advantage and checkmate, she'd stolen his heart.

Cav turned the horse onto Boiling Springs Road and headed out of town. Soon he'd be free of his duty tonight. He lined up a plan. Order up breakfast, dine in their master sitting room, and blurt his confession and pray she'd be receptive or, dare he hope, reciprocate his feelings. Then he'd lock the door and revel in their love.

Something drew his attention and he glanced to the left. Most likely, a large catalpa leaf. His eyes searched the vicinity. This had to be about the location he'd kissed Rhapsody that fateful day that had led to so much more. A grin filtered across his features.

As the horse clipped down the dirt road, they passed Preacher Dubber's homestead, nothing but two black burnt patches in the tall grass now. He slowed Number Three but didn't dare stop. Driving by this site always grieved his heart. He missed his friend. Yet Lazarus and the others were safe, and he thanked the Lord he'd delivered them. His wife's face, alight with the news cheered his heart.

Again a low set flurry blurred at his left. Had he seen something? Something running? No, just his imagination. If only he could hurry this task. Through his nostrils, he drew in icy air smelling of dirt and decaying leaves. If Rhapsody were indeed in love with him, perhaps their love would help her forget the melancholy of her parents' rejection.

Something darted in front of the horse, and the animal reared causing the wagon to shutter and nearly stop. Cav looked around wondering what sort of animal had charged across their path. Were there cougars about so close to the city?

He set the reins against the horse's back, murmuring to calm the usually composed animal. It only took a few moments to get back up to speed. Yet, Cav swung his head about trying to get a fix on whatever had startled Number Three. He grabbed his rifle. Then, three large hounds bounded from the woods, snarling and baying. The blood-red dogs leapt at him, aiming for his chest.

Cav managed only a grunt before he shot backward, grinding his back into the wagon bed, rifle flying, dogs baying and nipping. Teeth seized him in every direction while he warded off a powerful set of jaws snapping at his neck. He shoved, pushed and booted anything that drew near. Yet, sharp bites littered his body. In the mauling he realized Number Three had given a shrill whinny and now trotted at a blazing speed which whipped him from the wagon. He hit the dirt on his back, legs over him, with a painful crunch and life blinked white and fuzzy for a moment.

Strong teeth chomped at his arms and legs, vying for his neck. Cav kicked and hollered, mindful of the blistering pain in his chest. He rolled over, dug his forehead and knees into the ground, and wrapped his arms about his head, trying to protect himself the best he could.

"Heel."

The deep command stopped the battering as immediately as it started. Cav stayed curled in a ball, heaving in breaths. Only then did he register the curse directive. Catchers. Dogs.

"Roll him over."

Something struck his side and he sucked air at the pain, flipping to his back. Agony screamed from his chest.

"Sympathizer. You'll rue the day you were born," a voice, dark and gruff permeated his senses.

Two hurricane lamps shoved toward his face, and Cav flinched, eyeing the numerous ghostly faces circling him, two of which he thought he recognized. The same two he and Rhapsody had met on this very road. "What's going on?"

"You'll be helping no more runaways. Got it?" the voice growled. "Finish him."

A fist snapped Cav's head to the ground, and wooziness deflected a miniscule amount of pain that pulsated through his head. Then more punches from the left, the right, in his flopping face. Though he brawled like the devil, each swing took his breath with the blinding pain in his chest and the blows that each man landed. Unconsciousness reached out to claim him. If not for fear of Rhapsody's safety, he would've welcomed relief from the agony. But one last punch to his jaw shut out his lights.

Rhapsody shifted and groaned, resisting the pull to waken. Pounding on the bedroom's door ripped her from sleep. Silent tears had kept her awake till late in the night. Still, Cav had not arrived home. He'd promised they'd discuss where they were. Well, his absence screamed it loud and clear. She shoved the wretchedness aside. How she hated to face the day. Perhaps she could lounge in her bed and feign an illness. But from the sounds of the pummeling fists at her bedroom door, that wouldn't be happening today.

"Enter," she grunted.

Lissy spilled forth, a mass of hysteria. "It be da Mister, Mum. He all kinds o' beat up."

Rhapsody scurried from the bed. "Calm down. What are you saying?"

"Mr. Cav. He hurt."

Terror throttled her throat. She grabbed the bed jacket and slipped it on, not taking the time to even cover her feet and rushed after Lissy. Downstairs two strange men set a blanketed limp figure on the Chesterfield. She clutched the jacket to her throat, the consciousness of her state of undress sliding away as she recognized the form.

A shudder and a gasp ripped from her throat. Cav's face, swollen and bloody, was nearly unrecognizable.

"What—Oh, Cav!" She fell to her knees. "Lissy, get a wet rag. Have Barton run for the doctor."

"We've already summoned the doc," the larger man, bearded, with kind eyes answered. "I'm Heaker Thomas, ma'am, and my neighbor Abel."

"What…happened?"

"Not sure. Cav had borrowed my horse and wagon for the night, and they ended up near the house this morning. That set me to searching. Found him north of town. I think he may have been lying there for some time."

Rhapsody scrambled to her feet. "I don't understand. Who would hurt him?"

The deep look in the man's eyes made hers widen. She whispered, "Catchers?"

The big man shrugged.

One hand covered her mouth and with the closing of her eyes, her other palm slapped over the first. He'd been out. Helping others. Doing his good deeds for liberty and justice. And he'd been the one they'd caught. For all his covert plans, he'd been discovered and suffered the consequences.

"Lord, deliver us." She sank to her knees and pressed her head to his chest. They weren't safe. What if these horrible men returned? She lifted her head and forced herself to stare at his gory face. Tears leaked down her face.

Lissy arrived and squeezed out a warm rag into a metal pail. Rhapsody took it and wiped fresh and dried blood from his face. As she cleaned, purple bruises littered his features and his nose sported a bloated lump in the middle. Sobs shuddered her breath as she continued to wipe his cold skin. Punctures oozed blood at his neck and shoulders. Bites?

"Oh, Cav," she sniffed, dipping the rag once more into the water to rinse it. "Dear God, help him."

"Should we move him to a bed, Ma'am?"

She shook her head. "He's not going anywhere until the doctor gets here."

His lashes fluttered and a groan rumbled from his chest.

"Cav?"

He winked a few slow blinks. "Rhap…sody?"

Her tears blinded her. "Yes. It's me."

For a moment he seemed to drift off, and she swiped the cloth against his hairline to remove the dirt lodged there.

"We…need…to leave," he pushed the words out. "Catchers got me."

Fear pounded her brain and she caught her breath. He was right. If they followed him into town, they would kill him. And from the look of it, it wouldn't take much to do that. The door opened. The same older doctor who'd tended Preacher Dubber stepped in. Rhapsody rose to greet him and swipe at her tears.

She tugged Lissy aside, out of the men's hearing as the doctor examined Cav. "Pack a trunk for us. You, also, must be ready. I will need Barton to accompany us as well. Mabel and Mr. Wadell will stay here and tend the house and horses. Understand?"

Lissy nodded, all eyes, and then scurried off to do her bidding."

She beckoned to Barton who'd entered behind the doctor. In whispered tones she detailed a plan for Barton to retrieve four steamer tickets and to be ready to depart as soon as the doctor cleared him to travel.

The doctor rose. "He's been in a tussle, all right, with very uneven odds. Most likely he's cracked or broken his sternum and a rib or two. He has a severe concussion, but no other bones appear to be broken. He has bites and bruises all over him, indicating both man and beast has mauled him. Spending several hours in the cold might have actually done him some good, keeping the injuries chilled and the bleeding at bay. Nevertheless, he's in grave shape."

"Can he travel on a steamer?"

The doctor's white brows descended, and he glanced toward his patient. "Not the best option, but I see where you might be going with this. So, under the circumstances, I'd say with much care."

She nodded and looked at the two men. "I hate to impose on you further, gentlemen. But I ask your help to carry my husband aboard. We'll take a carriage there, as early as possible. We'll cover him and carry him to our stateroom. I must get him away from anyone who might still be tracking him."

"We'd be glad to help," Heaker nodded.

The doctor stepped forward, pulled some bottles from his case. "I'll get him bandaged up and leave some medication with you to use on your way.

She nodded. "And please, for the sake of my husband and your own lives, we must keep this as quiet as possible."

Chapter Twenty-Four

Late the next day, Rhapsody gave a sigh of relief as Lissy poked her head into the tiny stateroom with its two narrow bunks.

"We's here, Mum."

She nodded, dabbing Cav's forehead as he lay propped up against the luggage. He'd been unable to sleep prone and neither had rested well throughout the harrowing night. He'd woken her several times with groans of pain. "Good. Does Barton know what to do?"

She nodded.

"I can walk," Cav's voice came in a croak.

Rhapsody laid a hand to his sleeve. "It's easier to hide you beneath a blanket. Please, indulge me just this once."

Cav merely closed one eye as the other had swollen shut in the aftermath of the attack. His entire face was a mass of swollen purple flesh. She prayed his skull hadn't suffered any breaks. She grasped his hands and winced at the teeth marks that had round angry rings around each one. Dear Lord, how would he ever heal from so many injuries?

The boat slowed beneath their feet, the unending grinding sound eased, and Rhapsody waved Lissy in, handing her the lighter luggage. Nearly a half hour later, two rough characters toting a long wide board between them showed up at the door. Barton stood behind them while they loaded Cav, amidst much pain grimacing across his face, onto the board and carried him from the large steamer.

Barton had secured a battered black carriage and with much care and a few onlookers, they loaded Cav into the waiting vehicle. Most of the passengers had made their way up the stone gravel wharf and only a few weary stragglers cared to take the time to cast a nosey stare in their direction. Rhapsody snugged the cloak around her, the chill in the air nipping at her cheeks. She glanced around from the muddy river to the red banks lining the landing of Henderson, Kentucky. A large wharf, new and at least fifty foot wide. Impressive.

Although running scared was not the best introduction to a new city, it couldn't be helped. The deciduous trees around the area and across the river threw their naked arms up to the sky. Visiting in the summer would have gentled the harsh November surroundings, but this was no ordinary social call. Besides, it was time to get out of the weather and find Cora Gentry. The woman was about to have company, whether she liked it or not.

A moan drifting from the carriage interior sent Rhapsody scurrying to get inside. She thrust a couple of silver coins at the men who'd toted Cav, and then Rhapsody stuffed the case she carried behind his back with care. He had to sit up to find any comfort. The steamer had been a luxury ride next to the one poor Cav would experience now. His labored breath brought a billow of fog to the icy air.

Barton, bundled up in a long wool coat, scarf, and top hat nodded to a couple of dark-skinned men who pointed and explained. Hopefully, he'd get the right directions. Poor Barton. He'd have a cold ride ahead of him as the driver of the transport. But they had to find the Gentry farm. She didn't feel safe in the city.

She and Lissy settled on the opposite bench seat facing Cav tucked in with blankets. He seemed to be dozing now that the jostling had stopped. But his eyes blinked open once Barton had boarded and set the shabby carriage in motion.

The worn springs of the carriage did little to lessen the jolts of the two-hour journey. The city soon disappeared into the flat country of trees and pastures. Cav moaned off and on and vomited once, but seemed to weather the trip as well as he could. Barton slowed the carriage to a stop and Rhapsody huffed into her hands to warm them. The weak sun tickled the tops of the trees on the western horizon. The dinner hour had arrived. She couldn't imagine the toll the ride had taken on Cav. Personally, she was freezing and exhausted. She prayed Cora had been serious about entertaining them.

Barton appeared at the door and swept it open. Rhapsody exited to a white two-story farmhouse Freshly painted and trimmed in blue, it looked to be a fairly new structure. Beyond, she could see a huge red barn and yet another two story house. A mixture of horses and mules milled in the corrals surrounding the structure. The door opened on the quaint porch running the length of the front of the house, and a man stood there pulling on a coat. Very tall and dark-headed.

Rhapsody gnawed her bottom lip while Lissy exited the carriage with Barton's assistance. Well, no time like the present to announce their plans to stay not only for the dinner hour, but indefinitely. As she strode to the porch, another person, also tall but female, stepped beside the man. Cora, very pregnant, in a black cape. Thank God. They'd found the right place.

"Rhapsody?"

Cora's voice contained both surprise and trepidation. Rhapsody stiffened her back and gave a small wave. Please let her be accommodating. *Please.* The woman stepped down the stairs followed by the man. They met on the stepping stone walk.

Cora's face wreathed in smiles, her breath coming in frozen puffs. "I can't believe you are actually here. Welcome. Let's get you out of the cold."

Tears The very thing Rhapsody had buried deep inside for the last day and a half stung her eyes. She blinked to disperse them, but it was too late. One rolled down her chilled cheek. Cora stepped forward, shrewd eyes missing nothing.

She patted Rhapsody's hand. "Whatever it is, it's going to be all right."

"Thank you." She took a steadying breath, dabbing at the traitorous tear. "I am sorry to greet you in such a way. And at mealtime to boot. But I hope you'll be able to accommodate us. I know I'm being quite forward, but my husband is…injured. We had to leave the city for a time."

Cora nodded and gave a small smile. "Well, you came to the right place. This is Trigg, my husband. The rest of his clan live in the other house, and they'll be over for supper soon. You all are welcome to stay as long as you need. We have plenty."

It was simply lovely having others around to help bear the burden of caring for Cav. Trigg's brother Roe and sister Bliss arrived shortly after, and the two men helped Cav into the bedroom on the lower level. Lissy was installed nearby in a small bedroom, and Barton took a room above the huge barn. Rhapsody caught the uneasy glances the men shot each other at Cav's injuries but said nothing. Cora served up a meal of stew and homemade bread. Rhapsody ate a small portion before excusing herself to feed Cav.

He ate very little and drifted off to sleep. Rhapsody knew Cora would understand if she didn't reappear for the night so she prepared for bed. She lay in the rough cotton sheets, grateful to be away from New Albany. Hopefully, they would be safe while Cav healed.

Cav blinked and opened his eyes. He reclined on several pillows, with one beneath his knees as well. He moved his arms and felt the painful tug in the center of his chest. He must have done that…when? Somehow he'd lost his train of thought. He brushed his fingertips across his face. At least there was no wetness there, and his one eye had recovered enough to open.

He sensed a presence next to him, and he turned his head. Ah, Rhapsody, breathing gently, a crease between her brows. She worried, even in her sleep. About him? More than likely. He'd slept more than when he imagined he had as a newborn. But he finally felt awake. And a bit stronger.

Had Rhapsody told him where they were? The room's ambiance in the dark seemed unfamiliar. Wait, yes. At a friend's house? Sarah? No, Cora. Cora something. And somehow Rhapsody knew her, but he couldn't recall how.

Cav inhaled a deep breath as the sunrise lit up the room. Besides his fuzzy memory, his chest still hurt like the dickens. Rhapsody had wrapped it faithfully each day, making sure it was tight enough to support whatever was broken, yet loose enough to breathe and circulate.

It had been over a week now, and he'd progressed to getting out of bed. Today he had goals of walking around the yard. Trigg and Roe had been more than helpful with their assistance, but he had to regain his strength. He'd denied any painkiller except at night. But eventually that too had to go.

His wife beside him inhaled and rolled to her back. Her eyes blinked open and stared at the ceiling for just a moment before turning to him.

"Oh, you're already awake."

Her voice was soft and sleep-wispy. He may have forgotten a few things, but one thing he hadn't forgotten was the love that coursed through him at the sight of her.

He tugged a small grin. "Yep, ready for a full day of…" Shoot, he hadn't meant to forget the new day's activities.

She sat up, a troubled crinkle at her brow. "Nothing. You're doing nothing for right now."

"Where did you say we were?" From the look on her face, he knew he shouldn't have asked.

"Don't you remember? I told you yesterday and the day before that. Henderson."

"Kentucky?"

His question made her face scrunch up. My, he didn't mean to make her cry. "Oh, sure. That's right. I remember now."

She reached out and rubbed his shoulder. He suspected it was because she couldn't speak for a few moments. He'd disappointed her again. Then there was no use asking her how he'd been injured. He suspected he'd already asked. Maybe several times. Once more might bring her more tears.

"That's fine. The doctor said you may have some memory issues for a while."

He nodded, unsure if she spoke the truth for her gaze tinged so sorrowful.

"I need to get dressed so I can help Cora in the kitchen."

Ah, his favorite part of the day. Watching her dress. She stood and fumbled in the carpet bag, bringing forth a brown skirt and blouse and laid them across the chair. Rhapsody turned and shot him a pointed look, one hand planted on her hip.

"I'd tell you to close your eyes, but you never listen." A dimple sank in the corner of her mouth.

He let a wolfish grin cover his face. "We're married, remember? I have certain privileges."

Her face sobered. "Yes…I remember."

She was anxious about his lack of memory. That was clear. He would have to avoid using that word. Nevertheless, she spun and quickly made short work of shedding her night clothes. Hmmm. He was anxious to feel healthy again. She slipped on her underclothes and skirt and then wrestled the corset's ties. He hated to stop the show, but he knew she needed help. His hand pulled aside the blankets, and he set his feet on the floor.

"Don't you dare get out of bed, Cavanaugh Blackledge, and I mean it."

His painful echoing laughter was his only answer as he worked around the bed to her. He shoved her groping fingers aside and grasped the ties and pulled them snug.

"This isn't proper, you know."

He grunted. "Why not? I'm your husband."

"It's Lissy's job," She sniffed.

He turned her, his hands gentle on her bare shoulders. Leisurely, he took his fill of her, both shaped and exposed in the tight garment. She crossed her arms over herself.

"Cav. Stop."

Her voice came breathless, like she preferred he do the complete opposite. A chuckle slid forth from his chest, and he eased her into his arms. He tucked a kiss in the hollow of her neck. "Please don't ban me from enjoying my beautiful wife. I know I'm a battered mess right now, but you, my darling, are irresistible. Even when I can barely stand up."

Her soft giggle made him catch her earlobe in his teeth and tug before lining a row of kisses along her jaw. But he pulled away with only one more peck to her lips and limped back to the side of the bed. That small bit of sporting with his wife had wiped his energy stores. Rhapsody stepped forward, face puckered. She put a hand to his head and then probed his eye and the other points of injury before moving to the punctures on his neck.

Her lips trembled when she met his eyes. "You haven't got a fever, so that's good news. But the punctures at your neck seem a little swollen. Let's get you back in bed and after breakfast, I'll come wash them and apply Doc's medicine."

"Hmmm. A spit bath. I can't wait."

Her lips curved into a smile. "You are the limit, Cavanaugh."

"I try."

She slipped away from him and pulled the under petticoat and shirt waist on. Her quick fingers buttoned the frock up to her throat. She waggled a finger at him.

"Now, no more foolishness. Let me help you get back in bed."

He shook his head. "I can do it myself. And I'm getting out to walk today. It's time, Rhapsody."

After a moment's pause, she nodded. With a wave she left the room.

He needed paper. Then he could write everything he seemed to forget every day. He had to get back to normal, whatever that was. Breaking Rhapsody's heart every morning hurt him like a punch to the gut.

Punch. Yes. That was it. He'd been attacked, and his resourceful wife had brought them here for safety. He let out a rush of air between his lips. Maybe his brain was healing. He'd remembered something. Now, who'd attacked him? He shook his head slightly, but it brought on a nauseous dizziness.

Lissy? Her name brought a spark of memory, too. He'd have to work on it. Rhapsody had shouldered the burdens of this whole…ordeal. Whatever it was.

Somehow in his gut, he sensed a very real danger. However, not knowing made him hesitate, and that wasn't like him at all. At least he didn't think so.

He had to get back to good health, both mind and body. For it was impossible to protect Rhapsody if he didn't even recall the threats that faced them. And not knowing much of anything was mighty dangerous.

Chapter Twenty-Five

Darling. He'd called her his darling. A smile tucked in a corner of Rhapsody's mouth. It had to be a positive sign that he was falling for her, right? She'd seen love in a few women's eyes. But she'd never dreamed of it for herself. Mother had trained her to understand a marriage was a match for the benefit of both parties. Miss Bickle, also, had her silly quotes to the same effect. Thus why she'd married Devlin instead of Miles. Not that she'd loved Miles, either, but Devlin had been a better selection, both financially and socially.

At the tea, Rhapsody had witnessed firsthand, Cora's adoration of her husband. Love fairly lit up the woman's face. And since then, Rhapsody herself longed to experience the emotions of being totally in love with a man and to have that love returned. Now she understood the tenderness in her friend's gaze as she talked of her husband.

Rhapsody wound around the hallway of the cheery house that still smelled of fresh wood and entered the kitchen. She skidded to a stop. At this point she should be used to catching Cora and Trigg in the kitchen, hands clenched, heads bowed, praying. Cav's name came softly from Trigg's lips as he beseeched the heavens for healing and restoration. Rhapsody rolled her lips inward to stem tears, grateful for their prayers yet hesitant to intrude.

When her host ended his petitions, he kissed Cora thoroughly with a chuckle and circled the table to exit. With a wave at his wife and a smile, he disappeared. Lissy appeared at her side, waddled into the kitchen, and took a cast iron pan down from the rack of utensils. She greeted Cora and went right to work on cracking eggs. Rhapsody stepped in, never quite at home, but knowing Cora could use the help with so many to feed.

"Good morning," Cora grinned. "How's Cav?"

"Better, I think. Although I'll need to swab his wounds some more."

The woman nodded, busying herself with slicing a slab of bacon. "Help yourself to coffee. You know the routine by now."

Cora's laugh lit the room, and Lissy scrambled to fetch a cup. The thick pottery felt heavy in her hands. Rhapsody couldn't help but compare it to her own dainty bone china. She glanced up as her servant carried over the pot of coffee. Lissy, always rushing about to do for her. Rhapsody sighed as the competent woman poured the brew into her cup. She preferred tea to this terrible stuff, but Lissy dumped in enough sugar cubes to make it drinkable.

This was definitely a different way of living. No slaves worked the Gentry farm. Cora, even expecting a baby in the next month or so, while Bliss tended the kitchen and laundry duties. Trigg and Roe tended the animals and the work on the farm raising and breeding the mules. Though the work was grueling, they seemed happier than most of the people Rhapsody was acquainted with. Perhaps because Cora had come from a farming background? Either way, it intrigued her.

"Surely there's something I can help with?"

Both women turned and stared. Rhapsody blinked. Was that doubt in their eyes?

"Why, yes, you could slice the bread," Cora interjected into her look of hesitation.

Rhapsody nodded, looking to the bump under the kitchen towel. "Excellent. The bread."

She laid the cup on the counter, and walked to the table. Cora turned, sporting a rather large serrated knife.

"Oh," the strange sound oozed from her throat as she fingered the daunting tool. She could feel Lissy's dark eyes dissecting her.

"You'll want to break through the crust and make a sawing motion to glide it through."

Rhapsody nodded, positioning the knife's point away from her on the table. Then she uncovered the mound of bread. This couldn't be that hard to do. She gripped the intimidating blade and slid it over the crisp top of the loaf.

"You'll want to start at the edge and make them about yay big."

She froze with the knife blade poked mid loaf and threw a glance at Cora's fingers pinched into a small space. Made sense, except she'd started in the middle. "Thank you. I'll try that."

Once she hacked through the bread, the slice smashed a bit, she looked at the two other women. But they were busy at their tasks, so Rhapsody returned to her slicing. Starting at one side of the half-loaf, she began again. Crumbs grinded from between the thick slices. Surely the other women wouldn't have such a mess when they finished. But she gritted her teeth and completed the assignment.

When she finished, she stepped back. Well, they weren't the best slices she'd ever seen on a silver platter, but they would do. A smile snaked across her face. An odd sense of accomplishment bloomed in her chest with her first stab at slicing bread. So this is what Cora felt as she completed her mundane tasks.

"Jam and butter are in the cold box," Cora said as she laid the meat slices in a black iron pan.

The sizzle set Rhapsody's stomach to grumbling. Cold box? Cora gestured with a fork to a small door next to the window. With a nod she marched over and unlatched it. Inside a small crate, cold with the November weather, lay a pitcher of milk, butter, and strawberry jam. Thrilled by now to step into a country wife's shoes, she collected the items and set them on the table, turning them this way and that for aesthetic flair, then deciding it didn't matter.

In the next half hour the ladies worked together to put the finishing touches on breakfast. Bliss arrived and started the gravy and the men returned from the barn. Cav appeared at the door, looking better but battered. He sank into the bench seat and Rhapsody fetched him some coffee. Lissy's wide eyes and gaping mouth showed the woman's surprise and Rhapsody could't help but grin at her.

She turned her attention to her husband. "Sugar?"

"Yes, please."

Cav's brows lifted and he winked at her. Her face flamed. Country indeed. Cav would fall right into place, the rapscallion. Lissy filled two plates and disappeared to tend to Barton. She seemed quite eager to do so, which put to mind that the woman might enjoy his company a little too much.

With everyone gathered, Trigg said grace and the usual cheerful morning chatter scattered about the handcrafted pine table. Talk of mules and chores. A story or two. Some anecdote of New Albany and Louisville. Rhapsody rather enjoyed the comradery sitting next to Cav, his leg against her, and Bliss to her left. That is, until the meal concluded and Trigg set his napkin on the table and cleared his throat.

"I feel it's time to bring up a few topics that thus far, I've avoided. But I feel the Lord's hand upon me to broach the subjects."

His dark eyes assessed both Cav and her.

Cav straightened. "You've been a most kind and gracious host, Trigg. Rhapsody and I can't thank you enough. I'd be happy to answer any questions you have."

With a nod, Trigg continued. "Perhaps it shouldn't be spoken about, but I can't help but wonder how this beating came about. I mean, you haven't come out and said you've been attacked. But I think it's most obvious, if you'll pardon my notice."

Cav shrugged. "I think it's clear I was jumped. Out on the road alone."

Trigg's eyes narrowed and he dropped his gaze to Cav's neck. The puncture wounds. They told a story of their own. Had Cav forgotten or was he still concealing?

Rhapsody laid her hand on Cav's arm, studying both Cora's and Trigg's eyes. Could they be trusted? "No. He doesn't remember. He was attacked by…catchers. Slave Catchers."

Trigg nodded and Cav's face swung her way, puzzlement and then dawning widening his eyes. She reached up to stroke his face. "Do you remember?"

Cav's head gushed warm. Dogs. Late night. Cold. He'd tumbled to the back of the wagon. Heaker Thomas's wagon. He'd heard a snap in his body. Then there was a circle of men, one, two—no—five in all. Their fists came at him, over and over. In the midst of it, he'd blacked out. Then—here, somehow.

A groan slid from his throat. Rhapsody's eyes widened.

"You do, don't you?"

"Yes," he whispered.

"Catchers chase runaway slaves. Why would they bother with you?"

Cav swung to gaze in his new friend's eyes. The only dark-skinned workers on this farm were Barton and Lissy. Yet they were in Kentucky. Despite a shard of doubt, Cav knew Trigg deserved answers.

"I'm a safe connection for fugitives. I deliver them to their next station," Cav murmured.

Trigg leaned back. "I see."

Rhapsody bent forward. "Please, our very lives are at stake. It's imperative you keep our involvement a secret."

A grunt tumbled from Roe, next to Cora who sat transfixed in the middle of the men. "You don't have to worry about that. We don't want those thugs here."

"Here?" Rhapsody shifted to peer at Cav. "Would they dare follow us?"

But it was Trigg who answered. "Not likely, though they do track their quarry for quite a spell. Hopefully, they don't know where you've gone. Let's pray over it."

The six of them joined hands in the center of the table. Pray? Cav guessed they could do a lot worse. He grasped Rhapsody's chilled hands and added their hands to the pile.

The man called on the Lord in a reverent tone, but with a familiar quality, like speaking with an old, trusted friend. Like he'd spoken to Preacher Dubber. And as Trigg called down God's protection and guidance on all of them, Cav envied the man's connection with the Almighty. As much as Cav liked to think he could package the world with a good length of string and a wad of thick paper, he sat here, aching with the pain of an assault that had taken him by surprise.

He'd never thought of himself as a lost soul, bumping around life with no wisdom and direction from the Creator. But he didn't have *this*. An understanding and acceptance that God held all the answers. That the Lord Jesus was true strength. That dealing with life wasn't just about leaning on his own human might. It was about the realization that God's Son had suffered a much worse beating of His own choice and died so that Cav's sin and pride were forgiven. Comprehending this wonder filled him with a different kind of amazement and a new kind of power through Christ's saving grace.

As Trigg finished his prayer, Cav breathed one of his own. To draw closer to God and lean on Him for direction and quiet strength. His body relaxed, and he felt the Lord's comfort settle over him. No matter what happened, good or bad, the Lord would be near his side. Preacher Dubber had been right. That righteous man hadn't lost everything when he'd been beaten and died. He'd gained heaven's reward. And he'd brought Cav into the fold.

Thanksgiving came and went. Eating the humble turkey and fixings country style helped stifle Rhapsody's longings for home. Cav had sent telegrams of apologies to both his and Rhapsody's families for missing the usual holiday, but insisted they were on an extended visit with friends.

Rhapsody took ill shortly afterward and confined herself to her bed, frightened her illness would affect a very pregnant Cora. Slowly, surely, Cav's face transformed from the beaten pulp to his handsome features again. Rhapsody knew once she recovered fully, it would be time to decide what to do. They couldn't stay with the Gentrys forever.

By the next week, she felt human again and shifted to rise from the bed. Cav had taken to helping Trigg and Roe with the animals. In the cold, it made shorter work for all of them. She wandered into the kitchen, where the smell of yeast tickled her nose.

Cora stood at the table, kneading a huge wad of dough on a floured board. The woman pulled a quick welcoming smile and shoved the white mound into itself and added a sprinkling of flour.

"Ahhh, feeling better I see."

"Yes, thank you." Rhapsody breathed a sigh. "I have much to thank you for."

Their eyes met and connected. Cora understood very well.

"I only feel a little unwell in the mornings. Once that's passed, it seems I do much better. I'm sure I'm over whatever was plaguing me."

Cora's arms stilled, her gaze intense. "The mornings?"

Rhapsody nodded. "But I'm sure it's nothing. I wanted to be extra careful with you in …your condition."

Cora spouted a laugh and rubbed her rounded belly. "Sounds like you'll need to be careful in your own condition."

Her brows gathered in a knot. "What?"

Her friend shot her a look with a doughy hand to her hip. "Do I have to spell it out?"

Rhapsody's mouth dropped. "You think I'm with…child?"

The dough received another rough shove from Cora, while shooting Rhapsody a raised brow. "Sure does sound like it."

With a fluttering hand, Rhapsody settled her palm against her lower belly. Could it be so? She settled back onto the bench glowing with wonder.

"Glory Hallelujah, it sort of knocks your socks off, doesn't it?"

Rhapsody giggled, not only from Cora's amped-up southern slang, but from the delight of carrying Cav's child. "Oh, yes. I'm afraid I'm quite…shocked."

Cora snorted. "From the sizzling looks your husband throws you, I'm not a bit surprised."

Gracious. Cora didn't mince words. "I'm not sure, I mean how can I…do this?"

She rose and paced the room, her breath coming in small gasps.

"I reckon like the rest of the women in the world." Cora's voice seemed to come from far away. You'll carry the child, give birth, and raise him or her. Just like your own mother."

Her own mother? A moan tore from her. Heaven forbid. And her heritage. What if the child reflected her ancestors? The child would be ostracized. She, herself, would be marked forever. Her hands flew to her mouth. This couldn't be happening.

Cora stepped in front of her and eased Rhapsody's hand down with floury fingers. "Hush now. You're getting in quite a state. It's just a baby. Pure and innocent."

Rhapsody shook her head. "You don't understand. I can't be like my own mother."

Cora shrugged, her eyes fastened to hers. "Then don't be."

"What if the child is…shunned?"

The face in front of her puckered. "Now you're just out of your head."

"No, I'm not. I'm…adopted. A child of an…exotic paramour," Rhapsody whispered, shocked she'd allowed the confession to tumble from her mouth.

"Come on." Cora led her back to the table, pressed her to the bench, and seated herself opposite. "God knows what's in store for your little one. And He's given you a heart of love for this precious child before he or she is even born. The Lord already has plans in place."

Rhapsody swallowed. "How can you be so sure?"

"I know my God."

With a nod, Rhapsody huffed small breaths. Cora did know God. The proof lay in the surety in her eyes, the prayers on her lips, and her full trust that she displayed right now. Mother's trust had been in society and all the ramifications of what others thought and whispered. Cora was right. She had a choice. She could be a parent like Mother, or she could choose a different way. Maybe one like Cora's? Trusting that no matter what, God had everything in His hands?

A tear slid down Rhapsody's cheek and heat rushed to her face. A rush of emotion churned in her gut. She already loved this child. Yes. She wanted her babe, no matter what skin he or she was dressed in, to come into this world with plans orchestrated from an ever-powerful, loving God who looked beyond a human's viewpoint. Who cared for the child's very soul.

"Yes," she murmured. "I want to know your God, too. Please, Cora, tell me. Tell me everything."

Moisture gathered in Cora's eyes and a grin snaked across her face. "It would give me no greater pleasure."

Chapter Twenty-Six

His wife slid a brush through her hair. Her movements transfixed him. Yet, Cav couldn't lose focus. It grew late and he had so much to tell her. He shrugged out of his work smock and laid it on the guest bed. He left his trousers on, but didn't bother to grab his night shirt. Chest naked, he padded to his wife sitting stiffly in the straight back chair. He stepped behind her and eased the brush from her hand. After a few strokes through her golden hair, he found his attention being stolen by something even more arresting. No. They needed to talk.

He propped his rear on the end of the bed. "Listen, Rhapsody. I spoke with Trigg, well, several times actually. I'm quite taken with the notion of drawing closer to…God. No, not just taken. I'm compelled. This whole incident has shown me I can't run my own life without God. I—We need the Lord's hand upon us. In all things."

To his surprise her eyes filled with tears.

"There's more." He rose and grasped her hands in his, took a breath then fixed his eyes on hers. "There's no other way but to say it plainly. I love you. I want our marriage to be more than suitability and convenience. More than the mission, more than—"

Rhapsody's head popped up. She threw her arms about his neck and sobbed against him. With a wrinkled brow, he held her, his skin reveling in her touch. He closed his eyes, running his hands across her back and wondered at such a reaction. Surely, she seemed elated. Finally she pulled from him and cupped his face in her hands.

"Oh, Cav. I've fallen in love with you, too. And I'm…" Her face shone through her tears, and her chin jutted out slightly, "carrying your child."

Cav blinked. Had she truly said what he'd thought she had? He shot upright. "You're with child? Right now?"

She nodded, a smile wreathing her face, her blue eyes awash with adoration. He could barely breathe. Yet he could read the truth in the eyes he so wished to drown in. Cav cradled her back into his arms and nuzzled her head in the nook of his neck. He'd only desired her love and the Lord had delivered that plus the blessing of a child. How could he ever doubt God's generous providence again?

He soothed her shining hair behind her ear and kissed her cheek, basking in their blessed love. Rhapsody gave a small coo of satisfaction, and he tightened his arms. "Rhapsody, I love you so much I ache with it."

"Hmmm."

He perched on the bed and drew her on his lap. Desire could quickly light a string if he didn't ease back. As he stroked her arm, he continued to gather his thoughts. "And that's not all. I feel like it's time to go home."

She caught her breath and pulled away to gaze at him.

But he nodded at her. "It's time."

"The catchers."

He clamped his teeth. "I'm not afraid. Preacher Dubber wasn't as he served his God. I won't be either."

Rhapsody laid a hand to his cheek. "Perhaps we could relocate?"

"No. I have work to do there. And I will do it."

A sliver of fear chased its way across his wife's precious face until a steely look of determination settled there. "Yes. We have much to do."

"The freedom fight will continue to escalate. I'm sure of it. We must be extra cautious but aggressive. I know, soon, there will be a clash. This issue will not go away silently. I fear it will be violent before our nation resolves it. And I want to be on the side of righteousness when it does."

She grasped his hand and pressed it to her belly. "This child will know freedom with every breath of my soul."

A fierce sense of protection and love gripped him. Giving God the ownership of both his wife and child would prove challenging. "And I will give my life to make that freedom a reality."

Despite Rhapsody's convictions to God and the child that grew within her, stepping off the steamer at the New Albany wharf sent ripples of uncertainty down her spine. But Cav's strong hand upon the back of her waist steadied the unstable emotions. He leaned his head down, face completely healed and whispered against her ear.

"All will be fine. God will see to it."

She nodded, wishing they could grasp hands and pray together just as the Gentrys had done in their country kitchen. Instead, she sent a silent prayer upward, resting in the knowledge that Cav would be too, and that God would safeguard their way. She could see Mr. Wadell aboard their larger carriage up on Water Street. He'd received their telegram of arrival. Soon they would be…home.

Funny how Cora's country house had emulated more warmth and welcoming than her own mansion decked with trimmings of her every whim. Love and industry lived in every nook and cranny of the Gentry household, while hers rang empty and impersonal. Suddenly the thought of leaving didn't pain her as it would have previously. In fact, a smaller, cozier home might be just what she really craved.

Barton and Lissy trailed them as they reached the curb of Water Street. The men loaded the luggage and Cav assisted her and Lissy into the carriage. Rhapsody couldn't help but smile at Lissy's longing gaze shot Barton's way. But the man disappeared into the front seat with Mr. Wadell while Cav climbed inside the cabin.

The house smelled stale as the door flew open. But obviously, Mabel had dusted and aired the rugs and linens for the place sparkled. Cav carried the carpetbags up the stairs, and she had no option but to follow.

The rest of the afternoon was spent reorganizing their clothing and other luggage. Cav had excused himself to tend to business and meet with Mr. Albridge. By early evening, she'd ended up on the fainting couch in the master sitting room, quite exhausted. Cora had warned her of the fatigue of pregnancy. Traveling and arranging everything had zapped her strength.

Rhapsody was just drowsing off when a knock sounded on the outer door. With a long draw of air, she rose and walked through to the bedroom.

"Enter."

Lissy's bright face popped in. "Guests, Mum."

To borrow from Cora, Glory Hallelujah. Now was not the time. "Who is it?"

The big woman slipped into the room and pressed the door closed behind her. "Da Blackledges."

Rhapsody shut her eyes for a moment. Shunning them due to illness was out of the question. "Where's Cav?"

"He downstairs wit 'em."

Well, at least she had an ally. "Very well. Would you help freshen my hair?"

The maid bobbed as Rhapsody settled into a dressing room chair. Lissy made quick work of the flyaways and pinned the curls tighter. She fetched Rhapsody's new white crocheted wrap, a gift from Cora's own hand.

Rhapsody stood and tottered a mite. Lissy's eyes widened.

"You's sick, Mum?"

She laughed, "Oh, no, Lissy. I'm with child."

Her servant's eyes widened round and white. "You is?"

Rhapsody gave a small giggle. "Yes."

"Oh, dat's good news, Mum. Good news."

The woman's dark eyes danced with joy. Rhapsody marveled at the woman she'd ignored and used for so long. How faithful she'd always been. Never a sharp word, always there to tend to Rhapsody's every need. A throb of emotion bubbled up her throat. She leaned forward and wrapped her arms around the maid's plump form. Tears sprouted in Rhapsody's eyes.

"Thank you, Lissy. You mean so much to me. I know I've never said it, but it's true."

A cloud of doubt gathered in the woman's brows. Lissy pointed to herself. "Me?"

Rhapsody laughed again and gave a small shake as she gripped the woman's arms. "Yes, you. Now, please pray for the mister and me. I'm not sure what God's planned for us, but we're determined to meet them head on."

With a stiff nod, Rhapsody strutted to the door and exited. Her resolve stayed firm until about the third step from the bottom.

Mrs. Blackledge's voice floated to her. "There she is, looking beautiful as always."

Cav, who'd been lounging against the newel post, straightened, gave her a covert wink, and held out his elbow to her. She took it like the lifeline it was. Mr. Blackledge rose from the wing chair and came forward with a bow while clutching her hand. Mrs. Blackledge stood from her spot on the Chesterfield and glided forward to her with an air kiss to her cheek.

"I'm relieved to see you're up and about, my dear, after my ruthless son has carted you all over creation, causing you to miss the roast duck and trimmings we had a few weeks past." The stately woman cast a playful glance at her son. "Even Shafer and Eunice made the trip. We were quite startled to receive your telegram."

The false-front smile came easily. After all, Rhapsody had been doing it her whole life. "I assure you, Mrs. Blackledge, that the journey was entirely my idea. And, I remind you, what a delight your son is to me. I love him so and he adores me, so it wasn't a hardship at all. We did miss you all, of course."

The last part Rhapsody delivered with a quick glance at Cav, now seated to the right of her place on the Chesterfield. Although her fixed high society smile had smacked artificial, there were no truer words.

Mrs. Blackledge, dressed in a beige creation of organza now spread across the leather cushions, chimed in with a calm smile. "I did so miss you both. But I agree wholeheartedly. My Cavanaugh is indeed a delight. And, please, Rhapsody, call me Forsythia."

Mr. Blackledge cleared his throat and crossed his legs in the other wing chair opposite of Cav. "Now, let's resume our business."

"You mean, inquisition?" Cav cut in smoothly.

Rhapsody swallowed.

"What of this rumor that I've heard circulating. Were you indeed accosted?"

The judge sat high in his chair, feet planted on Rhapsody's hand-knotted Persian rug, hands gripped on the wing chair's padded arms. As if holding trial. She squirmed and then tensed, her pinky and ring fingers digging in tight.

Before Cav could answer, she rose, blinking at the dizziness that swarmed her vision. The men stood as well. "I apologize, gentlemen. But I must see to the refreshments, if you'll excuse me."

As she fought not to hurry her steps, Mrs. Blackledge's lowered voice drifted toward her. "Surely there's a servant's bell here somewhere about? In a manor of this sophistication?"

Rhapsody slid into the kitchen and gripped the low table to steady herself. The smell of tea brewing eased her jangled nerves. Although her equilibrium screamed at her to sit, the tension in the room had sent her fleeing. Mabel looked up, a tray of delectable appetizers resting on the table in front of her. Tiny sandwiches of meat and cheese, topped with sprigs of parsley, decorated the plate.

"Miss Mabel," she dipped her head. "I'm glad to see you."

The old servant dipped her head, her coarse white hair secured at the nape of her neck. Like always. "We'll need tea as well."

"Of course, Mum." The woman probably thought she'd lost her last marble, coming to alert her to something she'd obviously already begun.

With a fortifying gulp of air, Rhapsody swished back through the door and traveled much too quickly through the dining hall and music room to arrive back at the drawing room. Mr. Blackledge's voice rang louder in intensity than when she'd exited. She leaned against the small table where the ornate golden candelabra rested, contemplating excusing herself once more.

"I declare, Cavanaugh, I mean to have a straight answer and I'll have it now."

"Fine. But I'll not have you upsetting Rhapsody. She's in the family way."

Cries of surprise and delight emitted from Mrs. Blackledge who floated to her and gathered her in a light hug. "How completely wonderful! I shall have two grandbabies very close in age. What a delight for them to grow up together. Oh, Cavanaugh, you rascal. Is that why you went away? I assure you we can find a qualified doctor to tend Rhapsody in Louisville. She does look quite pale."

Mr. Blackledge rose and nodded, offered congratulations even though the malevolent glint in his eye didn't vacate. Rhapsody turned her gaze upon Cav. How could he just spring that bit of information in a room rife with strain?

Not that she could blame him. The judge seemed quite focused on his line of questioning, perhaps eventually forcing out the exacts of the attack, thus jeopardizing the mission. And they couldn't risk further exposure. No doubt her father-in-law was quite gifted in discernment and the rhetoric of direct examination to squeeze out the truth. Especially from his own son. Perhaps her news had saved a confrontation.

For now.

Chapter Twenty-Seven

"Quite a prosperous community," Fulton Mantleroy said.

Why the man insisted on a tour in early December befuddled Cav. Surely the man could have restrained his need for a financial investment until spring. But the New Yorker had heard the winters were less severe in Cav's neck of the woods. And the current day had certainly welcomed the stranger in, hovering at the fifty degree mark.

He pointed to the Lennox Steamboat Works, the hull of a huge sidewheeler taking place. "I'm most fascinated with the engineering of such marvels. Nothing but a flat box in the water, yet it stays intact. If not for the boiler issues on such crafts, they'd take over the world of transportation."

The laugh the older man gave put a genuine smile on Cav's face. Seldom did he entertain a prospective client, but Holden insisted on hobnobbing with the man. Yet, Cav found that Mr. Mantleroy's demeanor and principles reminded him of himself. And now, he'd confessed an interest in the design of steamboats. "I agree. Although I think, as we've discussed, the train has an advantage as it can travel anywhere whereas the steamer is confined to waterways."

"All the more a shame." Mantleroy's graying mustache parted in a smile.

Cav supposed the man would be considered handsome by most women. Salt and pepper hair, an intelligent brow with shrewd, wiry brows. The man had come into old money and refreshed it with his own new investments. And now he endeavored to come west, centering his business in Louisville, though he seemed keen on touring New Albany. Mantleroy certainly embodied a suave sense of dress and movements. But then, the man was used to the finer things in life, given that Cav himself was spending the afternoon encouraging the man to invest in his bank.

"Though I will center my investments in Louisville, I prefer to live on this side of the river. Quite quaint. Lovely homes. As a matter of fact, we passed one not long ago that I believe would suit my wife." Mantleroy tapped his cane against the carriage floor.

"Is that so?"

"Yes, located on Upper High Street. I believe it might also be called Upper Main."

Cav raised his voice to Barton in the front seat. "Back to High Street, my man."

Barton gave a brief nod and turned at the next block. After a few blocks, Mantleroy leaned over and nodded toward Cav's own house. Cav rapped on the side of the carriage, and Barton slowed the horse.

"The exact one. A rare beauty, even in a city with so many grand homes rife with the latest architecture."

Cav stared at his own white gables and wanted to rear his head back and laugh. So, the man desired his house. He had a knack for picking the best of the lot.

"I'd appreciate it if you'd get with my associate as to the owners of the home. Then I can be moved in by summer."

A wry smile rose to Cav's lips. "Perhaps the owners would be unwilling to part with such a jewel?"

Mantleroy threw back his head. "Ha. Everyone has their price."

"Indeed." He wanted to scoff at the man's audacity, but chose instead to let it pass. The man would find out soon enough that the house was not for sale. Perhaps this was Mantleroy's weak underside. He desired. He took. How would he react when he didn't obtain his desire? Somehow Cav thought the man seldom saw that possibility.

He tapped the side of the carriage, and Barton sped up. Fifty degrees or no, he longed to warm his toes inside the office, and a long, chilly ferry ride across the Ohio stretched before them. Cav glanced down Boiling Springs Road, knowing tonight he would have a meeting of quite a different tone.

But first things first. He'd welcome newcomer Fulton Mantleroy into the Louisville Southeast Bank and let Holden do his magic to use the man's money to their advantage. Then, he'd meet with his new partners to start planning for the last fugitive delivery before Christmas. If this delivery was successful, they had time to plan for a busy spring.

The man beside him chattered on as Barton drove the carriage onto the ferry. Cav nodded appropriately, yet his mind wandered to Rhapsody. She would be disappointed not to be involved, but including her now during her delicate condition was out of the question. He'd even set the meeting time for the evening, shrouding his appointment as a bank meeting, although it would take place in the city at the new Second Presbyterian Church.

The place backed up right to the river and very near the Portland ferry. What better place to conduct a little enterprise of special packages? And with numbers came safety. He would not be caught out alone again. Although Holden covertly searched for his attackers, Cav knew it best to let it ride. Instead, he'd group up with others of like minds for means of protection and improved success rate. If the investors' increased backing made his bank grow stronger, then a larger group of abolitionists could make the Underground Railroad more successful, too.

At least, that was his hope.

Rhapsody stared hard at Mr. Albright and shoved the stack of bills closer to the man behind the desk. "Cav doesn't need to know."

The man's shrewd green eyes narrowed. "You know I can't do that."

She gave a very unladylike sigh from puffed cheeks. "Then I'll go elsewhere. Possibly to someone who has no loyalty to my husband. Who could perhaps learn of his underhanded maneuvers and leak information that may get him or me killed. And then, Mr. Albridge, you will have our deaths on your conscience."

The momentary close of the compact man's eyes either told of his disgust at accepting blame of their imagined deaths or his impatience at her fanciful drama. She couldn't be sure of which it was.

"Nevertheless, I must, by moral virtue, inform Cavanaugh of your intentions. Which you could so easily do yourself, and then I would be happy to purchase the land, Madam."

Rhapsody wanted to beat her fist against the man's desk. The rest of her personal money from the safe combined with the sum of the clothing brigade money sat in a fat pack, ready to purchase land for fugitives to settle on. Why couldn't he see the wisdom in this plan? Then, people like Lazarus and Adalia wouldn't have to take the arduous journey to Canada and settle in a completely different country.

There were black communities popping up all over Indiana, and the land she'd secured near the White River would be perfect. All she needed Mr. Albright to do was make the transaction. But he was being so incredibly stubborn. Yet loyal. She did appreciate the latter.

"And I will tell him. But he's been so busy of late, including both appointments with investors and evening bank meetings. But this opportunity needs to be taken care of now. Please."

The man took a deep breath and leaned forward. "Very well. I will see to it. But, I will mention it to your husband at the first opportunity. Let that be a warning. I see no reason to keep any type of business merger or acquisition from him. We are partners."

She nodded. "Please don't mention it before the holidays. I intend it to be his Christmas present."

One of Mr. Albright's brows rose. "Quite an unusual gift."

Suppressing the smile of adoration that parted Rhapsody's lip was impossible. "Cav is quite an unusual man."

Rhapsody rolled out the map she'd kept in her lap. "Here, below Washington, Indiana. It will be a farming sanctuary. Mrs. Cockrum assures me that it's perfect for crops. So this is what I purpose..."

With a hand to the newel post, Rhapsody inhaled the spices of what she suspected was pumpkin pie. Mabel spoiled them. Christmas was still a full week away and she continually baked special treats. At this rate, with the baby growing, she'd be doubled in weight by the new year. She snugged the black wool cape around her shoulders. Lissy and the two new household servants draped the greens across the veranda. She couldn't wait to see the festive decorations.

After last week's unseasonably warm spell, winter had returned with a snap to remind all of red noses and cutting winds. She slipped through the front doorway to the three women scurrying about, fir branches tied with strings along the top railing. An age-long sense of peace and joy shimmied through her middle. This Christmas boasted a special enchanting quality this year. Whether that came from the stirring love of her husband, or the life that grew within her, Rhapsody couldn't say.

But when she backed away from the house, candles alight in the windows, the green boughs of the holiday adorning the veranda, a quiver lit across her lower belly. She caught her breath. That was more than the blessed delight of the season. It was…her child. Tears pricked her eyes. There, again. Just the softest flutter.

She pressed her hand to her belly and before she realized it, Lissy was there, hand on her shoulder, eyes full of concern. Rhapsody pulled a watery smile. "I'm fine. I can feel the…baby."

Lissy's eyes grew wide with wonder. "Dat's good, Mum."

"That's very good." A giggle popped forth. And on impulse, Rhapsody hugged the chunky woman. "Come, I have something to show you."

She grabbed the servant's hand and swung toward the house. "The greens are perfect, ladies. You've done an outstanding job."

Rhapsody turned a sunny smile toward their hesitant ones as she pulled Lissy through the front door. She continued up the stairway and on to her fugitive wing, opening the door of the empty guest room.

"Now, I know I am early, but I just can't wait another day." Rhapsody grinned and strode toward the armoire and flung the doors open. Inside a large square package rested, wrapped in bright red with a green bow. "I can't lift it. Would you mind?

Lissy hesitated by the door before going over and pulling the large box from the closet.

"Here, you can set it here on this chair and then open it."

The woman froze. "Me, Mum?"

A laugh tumbled from Rhapsody. "Yes, silly. It's for you."

With puzzled eyes and mouth agape, Lissy set the package on the ladder-back chair, rubbing her hands along the fine wrapping.

"Tear it open, Lissy."

"Oh, Mum. This is da finest package I's ever got. I's need to rub it a minute or two."

Rhapsody tucked her smile in, letting the maid enjoy the moment. With tentative fingers she undid one fold and then another, almost unwrapping the item without tearing any of the paper. She eyed Rhapsody once more before pulling the top off the wooden crate. With a cry, Lissy lifted a tiny teacup with pink roses all around the top and a delicate silver-striped handle and cradled it in her big hands.

"I doan unda-stand, Mum?" Lissy stared at her, mouth open.

She stepped forward and laid a hand to her arm. "They're yours. When you and Barton make a home together, you'll have your own dishes."

"How'd ya know I's sweet on him?"

Soberness poured on Rhapsody like a douse from a waterfall. “Because I’ve had my eyes opened, Lissy. I used to not see you. Not really at all. You fetched things, dressed me, fixed my hair. By the Lord’s grace, I see the error of that way of thinking. Someday soon, you will have a home of your own. And these dishes are your start in a new way of life.”

The woman’s eyes grew round, then teary. “Home o’ my own?”

Rhapsody nodded, dashing the moisture from her own eyes. “Yes.”

Lissy pressed a hand to her breast, shaking her head. “How dat gonna be, Mum?”

Gentle hands took the teacup from the servant’s hands and pressed it back into the straw packing. Rhapsody then grasped the dark hands in hers. “It will be, Lissy. It will be.”

This cold snap had put a major snag in this operation. Specks of snow flew through the dark night. Cav rubbed his hands together and eyed the young dark man wrapped in a gray scarf guiding Number Three. Known only as Parvey, he was a quiet sort, thin and raw-boned.

Tonight, three wagons were due to arrive at the church, load, and head for safe houses. Of the three, he remained only one of two white men, Harlan Whitson being the other and on a different wagon. All were armed with the gossip of catcher raids on the rise in the county.

The packages had stayed for a time at the church, wearing the clothes Rhapsody had collected and integrating into the freed Black community. Now it was time to move them on before word got out. The catchers, despite the cheering holiday season, patrolled the streets in sulking diligence, forcing others to help in their sinister searches.

Cav wrapped his own scarf up around his face. They would be stopping soon. He checked the wood stacked behind him. All was ready to take on the next three bound for Canaan's land, the land of freedom. Canada.

His driver steered off High Street, and Cav breathed a sigh of relief. Being smack dab in front of the busy Depaw House where many prominent citizens boarded, not to mention housing the telegraph office that never slept, set Cav's nerves on edge. The last thing they needed was Mr. Johnson alerting the entire building of the unusual wagon traffic at the Second Presbyterian Church.

Third Street headed toward the Ohio River, affording a bit more privacy and cover than the main thoroughfare. Here, on the side street, several widows' homes lined the road, their windows dark and shrouded. Hopefully meaning the old dears lay snuggled fast asleep under their home-tatted quilts, not perched near the lace curtains spying at the middle-of-the-night activities.

The plan? Load from the side of the church and scurry west on Water Street trailing the river. Then veer north on Boiling Springs Road and disappear six miles north to Floyd Knobs. There, his "packages" would vanish into the free black population to be delivered north or risk the dangerous path of being declared free through the fickle court system. All that with no one the wiser.

Thoughts of his previous attack made Cav finger the .34 caliber Allen and Thurber pepperbox pistol in his pocket. A six-shot, the weapon was loaded for bear. He would not be caught unawares tonight.

Parvey slowed and Cav jumped off and dropped the tailgate. Within moments, three shadows loomed closer. He pointed to the empty compartment beneath the wood and they wiggled in. They had no sooner pulled in their clothing brigade leather shoes than Cav had fastened off the back and leaped aboard. Smooth as his grandmother's banister. The brisk icy wind helped hide both the clank of the wagon's hardware and the tread of the wheels and hooves.

The driver eased the horses toward Water Street when a form rushed out in front of them, waving arms in the air. Cav tugged out the pepperbox and aimed.

"Stop, Parve."

The horse danced to the side. Not a catcher after all. Only Deacon Willem's portly shape. He scurried up to Cav's side. "You got to take on three more. We got word the catchers are just four blocks away. The next wagon will be too dangerous."

"We can't. We're full." Cav whispered back.

"You have to. Or our goose is cooked."

Cav studied the bald-headed man, breathing hard, the white at his temple visible in the muted moonlight. Tonight he'd be at double capacity.

Parvey leaned forward in a quick mumble. “Bring ’em out. We’ll deliver the extra packages.”

“Best hunker down for the night and head out with the six tomorrow,” Deacon returned.

Cav blinked. “What? Hunker down where?”

“The emergency station,” the old man hissed.

All the air rushed from Cav’s lungs as three more figures rushed from the back door of the church. The emergency station was his house. Only to be used when no other escape route was available. This was not how two days before Christmas was supposed to go. No time now to contemplate. Cav leaped from the wagon. They would have to lay on top of the wood pile.

He tugged the canvas back and Cav and Deacon helped two aboard. The third, a small woman, took hold of Cav’s arm in a vice grip. Didn’t this woman know time was of the essence?

“Please, sir. You have to help me.”

“Shhh. Get aboard.”

“No.” Her voice rang out, bold as a skunk in the kitchen pantry. “I must find my daughter.”

Cav tugged the woman’s hand from his arm. He had to get her on the wagon and fast. He froze. Her skin glowed nearly as light as his own. His eyes met hers. “Lady, I can’t help you there.”

A shot rang out behind them. They were coming. The catchers were close enough to sight in their rifles. They had to go, and go now. But the light-skinned woman grabbed the arms of both his sleeves and shook him.

"Yes, you can. Do you know a man named Grafton? I'm looking for a child."

"We've no time for this. We've got to—"

But the woman yanked away, lifting her chin. "A girl child named…Redemption."

Chapter Twenty-Eight

Parvey slapped the reins down and Number Three shot off, leaving Cav and the woman standing in the street. Great, now they had no defenses. He yanked the woman toward the church, circling around the building as the catchers rushed past. They would beat Parvey to the intersection of Boiling Springs Road. Then, he'd be caught. Him and five other fugitives. That could not happen.

He kept his fingers around the woman's delicate wrist and pulled her across the bricked pavement. In the middle of High Street, he pulled his pepperbox and thrust it into the air and fired three times. The explosions rocked down his arm and pounded his eardrums. If the catchers didn't hear that, their ears had fallen off.

He pressed the weapon into the back of his waistband and then shoved his hand into his pocket. His fist tugged out a handful of capsicum pepper and sprinkled their pathway across the street. The baying of the dogs echoed louder. Perfect. They'd turned back.

Cav lunged behind a thick stand of bushes, thrusting them both to the cold winter grass in the Depaw House's front lawn. Stretched out on his belly, he flung the rest of the brown powder across their bodies. Then, Cav gripped the pepperbox, pushing the woman low to the dirt. The noise of the speeding wagon had long drifted away, bringing another sound. Numerous hoof beats. They thundered by and Cav tensed. Had he given Parvey enough time to escape or had he turned back toward the mansion?

"Mister?"

"Shhh." Didn't the woman know both their lives hung in the balance? Anytime, one or more of those savage hunters could double back to search the area. And if they did, he knew they wouldn't come alone. He rose slowly, listening in all directions. Already a couple of lights flickered to life inside the big boarding house behind them. "Follow me and don't talk."

He crept to the trees lining the huge manicured lawn and dipped behind the big house. With stealth, he slunk through the back yards of the manors that stood sentry in the dark night. He knew every tree, bush, and wrought iron fence by heart. It was necessary. He couldn't afford to get locked into an enclosed area if the catchers returned. He circumvented a tub of dead flowers, frozen with a layer of frost, and snuck behind an arbor just as the low light of a lantern lit a nearby window.

When at last he wound around behind his own carriage house to his own back door, he knew. Parvey and others weren't here. Had his diversion allowed enough time or had they been captured? A wagon load of people couldn't outdistance men on horses for long.

With a groan, he turned the handle. *Please, Lord, don't let Parvey get caught with five runaways. Let them escape.*

With the door pressed closed behind them, he grabbed an unlit candle from the long pine table in the kitchen and inched through the house, avoiding the squeaks in the floorboards. His moon shadow followed faithfully up the stairs, and without a word, he led the woman down the westerly hallway to the fugitive bedroom on the right. He swung the door open, swiped a match, and touched it to the wick. It was the only safe room for lights since the windows were still covered with thick black blankets.

The woman walked in behind him, set her hands on her hips, and spun to stab him with steely blue eyes.

"I don't know what you're planning here, Mister. But I'm not jumping from the frying pan into the fire."

Her dress below the fine black cape looked to be silk covered in lace. That garment had definitely not come from Rhapsody's clothing brigade. And her blue eyes reflected the color of the dress. Blue eyes? He studied the fancy's features. Pearl earrings hung from her finely formed ears to match the glowing beaded necklace, an ensemble he knew had cost a good penny. A good many pennies. Dear God, if not for the creases of age, the dark curling hair, and fuller lips, it could be Rhapsody standing in front of him.

She tugged white gloves from each finger and pulled the lace gloves from her hands. Her finely chiseled jaw swung a disdainful arc. "Did you hear me, sir?"

He nodded, transfixed. So, this was his wife's birth mother. There was no other explanation that made sense. Grafton had indeed selected a beauty for his closeted fancy, for the woman appeared an older, darker version of his gorgeous wife. And if that weren't enough to reveal her true identity, she knew Rhapsody's forbidden middle name.

"Cav?" Rhapsody's voice floated from down the hall. Suddenly the footfalls hurried. "What's happening? I heard noises."

His wife appeared at the door and entered. A gasp tore from his wife's throat. She stood agape, gripping her white night jacket, chest heaving to gain a breath.

"Redemption?" The woman moved a step closer, her eyes narrowing in the dim light.

The bold woman yanked the candle holder from Cav's hand and tiptoed forward. Rhapsody shrank from her. "How…how do you know that?"

Dizziness rose up to greet Rhapsody, and the room tilted. Cav stepped forward to encircle her waist.

"You must sit down." He led her to a chair near the door.

Rhapsody raised a hand to her throat, keeping the woman within her sight. "You're…Mr. Grafton's paramour, aren't you?"

The fancy woman squinted her startling eyes and scowled. "I've never been his anything and never will be."

"Why…why is she here?" Although she addressed Cav, her eyes fixated on the woman. She panted a few breaths but couldn't seem to fill her lungs. Why couldn't she breathe?

"I had to bring her here. The wagon drove off without us. Did anyone else show up?"

She shook her head as trembling took hold. "No one else came."

The clatter on the veranda froze them all.

"They've followed me," Cav said.

"Who?" Rhapsody clutched Cav's wool coat sleeve. Why couldn't she think?

"The catchers most likely."

The woman holding the candle shuddered and cast glances about the room. "I won't go with them. I'll kill myself first."

Cav pulled a pistol from his right pocket and hurried through the door.

The woman scurried across the room, yanked the water closet door open, and dipped inside before popping back out.

Rhapsody stood, closed her eyes for a moment until the dizziness passed. Then, she held out her hand. "Come. I know just the place."

She hurried down the hallway, clutching the woman's fingers tight. This was her…no, she couldn't think on this now. Instead, she had to focus on concealing the woman's presence. Coming to the end of the hallway, next to the door of her bedroom, Rhapsody dropped the woman's hand and grabbed the small ornate table resting there. "Help me. If they're here, we have little time."

The other woman clutched her end of the small but bulky marble-topped table and heaved it out from the wall. Rhapsody brushed her hands beneath the hanging tapestry and pressed the wainscoting. The panel snapped forward and opened. Inside, a small space, only enough room for a hunkering person.

Rhapsody clutched the candle holder and the woman yielded it. But her blue eyes stayed fastened to hers. "You are Redemption…Grafton, aren't you?"

She nodded.

"I'm—"

A gun blast below blocked any words. *Cav.*

"I know." Rhapsody hissed. "Get inside."

The woman scrambled into the dark alcove, tucking her fine cape and dress around her, and Rhapsody pressed the panel closed, letting the tapestry fall into place. Gritting her teeth, she thrust the heavy ornate table into place. Then she grabbed the small silver box atop the marble slab top, opened it and sprinkled the powdered contents at the base of the table.

Breathing heavily, she hurried into the master bedroom and grabbed the fireplace poker hanging near the banked fire. She reached up to secure her bed jacket, slipped on her night cap, and rushed through the door. Lissy, still in night clothes, appeared at the end of the hall.

"Mum? I's heard sum'um." Her hiss relayed panic.

Two servants materialized behind Lissy, huddled together, fear live in their faces, gripping their gray bed jackets.

"Pray, ladies. It could be catchers." Rhapsody scurried down the stairway.

Halfway down the stairs, she caught sight of two scruffy men on either side of Cav, gripping his arms behind him. One held a gun to her husband's temple. Cav sported a black eye and a growing blood stain on his upper arm. She struggled to hold her voice below a screech. "What's the meaning of this, gentlemen?"

"All is fine." The deadpan voice came from Cav, whose expression matched his voice. Except for his eyes, live with secret warning. "These good men are searching our home for an escaped runaway. And, of course, we're cooperating fully."

So that's the way it had to be. They would act like proper outraged aristocracy following the rules of extreme civility while blood spurted from her husband's arm. She shoved the fear of Cav's bloodstained arm aside and stomped the rest of the way down the stairway, wielding the poker with both hands. "Sheath those pistols, sirs, or I shall alert the sheriff of your reprehensible conduct."

The shifty-eyed catchers lowered their weapons, looking behind her. She spun. A tall man with oiled hair stood behind them. He gave a slow smile, showing one missing front tooth. Beyond him, three other men circulated the house, none of which she recognized, opening doors and pulling things from closets. Something shattered in the kitchen, and Rhapsody closed her eyes momentarily.

"This must be the fine missus." The tall man advanced.

Dear Lord, help us. She lifted her chin a fraction and gripped the poker. "That's right. I'm Mrs. Cavanaugh Blackledge, and you're violating my home in the middle of the night. We're respectable citizens in this city, and I demand you treat us with some dignity."

His grin never wavered, and he moved close enough for her to smell his foul breath. "Ma'am, as you fully know, we're within our rights under the Fugitive Slave Act whether it's the mid-afternoon or midnight."

He grasped the poker in her hands and easily pried it from her. "Now, go sit on that fancy settee with your husband while we conduct our search. I'd sure hate for you to get hurt…Mrs. Cavanaugh."

He gave a short laugh as she stumbled to the Chesterfield and collapsed. The other two shoved Cav to the cushion next to her, but the horrid men kept a vigilant stance nearby.

The door burst open bringing the cold and four redbone dogs nosing through followed by a man fisting their leashes. The twitching excited dogs yanked the short, sandy-haired man through the drawing room and dining hall. Then they disappeared through the kitchen door. Rhapsody grasped Cav's hand like it was the last life preserver on hurricane-tossed waves. Trembling, that had nothing to do with the freezing air rushing through the open doorway, racked her body.

The oily-haired leader sauntered to the door and slammed it closed. Then he tossed a log on the low-banked fire and jostled the coals with her poker. Fire licked around the log. Once finished, he took a leisurely stance near the fireplace.

The dogs reappeared, a couple baying, and the man scuttled by as the dogs leaped up the stairway. Rhapsody closed her eyes and prayed. *Please let the capsicum work.* When she'd begun the clothing brigade, she'd stolen Cav's idea of the peppered flowers he'd pressed into her hand the night he'd first kissed her. The night her life had changed forever. Now, little silver boxes lay discreetly hidden in every room.

Dogs sneezed on the landing above. The man near the fireplace leapt up the stairs two at a time. Then a bark. More sneezes and blowing. Shuffling, doors slamming. She swallowed and clutched Cav's hand tighter. Time ticked by in agonizing slowness. Would they never finish? Thumps sounded above, and the servants, eyes wide with fright, thrummed down the stairs with a man behind them. They crossed the room and huddled in the far corner.

Rhapsody's eyes wandered to the clock on the mantle. Two forty-nine. Each tick set a new spark of dread through her. They obviously hadn't found… the paramour, for she couldn't think of her as her birth mother yet. How long would they continue to search?

The front door opened again. Barton and Mr. Wadell stumbled into the room as if pushed, their hands behind their heads. They stepped closer to the other servants as two more catchers trailed into the house, their dirty boots sending shards of clumped soil across her Persian rug. Ah, her old friends Mr. Bowles and Smitty. The ones who had instigated her impromptu marriage.

Nine men, if Rhapsody counted correctly. Someone powerful must have instigated such a large search party. Usually they only traveled in twos or threes. Could Mr. Grafton have funded this expedition for the express purpose of finding his long-time fancy?

Men tromped down the stairs, the oily-haired one last, looked around and then shot her a narrowed gaze. The group of unkempt men parted, and he stomped through.

"I know she's here." He pulled a chambered pistol from his holster and spun the barrel. "I don't suppose you'd tell us where you hid her?"

To her panic, Cav stood. "We've nothing to declare to you. You've assaulted and shot me, then forced your way into my house and found nothing. Unless you'd like for me to speak to my father, Judge Cavanaugh, about assault and the trespass on my fourth amendment right of an illegal search of my property, I suggest you vacate this building. Immediately."

The catcher pulled a tight smile and lifted a brow. He shoved the revolver back into the leather belt. "Try to make that stick."

He and Cav stared each other down until the man spun and made for the door. "Let's go. We'll be watching."

All nine men and four dogs shuffled out the door and shut it with a bang. Rhapsody covered her face with her hands until Cav's arms wrapped around her. She pressed her face against the strong column of his neck. Lissy and the girls sniffled from where they huddled in the corner. Barton drew them all toward the fireplace, gathering Lissy under his arm.

"Shhh. We made it. By the grace of God, we're safe," Cav whispered in her ear.

She pulled away, and eyed his face, her fingers exploring his eye. "Did they jump you? Are you injured?"

With gentle fingers she probed the spot on his upper arm.

"Just a graze."

"We need to tend it." She rose and hurried to collect bandages.

Cav forced himself to sit still while Rhapsody and Lissy fussed with the bullet scrape on his arm. It didn't hurt nearly as much as his pride. He'd been shot at and coldcocked leaving Rhapsody undefended. His expectant wife. The woman he loved with all his heart. No matter how he added it up in his head, he couldn't have taken all nine men. His pepperbox only held six shots. Besides, murdering nine men wasn't high on his list to accomplish in his lifetime.

He had to think how to stay involved yet keep his growing family safe. And right now New Albany had become a dangerous place for them to be. How they didn't find the fugitive was beyond him, but he wasn't about to ask Rhapsody what she'd done with her with a room full of servants who still circulated in fearful distress.

No, it was time to vacate. Where to go was beyond his comprehension. There were really no safe places to operate his mission. But he knew one thing. He had to pull back his active involvement, if only for a time.

His mind drifted back a few weeks to a certain investor. An investor who'd been enamored with the huge manor that they all hovered in, fighting waves of panic. Perfect. Fulton Mantleroy was about to be a proud owner of the largest mansion in New Albany.

Chapter Twenty-Nine

Christmas came and went, hushed and foreboding. They'd celebrated with his parents, gleaming with false smiles and fear of leaving the paramour locked in her safe box too long, but Rhapsody's mother and father let the holiday come and go without communication. With it being too dangerous to move Zoya, Rhapsody's birth mother, they continued to hide her in the fugitive's bedroom and freely brushed the capsicum powder throughout the hallway carpets.

Cav now, resting his forehead against his wife's in the master sitting room, whispered plans furiously. "The house is sold."

She caught her breath. "Already?"

"Yes." He stroked her cheek when she pulled away and pressed a hand to her belly. "What's wrong?"

A tiny smile danced in the corner of her cheek. "Your child. I can feel him dancing. Perhaps he's anxious to leave the mansion."

He cupped both hands over her belly, but the child's movements were too slight to catch. Instead he pulled her close to him once more.

"Soon, you will feel him."

"A boy?"

Rhapsody shrugged. "Maybe."

Cav pressed a long kiss on his wife's lips. "Let's talk about this land you've invested in."

She grew quite animated. "I've heard about other places where freed slaves can go and own land and work it. Mrs. Cockrum sent a long letter about a month back about a free black community near them. A place called Switch Settlement. We could do the same."

He grinned at his wife's passion. How he loved her generous spirit. But his face sobered. "I want us to only be involved from a distance. I won't risk you or the baby again to a bunch of malicious catchers."

"But we could do just that. We could do it quite legally, buying slaves and granting their freedom. Perhaps Mr. Albridge could assist us from Louisville. Then they could be transported to the new town."

"Holden?" He'd always kept his best friend and partner detached from the movement, but perhaps it would be a way to keep his involvement undercover. Perhaps this new…community was just the thing to keep everyone safe, and at the same time, grant precious freedom.

Rhapsody stood next to the carriage, all her necessary possessions loaded onto the steamer at the wharf. She squinted at the huge mansion she'd called home for nearly four years. Most every memory from the home would not be missed a great deal. Except her time with Cavanaugh. And learning more about her…birth mother, for she'd spent considerable time in the last few months coming to know her.

The home she'd thought she'd wanted had cost her a great deal. A husband, a life. But she'd found those things within its confines as well. For that, she would ever be grateful. She pressed a palm to the roundness of her belly, Cav waiting by the door of the carriage, concern in every crevice of his dear handsome face.

She strutted to him and stroked his beard and curled a wayward lock behind his ear. "Don't worry, love. I won't miss it. Everything that is important to me is coming along for the journey."

His jaw pumped as his hands slid to her abdomen. The baby gave a kick, which brought a smile to his face. Yet his eyes reflected apprehension. "Are you sure we don't need to wait until after the baby comes? The doctor said your time is approaching."

"And he also said I was safe to travel as long as we go slow. And we are floating from the Ohio to the Wabash to the White. I'm not sure how much easier it could get." Her laugh lightened the look of unease in his gaze.

Despite Barton and Lissy looking on, he pressed a kiss to her lips. "Yes, my darling. I live only to make you happy."

She laughed freely as Cav handed her into the carriage to settle against the cushions. He'd taken to quoting that maxim from the night he'd felt the baby first move within her womb. How amazed and stunned he'd been. A smile vined across Rhapsody's face.

A blanket waited for her on the seat, given her propensity of getting chilled as her belly had grown. But this delightful April day had been the first clear of rain since the week before, and she took that as a smile from the face of God himself.

In less than a week, she would be ensconced in her new home, helping freed Blacks make a life for themselves, no longer enslaved by the erroneous laws of the country. She gave a sigh of happiness. Lissy and Barton had married in their home in a quiet ceremony. Rhapsody would never forget the look of complete exhilaration on her previous servants' faces. They would be the first to inhabit Redemption, the new community of free Blacks.

Rhapsody smiled and slipped her hand into Cav's as the carriage eased into traveling speed. From now on, she would live with no regrets, dedicating her life to the path the Lord had put her on. A path of freedom not only for those who had little chance of obtaining it, but freedom for herself as well.

A few months later, Cav stood in awe of what he held in his palms. A rosy son, wrapped in the softest quilt, squinted up at him, blinking his wide blue eyes. Rhapsody rested against the pillows, looking slightly pale but ecstatically pleased. Zoya sat beside her, squeezing her hand, bliss written across the older woman's face. Lissy fussed nearby, pressing a cold drink to his wife's lips and feeling Rhapsody's forehead before swiping away damp tendrils.

Cav rose from the rocker in the corner and navigated through the new Italianate home he'd had built before they'd arrived. It wasn't nearly the mansion they'd left behind, but already, it felt cozy and welcoming. He carefully maneuvered the stairway to the audience of dark-skinned guests in his gathering room, for Rhapsody refused to call it the parlor and heaven-forbid, the drawing room.

Barton drew near with the others, smiles wreathed on each face. Cav stopped near his carriage driver, now a farmer on the eastern side of Redemption, and held up his bundle.

"I'd like you all to meet Asher Jobe Blackledge. My son."

Six people moved forward, two women, four men besides Barton who now shared Redemption as their home. They offered congratulations and moved toward the front door, a standing rule at the Blackledge house. All guests, *all*, came through the front door. Only Barton remained.

"Mr. Cav?"

He let out a brief chuckle. That man just couldn't drop the formal address. "Yes, Barton?"

"There's someone here to see you. I think you'll be delighted." Barton disappeared to the veranda and brought forth yet another dark-skinned man. Moisture actually filled Cav's eyes as he came face to face with Lazarus, up from the dead so to speak.

Cav stood with his mouth open before throwing one arm around his friend.

"Yo been right busy since I been gone." His old friend pulled the blanket back to see the babe's face.

Asher slept on in peaceful freedom.

"You here to stay?" Cav could barely wrap his head around the fact that Lazarus stood in his house.

The big man nodded. "Hopin' to start a sawmill. Always been handy turnin' out wood."

Cav held out his hand and Lazarus took it in a long robust grip, pleased beyond words that he'd returned to settle amongst the new arrivals. "We'll need a good man like you, Laz." He paused and blinked. "Adalia?"

A touch of sadness creased Lazarus's face. "She passed. Sick to death of missin' Preacher. Guess now they together though."

"She was happiest tending to her man." Clearing his throat over the moisture that gathered, Cav nodded. "I'm sure I'll be seeing you about. Let me know if you need anything. Meanwhile, I need to get back to the wife. She'll be fretting without her cub."

Lazarus nodded, waved, and strode to the door.

With a deep, fortifying sigh, Cav climbed the stairs, sat in the rocker next to his wife's bedside, and nestled his son in the crook of his arm. The Lord had taken a very unlikely late-night rendezvous and had not only fixed an urgent calling on both of their lives, but He'd also granted them a blissful marriage. Cav's gaze brushed over his son's tiny face.

And a firm hope for the future.

"Hurry Cav, the walls are going up!" Rhapsody snatched three-year-old Asher's hand and tugged him away from the picnic area next to the church. They left the shaded area, and she sidled up next to Lissy, cradling her own infant in her arms, a smile and tears upon the faithful woman's face. Rhapsody grasped her free hand, and they stood, hand and hand as the men heaved.

Cav rushed over from the wagon and grabbed the rope behind a long line of men, both black and white. Slowly, the wall straightened, and the men rushed forward to secure it.

"My boy gonna be edu-cated." Tears formed lines of moisture down Lissy's face.

Rhapsody giggled. "Indeed he will."

"I's neva thought I's see sech a miracle, Mum."

"Rhapsody." Always, she reminded the woman. But change came hard. "And praise Jesus, author of redeeming grace, that redemption has touched us all."

Cav rushed over and pulled his wife beneath the shade as the men hammered on. "Well, wife. What do you think?"

"I think this is a good place. And I think you are a wonderful man." Her cheek dimpled. "A great husband and a wonderful father…again."

His eyes grew wide once more as he laid a hand to her belly. "You're expecting?"

She nodded. He leaned down and picked up his son, sunny yellow hair like his mother, grinning at his papa.

"Rhapsody Redemption Blackledge, look at all the Lord has wrought." Cav drew her into a circle with Asher and pecked her cheek. "How could I be more blessed?"

She laughed, stroked his beard, and leaned close to whisper for his ear only. "Maybe later I'll show you."

Cav's thunderous laughter brought the gazes of the surrounding people, but they only smiled and went about their business. They were used to the couple who had made this land possible, wrapped in embraces, whispering sweet secrets. For this place was built on sacrifice and love, of which its true spirit never dies, only swells and grows even through adversity and pain, much as Christ had done on the cross for all these precious souls.

And as for the Blackledges, love would continue to bloom as they fought to save the blessed few who would continue to hallow this ground. And other places like it.

A site of safety and independence. Home. A place where all would hear of God's love and His saving power. Where *NO* one was lowborn. A place for true…

Redemption.

About the Author

When Peggy Trotter's not crafting or DIY-ing, she's immersed in a story scene of some sort, always pushing toward that sigh-worthy, happily-ever-after ending. Two kids, two in-law-kids, and four grandchildren, the delight her life, as well as her Batman of 37 years rescuing his wife from one scrape or another.

Winner of the prestigious ACFW Genesis Award in 2014, she flip-flops from historical to contemporary to suspense, but always inspirational. But ultimately, it's always about Ransomed-Ever-After Fiction. Incredible characters and storylines reveal God's guiding providence and unending love.

My Note to You!

I hope you enjoyed *The Lowborn Lady* that it gave you clean inspirational entertainment or even helped you on your own life journey. Realizing your worth in Christ is Rhapsody's true message. But most of all, I wanted to stress the fact that nobody~NOBODY is an outcast to God, no matter how rejected, broken, or lowborn you might think you are, or are made to feel by others. ***God loves you.*** He sent his own Son, Jesus, to save each and every soul. Every person is precious in His sight. So precious, He died to save each wayward soul.

I love my readers and enjoy interacting with all of you. Please join me on my websites and sign up for my newsletter to get information on my next books. Oh, and there's always prizes!

Links:

peggytrotter.com

peggytrotter.blogspot.com

diamondsinfiction.blogspot.com

Twitter: https://twitter.com/Peggy_Trotter

Facebook: https://www.facebook.com/PeggyTrotterAuthor

Goodreads:

https://www.goodreads.com/author/show/13778873.Peggy_Trotter

Amazon Author's Profile Page:

amazon.com/author/peggytrotter.com

Instagram: https://www.instagram.com/peggy_trotter_author/

Pinterest: https://www.pinterest.com/PeggyTrotterAuthor/

LinkedIn: https://www.linkedin.com/in/peggy-trotter-44a29b95/

BookBub: https://www.bookbub.com/authors/peggy-trotter

MeWe: mewe.com/i/peggytrotter

Parler: https://parler.com/profile/PeggyTrotterAuthor

Usa.life: https://usa.life/PeggyTrotterAuthor

Gab: https://gab.com/PeggyTrotterAuthor

Don't miss the third installment of the Society of Outcasts Series *The Spellbound Schoolmarm* releasing 6/1/22. Keep reading for the blurb and the first chapter sample.

The Spellbound Schoolmarm

Society of Outcasts

Book Three

Rigidity, rules, and reason. Simple concepts that strict schoolmarm Sissy P. Eberlin utilizes to maintain classroom stability and whip her pupils into shape. Yet, internally she quivers in fear, dreading someone will uncover her scandalous past. Or even worse? Sissy's even more malevolent present. No one, absolutely no one, must break beyond her carefully constructed boundaries. Ever. Better to be lonely than hated. So, why does the widowed blacksmith, Heaker Thomas tug at her heart?

Careworn and exhausted, Heaker rustles every bush to find a mother for his five daughters. But with his youngest at death's door, no woman seems willing. Instead he's become the laughing stock of the community. To still the rumors, he swears off his search and vows to remain single. Yet, when his elderly nursemaid abruptly departs, leaving him in a desperate situation, he turns to the prickly new schoolmarm for help. After all, how can he resist a woman whose eyes betray a need for love as deep as his own?

Chapter One

1853~New Albany, Indiana

This was a huge mistake. Heak stood up. Courting shouldn't feel this….forced.

He nodded to the blond-haired girl who hadn't even reached her twentieth birthday. Today, he'd turned thirty-eight. Officially twice her age. How could he have considered this child to wife?

Because he was that desperate.

Miss Cora Taggart stood near the porch swing, gripping the lemon peel baseball in a leather glove, having snatched it from the air just moments before his realization. Or maybe exactly at the same time.

The pretty young girl appeared relieved, her shoulders now relaxed. And although she been too kind to express her lack of interest in him, her eyes had always dodged his to peer up the lane. Hankering for another man? Perhaps. But not him. Her discomfort had been clear from the start.

He paused at the steps. "I wish you the best, Miss Taggart. I'll let your father know of our decision."

She nodded. "Drive safely."

And don't come back. In her direct words, the unspoken message rang clear. To her, he was an old man. And maybe he was. But he needed a mother for his girls. Heak strode around the corner and hailed her father, a good friend of his. Perhaps, if he'd been paying attention, his first clue that marrying his friend's daughter wouldn't work.

He made the break in the courtship quick yet gentle. He waved and strode to his wagon. Already Miss Taggart stood in the front yard, tossing the lemon peel ball to her nephew. She paused long enough to throw up a brief wave before sending another rocket pitch to the blond-haired boy. With a heavy sigh, Heak leaped into the seat. Definitely not a woman ready to step in and mother five girls. And that had been the whole point. Now he was back, again, to square one. Heak couldn't get away fast enough.

Down came the reins and the faithful bay quickened her step. He needed to spell old Mrs. Grayson, for she was indeed old. Nearing eighty. Her son dropped her off every morning to care for his youngest daughter Tupie. Without her, blacksmithing in town would be impossible.

Some thirty minutes later, he pulled into his driveway. The girls lined the porch playing marbles and stitching. Only Cat and Tupie were absent. He pulled on the brake as he came to a stop and leaped down. As his boots thudded the earth, he prayed Mrs. Grayson had been able to get a few spoons of gruel down Tupie's throat.

He lit a hum in his throat, a phrase of a hymn of some sort laced with his own melancholy. The smell of something sweet lit his nostrils as Willow, Magnolia, and Chinquapin rushed to greet him with hugs and sweet girl smiles. He chuckled when the two younger ones latched onto his legs, giggling as he continued to walk with exaggerated steps. The eldest, Chinka by nickname, launched her tomboy body at him full force. The girls' corkscrew curls bounced in glee as they clutched Heak's legs and shoulders.

Suddenly Cat stood at the door with a tired smile. "Hi, Papa."

Heak knew she secretly wished she could launch into his arms just as her younger sisters had. But he suspected Cat had remembered the significance of the day and had spoiled her old Papa. The younger girls detached themselves from his legs to run to the porch, as if they'd just remembered their roles in the event.

On the porch they both threw their arms up and cried in unison, "Welcome home, Papa. Happy birthday."

Catalpa, Cat for short, eldest at nine, rolled her eyes. "You three were supposed to stay on the porch and sing."

The girls shrugged. Heak felt a grin snake across his face. His girls, his strong little saplings, all named for trees. His wife's effort to assure her girls would be stronger than she.

But bearing Tupelo had drained the last of his wife's strength. His youngest, Tupie, as she was known, had never become strong.

As much as he adored his four eldest and their resiliency, he wished Tupie had run from the house to embrace him as well. Or rolled her eyes in annoyance. Anything but lie in the bed growing thinner and thinner each day.

If only Flossie had lived. She'd died trying to give him a son. And now, all he had of her were the memories of her tall frame sweeping the walk in front of his father's general store. She'd given him a shy smile when he'd walked up. One of the few women who'd even noticed him. Even though many had claimed the young widow as plain, he knew he'd found a treasure beyond measure.

His throat grew a lump, and he swallowed as his four girls ushered him through the door. On the scarred table lay a lopsided cake, swathed in white icing. A lump of gratefulness ballooned in his chest. But one look at Mrs. Grayson who stepped from his bedroom deflated the swell of pride. He raised his eyebrows. The old woman pulled the bedroom door closed and shook her head.

But her weathered face drew up into a weary smile. "Looks like a real celebration."

Heak forced a smile to his face, much for himself as for the angelic faces staring at him wide eyed. "You're welcome to stay and have some cake."

Mrs. Grayson waved a pale, veined hand and set the full oatmeal bowl on the edge of the table. Heak pulled his eyes from the offending dish. "Best get you home then."

He aided the old woman down the steps, lent his arm as she tottered toward the wagon, and lifted her into the seat. Leaving the girls alone always tugged at his heart. He released the brake and pulled the reins to circle the wagon.

"In the house, girls," he rumbled with a nod. Cat gave a half-hearted wave. With it nearing dark, she would be counting the minutes until his return. Heak slapped the reins on his brown mare and she took off, aware of the familiar trail.

He saw Mrs. Grayson to her door and hurried back home. Tupie needed him. As well as his other girls, although he was sure they had no clue how much he loved all of them equally. Tupie took much of his days and nights.

Once back he drew the wagon into the barn and corralled the mare. Inside the house, he checked Tupie, asleep and swathed in blankets even in the early fall's heat. Then his four older girls sang to him, kissed his bearded cheeks, and hugged his neck. Their visible, visceral love glowing from their eyes, radiating from their tiny bodies eased his empty hollowness and filled him with warmth. Cat spoke first.

"How was Miss Taggart?"

Heak cleared his throat. "She's fine. But I don't think I'll be calling on her anymore."

The girls blinked at him, and Cat threw a fist to her thin hip. "She shun you, Papa?"

"Of course not," he shook it off lightly, quite a feat considering at least four other women had done just that. "I just think she's too young for me. That's all."

"But Papa," Chinka protested, "she can throw a ball better than the boys at school."

No denying that. He'd reached out to shield Miss Taggart from an errant ball only to find her catching it square in the center of her leather glove. It had been the last straw. The moment he'd known for sure she was too young for him. "I know, pumpkin."

Wills wedged into his lap. "Lettie Flanders said nobody wanted to marry you 'cause we gots too many kids."

"Willow!" Cat snatched the five-year-old from Heak's lap with a growl.

Heak laid a gentle hand to his eldest's shoulder while gathering Willow back into his arms. "None of that."

"And Harold and Grandle said you was too ugly to get a girl. But I beaned him with a rock when he said that." Noley nodded her head in satisfaction.

In a deep inhale, Heak eyed Magnolia and the rest of his brood. It seemed the whole neighborhood had taken to discussing his courting history. Even the children.

Cat threw an arm around his shoulder. "Don't worry about all that, Papa. They've got big mouths."

"We know you're the bestest, most handsomest daddy in the whole world." Wills squeezed his neck in a hug.

The others joined in, tugging and pulling at him. And despite the knowledge that the neighborhood children had taken up teasing his daughters about his courtship disasters, it warmed him to be surrounded by the ones he loved most.

But it made it clear to him what he should do. After striking out for one reason or another with four—now five women, it was time to call a halt. His desperate search to find a mother to care for the girls had failed. So, with the Lords help, he would extinguish the gossip and carry on himself. After all, he'd managed for nearly three years.

He filled his arms with his precious daughters and stared at the cake. The exhaustion throbbing inside his body mocked his new resolve. Yet he ignored it, just as he snubbed the wave of loneliness that rose to swamp him. The futility and fatigue of battling alone would continue. These small precious ones depended on him.

From now on, he'd add no more fodder for the gossip mills.

Sissy P. Eberlin stepped from the steamer with a stiff gait. As she straightened to full height, which wasn't much, she stifled a groan. The body aches screamed from her neck to her lower back. Her third employment, Boiling Springs Road Subscription School, New Albany. A new start. Everything else lay buried in the past. Where it belonged.

She motioned to the dock worker who chucked her trunk down with a thud. Good thing she'd sold the last of her mother's valuables. They'd be in pieces by now. Her slow creep west took her further and further away from the small town near Cleveland, Ohio. Away from the hostility and censure. That's all that mattered.

Her gaze swept the street above as she gripped the carpet bag in her hand, dreading the climb up the steep bank. A Mr. Abel Bradshaw and his wife, Aleena, were due to meet her. She hoped this family proved to be corporative yet not too meddlesome. And not of the hugging type.

With one last glance toward the top of the bank, she heralded a passing worker, not much older than a child. “I’m the new schoolmarm for Boiling Springs Road Subscription School. Could you tote my trunk to the street?”

“Cost ya a half dime.” The boy nodded, long hair flapping on either side of his thin face.

Sissy sucked in a quick breath, his likeness driving a spike through her heart. For a moment… She shook it off and tightened her lips. “For the life of me, I’ve never heard of such prices.”

The lad in worn clothing and trousers a bit too short, shrugged and continued up the haphazard planks to the street. Her eyes trailed the hauntingly familiar form. She turned away and stiffened her spine.

Who ever heard of such nonsense? A lad…earning a half dime for lugging a small trunk a few hundred feet. What kind of place had she landed in?

A man waved. Large, bearded, and grinning. And much too friendly. At his side a tall blonde woman in a white blouse and dark skirt strode beside him. Sissy had a sinking feeling these folks had come for her. And as one of the school trustees, Mr. Bradshaw appeared much too sociable. Gregarious, even. Yet, what luck. A jolly Goliath ready to tote her trunk wherever she needed without having to pay a penny.

“Miss Eberlin.” He raised his hand in greeting again, his arms encased in the rolled up sleeves of his brick colored shirt.

She set her shoulders. No use getting the welcome entourage up in arms about the new schoolmarm’s offish behavior. Her mouth worked into a semblance of a smile, and Sissy, S.P. Eberlin to the schoolboard, fluttered her fingers in an attempt at a wave. The woman beside him possibly would be more trouble than the grinning ogre. Her face remained flat and her eyes assessed Sissy's attire and luggage in one swift sweep. Then, the woman with the starched blouse nodded.

"You are Miss Eberlin?" the large man clarified, holding out his meaty hand.

Sissy bobbed her head once. No use wasting energy. "Yes. Mr. Bradshaw, I presume?"

His hand fell to his side when she snubbed it, but still, he grinned. "My wife, Aleena Bradshaw."

"How do you do?"

Mrs. Bradshaw inclined her head, a bit like royalty. "I am well, thank you. I trust you had a pleasant journey?"

As a matter of speaking, if one could consider sitting for two days on a filthy crowded vessel, dragging as slow as molasses on a scorching hot June day good, then yes, the travel had been…passable. Sissy merely gave her one nod.

"This your trunk?"

A nearly genuine smile crooked the edge of Sissy's mouth. Her lumberjack schoolboard member would save her a half dime. How efficient and thrifty. "Yes."

He hefted the huge crate. Ah, the benefits of an overgrown man. Then he reached for the carpet bag in her hands, but she drew it away. Sissy trusted no one with its contents. "I can manage."

The burly man shot her another grin and nodded. Then he launched into his welcome speech. "I think you'll enjoy our small community. The school is on the northwest side of New Albany. In a fine rural area, in fact. The Boiling Springs District. We've got some beautiful fields there. Woods and streams."

And where did he believe she'd lived before? The moon? "How lovely."

He grinned sideways at her, not even struggling under the full weight of her loaded box. "You'll love the youngsters as well. We've got ourselves a passel of young 'uns. Why we Bradshaws and Taggarts will near fill up your school."

Sissy inhaled to cover a sniff. Nearly, not near. The man didn't know his adverbs from his adjectives.

"But if you have any trouble with our young 'uns, don't hesitate to consult us. Our brood knows that we expect them all to behave and obey the folks in authority over them."

Well, at least that was something. Sissy offered a stiff smile, ignoring the horrendous slang. "That's helpful to know."

"I think you'll find most are willing to step up and lend a hand for our little school." He meandered toward a farm wagon and deposited her life's possessions in the back. At least he had the decency to lower it in carefully. He extended a brawny hand. "I'll assist you to your seat, Miss."

She clutched his hand, hiding her distaste. Once Sissy settled and the two of them rounded the back of the wagon, she wiped her hand with her fresh hanky.

With a guffaw, the grinning monstrosity of a farmer hefted his wife up like she weighed less than a sewing basket and shot a full grin at her. A strange burning sensation soured in the pit of Sissy's stomach. Touchy-feely people would surely be the death of her.

She studied the town while Mr. Bradshaw lauded the area's advances and superior resources. Sissy made a mental note of where key businesses were as they passed. They curved up and left the city behind on Boiling Springs Road and didn't have far to go before they came to a small schoolhouse on the left corner. Of all things. The school had to be on a corner. Uneasiness lanced through her chest. She clutched the carpet bag in her lap.

But its location might prove to be the lesser of two evils. The building's paint peeled in great chunks and cracks and missing chinks graced nearly every window pane. For people who thought a great deal of their small school, there seemed to be too many things to repair, even from a distance. The shabby shutters hung cockeyed, needing a coat of whitewash as well. As they drew closer, she saw the moss had nearly taken over the upper half of the roof section tucked beneath the twin maples in the back. The roof appeared to fare better under the huge tree at the front of the building.

As if the ill exterior condition wasn't enough, no separate building existed, which made Sissy's heart sink. So she would room in the back, behind the classroom, accessible to anyone who knocked upon the schoolroom door. That meant the space would be small, only room for a bed, a small stove, and some shelves.

Basic comforts, nothing extravagant. A shudder ran through her. This is what her life had been reduced to. She had no choice but to continue to bear the cost of her own curse. And she would bear her cross. But beyond the repairs, beyond the difficulties of dealing with new people and starting over, she knew one thing.

She had to keep the hounds of misfortune from finding her again.

www.ingramcontent.com/pod-product-compliance
Lightning Source LLC
LaVergne TN
LVHW050928080826
845145LV00001B/244

* 9 7 8 0 5 7 8 3 1 8 1 5 8 *